Gargoyles
From the Archives of the Grey School of Wizardry

By Susan "Moonwriter" Pesznecker

New Page Books
A Division of The Career Press, Inc.
Franklin Lakes, NJ

GARGOYLES
EDITED AND TYPESET BY GINA TALUCCI
INTERIOR ARTWORK PROVIDED BY IAN DANIELS, DAVID HAMILTON,
OBERON ZELL, AND SANDY CARRUTHERS
Cover design by Lu Rossman/Digi Dog Design NYC
Printed in the U.S.A. by Book-mart Press

To order this title, please call toll-free 1-800-CAREER-1 (NJ and Canada: 201-848-0310) to order using VISA or MasterCard, or for further information on books from Career Press.

The Career Press, Inc., 3 Tice Road, PO Box 687,
Franklin Lakes, NJ 07417
www.careerpress.com
www.newpagebooks.com

Library of Congress Cataloging-in-Publication Data

Pesznecker, Susan Moonwriter.
   Gargoyles : from the archives of the Grey School of Wizardry / by Susan
Moonwriter Pesznecker.
      p. cm.
   ISBN-13: 978-1-56414-911-4
   ISBN-10: 1-56414-911-0
      1. Gargoyles—Miscellanea. I. Title.

NA3683.G37P47 2007
729 ′ .5--dc22
                                                                    2006031782

Dedication

For my family, *ex amino*.

Acknowledgments

I want to thank my mother; if it weren't for her, I wouldn't be here. My children—Katie, Scott, and Erin have been shining examples, showing me how to reach far and strive for excellence. My sween, Bill, was a font of support, and my sage-poodle, Ernie, gave me an unending supply of unconditional love and wet kisses.

Thanks go to Oberon Zell-Ravenheart and Elizabeth Barrette, magickal mentors without whose help I probably wouldn't have been able to write this book.

I owe a huge debt to my writing teachers: Bob Hamm, I always told you that if I ever published a book, your name would be right up front. I'm also grateful to Emily Orlando, Amanda Coffey, Craig Lesley, Michael McGregor, Debra Gwartney, and the nonfiction M.A. writing program at Portland State University.

Thanks to my contributors: illustrators Ian Daniels, Xander Gael, David Todd "Cashew" Hamilton, and Oberon Zell-Ravenheart; and writers Elizabeth Barrette, Anna Fox, Kalla, Oranstar, S.A. Sherwood, and Estara T'Shirai.

And a heartfelt thanks to my students—both in writing and magick—who have taught me things I couldn't otherwise have learned. Teacher, student...student, teacher...just one more of life's beautiful cycles.

Many blessings!

Contents

Foreword

By Oberon Zell-Ravenheart

Gargoyles—what fascinating grotesqueries, and how irresistible they are to us. What is their mystery? Why are we so drawn to them?

Recently, I was at the International New Age Trade Show in Denver, Colorado, sitting at the booth of our publisher, New Page Books. A woman came up to me with a very concerned look on her face, wanting to ask me about gargoyles. Were they evil? Demonic perhaps? I assured her that no, gargoyles are on our side—they are the staunch guardians of all within the buildings upon which they perch. They are similar to junkyard dogs—hideous, fierce, and terrible to intruders, invaders, burglars, and thieves. However, devoted and loyal to those who dwell within the sanctuaries they protect.

"Horrific antefixes" have been a part of human architecture throughout time and across all cultures. Monstrous guardians are stationed under the eaves and over the doors of ancient temples, palaces, castles, cathedrals, and even private homes throughout the world. Their analogs may be seen in the dragon prows of Viking longboats, and the figureheads of sailing ships, going back to the *Argo* of Jason. Medusa, whose head was removed by Perseus, was featured on the shield and breastplate of the goddess Athena, and was one of many carved Gorgon masks commonly embellishing the temples of Asia Minor.

I first traveled to Paris 20 years ago; a highlight of my pilgrimage was climbing up the long, spiral stairs to the rooftops and bell towers of Notre Dame and other cathedrals and coming face-to-face with their legendary gargoyles. There, high upon the medieval parapets overlooking the City of Light, I stood side by side with these ancient guardians, their eternal vigilance for a brief moment. They did not feel like cold inanimate statues, but rather living beings of stone, immobile at rest, but ready to awaken and spring into action if the need arose.

Today, gargoyles have become immensely popular as small statues and figurines, which can be purchased at most gift stores and placed on your altar, mantle, bookcase, or banister. A marvelous animated movie and TV series featured these powerful but benevolent watchers and guardians, and greatly expanded their mythology. They were noble creatures of another dimension, enlisted during the Middle Ages to protect the castle against invaders. By day, they appeared frozen and lifeless, but at night they came alive, flying over the countryside in the service of the realm. Centuries later, they came to the rooftop of a modern skyscraper in New York City, where once again they were activated into their ancient functions. The writing for this series was quite intelligent, and many of the voices were provided by members of the cast of *Star Trek: The Next Generation*.

So, gargoyles have returned to us in large and small ways, exercising their ancient fascination and appeal to our Halloween love of the grotesque. While the originals still guard the medieval cathedrals of Europe, their descendants may now be found under the eaves of many modern buildings, and miniature replicas are joining countless households. Presumably yours is one of them!

Introduction

s with all good journeys, this one begins with a question.

What do Green Men, secret societies, gargling drainpipes, dragons, and really big chunks of rock have in common? The answer lies within the following pages. But before you dig in, I'd like to tell you a little bit about the book.

This book, similar to the gargoyles it will introduce, is a hybrid of sorts, a work that includes scholarship, folklore, pop culture, history, personal experience, and magick. I've tried to make the book interesting and accessible to a wide range of ages and interests. If you're looking for serious and carefully researched information about gargoyles, you'll find it here. If you're looking for a fanciful read, or a way to incorporate gargoylish ideas into your magickal practices, you'll find that, too. For those who want to have a little fun, exercises are sprinkled throughout the book to help you test your newfound knowledge. There's even a certificate at the book's end, to celebrate your progress.

How to Use This Book

The book has three sections: Part I is all about gargoyles and their golden era, the Middle Ages; Part II conjures up the world of magick; and Part III presents an abundance of resources to help you find out more about gargoyles...or just to find them!

For the best results, start with Part I and work through one chapter at a time. This is important, as each chapter in Part I builds on material presented in preceding chapters. It's similar to becoming a medieval stonecarver: You start with a big, blank chunk of stone—an unread book, if you'll forgive the metaphor. As you read through the chapters, imagine that you're picking up your mallet and chisel and carving the stone, adding details and watching as the meaning unfolds and the images within the stone begin to take shape.

Parts II and III are less structurally important—you can read straight through them or dip in and out at will. You'll also find a detailed glossary in Part III. Much of this book is either about the Middle Ages or magick, and both disciplines include unique vocabularies; the glossary will help you decipher some of this language, and I encourage you to refer to it often. I've also compiled a thorough reference list at the end of the book—a good place to start if you want to learn more about gargoyles and their stony friends, or if you want to find out more about magick.

Many chapters end with Try This ideas. While these are geared toward my younger readers, they should be fun for everyone, and some will help you learn more about magick. Bottom line: Reading a book should be fun, and that's how I want this to be. So please, enjoy!

A Few Notes on Convention

Rather than the Judeo-Christian numbering system of B.C. and A.D., this work uses a less encumbered system, with B.C.E. representing "before common era" (preceding our calendar year 0) and C.E. indicating "common era" (occurring on or after the year 0).

Throughout the text, I use the spellings "magick," "magickal," and so on, when referring to arcane practices. Magickal correspondences, seasons, solstices, and equinoxes are described in terms of their occurrence in the northern hemisphere.

Are you ready? Pull your stout woolen cloak closely around you as we enter the world of the gargoyle.

Part 1: All Things Gargoyle

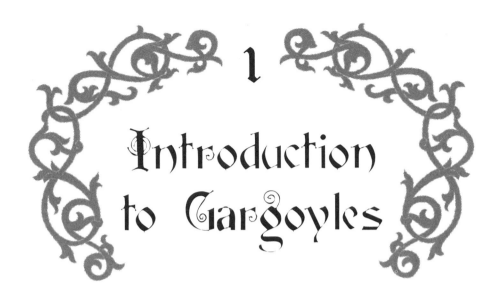

1

Introduction to Gargoyles

Picture an old, Gothic cathedral, its stone towers and archways reaching into the sky. Now, cast your eyes to the top of the eaves and the peak of the ridgeline. If you look carefully, you're likely to spot one or more creatures clinging to the side of the building, or balancing atop a needle-sharp spire.

Gargoyles!

Have you ever wondered why they were created, who made them, and how they got there? Carved sculptures of fantastic creatures appear throughout the history of human civilization. These figures stir our imaginations, as they stirred the imaginations of artists and craftspeople centuries earlier.

The story of the gargoyle will take you on a journey through bestiaries and traveling menageries, past grotesques and chimeras, through medieval guilds, and into huge, stone buildings. We will delve into the Middle Ages, explore historic models of arcane craftsmanship and architecture, consider the reasons that gargoyles came into being, and investigate the legend and myth of the gargoyle. We'll reflect on the role of the gargoyle in modern culture and examine the magickal implications of gargoyles and their stony kin, investigating ways to integrate these ideas into magickal practices. Finally, we'll wander through a "field book" of gargoyles—both old and new—that can still be seen today. But first....

What Is a Gargoyle?

You've probably seen gargoyles at one time or another, whether in pictures or in person. They're interesting creatures, often frightening and sometimes humorous as they haunt a building's highest reaches.

The word gargoyle shares a root with the word "gargle"; both come from *gargouille*, an old French word for throat and the French verb *gargariser*, meaning "to gargle." The word gargoyle is also derived from the Latin *gurgulio*, which has a double meaning: (a) throat, and (b) a kind of gurgling sound. The Spanish *gárgola* shares the same Latin roots. In Greek, gargoyles are known as *gargarizein*, again meaning "to gargle." In Italy, they are known by a more architecturally oriented phrase, *grónda sporgente*, or "protruding gutter." The German gargoyle is a *Wasserspeier*, literally meaning a "water spitter," while the Dutch version is *waterspuwer*—"water spitter" or "water vomiter."

Are gargoyles gurglers? Spitters? Vomiters?

The dictionary definition of gargoyle is a waterspout or drainpipe carved in the form of a decorative face or figure and projecting from a roof gutter. In other words, gargoyles are carved structures on the outside of buildings that work with the guttering system to carry rainwater away from a building, so that it doesn't pool up around the building's base, or run down the walls. Simply said, gargoyles are dynamic, decorated drainpipes!

According to Russell Sturgis,[1] writing in his *Illustrated Dictionary of Architecture and Building*, a gargoyle is: "A water spout, especially one projecting from a gutter and intended to throw the water away from the walls and foundations. In medieval architecture, the gargoyles, which had to be numerous because of the many gutters which were carried on the tops of flying buttresses, and higher and lower walls, were often very decorative, consisting, as they did, of stone images of grotesque animals, and the like, or, in smaller buildings of iron or lead."

When we look at gargoyles—either in photographs or in person—we almost always see them from below or from the side, and from that vantage they appear to be oddly elongated sculptures of exotic-looking creatures. From the top, the view is different. Medieval gargoyles are actually a kind of trough, open toward the sky to easily collect rain and snow. Water collects in the trough, which is slanted to direct the water toward and through the creature's open mouth. The water is then thrown several feet clear of the building wall and hits the street (or perhaps an unlucky passerby). Depending on how sharply the gargoyle is slanted, it might appear to drool, spit, or even vomit.

Most modern gargoyles are either fitted with drainage pipes instead of open troughs or are worked into the actual drainage system. Both practices minimize weathering and erosion, and prevent the collection of leaves, bird droppings, and other materials.

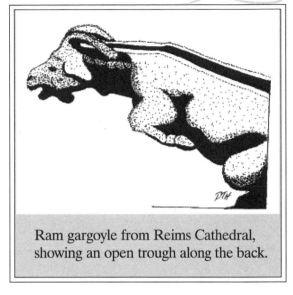

Ram gargoyle from Reims Cathedral, showing an open trough along the back.

Regardless of structure, water exits through the mouth of most gargoyles. Occasionally, the draining water pours out through something that is being held by the gargoyle. The Basilica Di San Marco in Venice features carvings of men who hold large urns, from which rainwater spills. Gargoyles on the Milan Cathedral hold animals and the water issues from the animals' mouths. In a few "defecating gargoyles," water exits through a different orifice, at…ahem…the other end of the alimentary tract. There are no known urinating gargoyles.

Grotesques

An unusual carved creature that looks similar to a gargoyle but doesn't have a drainpipe function is properly called a grotesque. Many carved faces, statues, and other architectural features that onlookers refer to as gargoyles are actually grotesques. Grotesques can serve a water "directing" function, in some cases channeling the water as it flows over or around them. This can be compared to the way water diverts around a rock or log poking up in a stream. However, unlike gargoyles, grotesques are designed solely for appearance, rather than function.

Chimeras

In classic Greek mythology, the chimera (KIH-murr-uh) combined a lion's head, goat's body, and snake's tail, with the ability to breathe fire. Eventually the term came to represent any sort of human/animal composite or any surreal

The gryphon, a well-known chimera.

creature that was not of this world and could not exist in reality. Gargoyles and grotesques were often chimeras featuring animal-human combinations or a combination of parts from two or more animals in a single sculpture. Some of the best known chimeras include the centaur, griffin (var. gryphon), harpy, and mermaid.

Medieval artists loved to create or invoke chimeras, and used them liberally in creating gargoyles and grotesques. In medieval times, the chimera often served as a warning as to what befell people who underestimated the Devil. It also warned of the consequences of indiscriminate sexual activity or physical deception, as well as being a symbol of the physical disorder that could result when the laws of nature and God were transgressed, or became tangled.

What motivated medieval artists to create chimeras? Some may have resulted from simple confusion, either in the correct makeup of exotic animals, or in errors in judgment between real and imaginary animals. For example, evidence suggests that the features of rams, unicorns, and rhinoceros were sometimes confused in bestiaries; if the bestiary, which formed a starting point for most medieval animal sculpture, was in error, the sculpture was likely to go wrong as well.

Isidore of Seville, one of the greatest medieval scholars, wrote that criminals were often forced to eat magick plants, which supposedly transformed them into animal-human hybrids (chimeras). Medieval people also believed in wildmen, who were said to be wild people living in the woods; they were regarded as a lower type of human that had allowed their inner beast to triumph and rise to the surface. Wildmen were a type of chimera in which the laws of civility and nature had become confused, creating a monstrous, fearsome race. Wildman gargoyles were giant humans, typically covered with long hair and sporting exaggerated extremities and fierce expressions. Some cryptozoologists believe that the Wildman gargoyles were representative of creatures akin to Bigfoot, Yeti, Sasquatch, and others of the mystery or "monstrous" races still thought to walk the earth today.

Medieval chefs had their own culinary chimeras: the *cockatrice* was a tasty beast created by cutting a suckling pig and a capon in half, stuffing them, and sewing them back together—each to the other's half. The delicious result featured two roasts: One had the front half of the suckling pig and the rear half of the capon, the other had the front half of the capon and the rear half of the suckling pig. The cockentrice was an expensive dish reserved for state occasions[2]. A modern version of this chef's chimera is the "turducken," in which a turkey is stuffed with a duck, which is stuffed with a chicken, which is stuffed with a smaller game bird (pheasant, quail, dove), which itself may be stuffed!

Most gargoyles are either *zoomorphic* (taking the form of real or imaginary animals), *anthropomorphic* (taking human or humanoid form), or a combination of the two. A few gargoyles, such as demonic versions, fall off into fringe groups.

In today's modern times, the term *gargoyle* is loosely applied to any sort of structural carving that takes the shape of these creatures. For ease within this book, the term *gargoyle* will thus be used to describe gargoyles, grotesques, and chimeras, unless otherwise specified.

Throughout the ages, gargoyles have given carvers and sculptors a chance to display their creativity. Artists apparently enjoyed creating these pieces, and viewers have always been fascinated by the results. But whom are these creatures creeping over the edges of medieval buildings? Who created them, and why?

2

The Beasts

Incipit liber de naturis bestiarum.
De leonibus et pardis et tigribus,
Lupis et vulpibis, canibus et simüs.

Here begins the book of the nature of beasts.
Of lions and panthers and tigers,
wolves and foxes, dogs and apes.

—*Aberdeen Bestiary*, c. 1200

In the Middle Ages, people came to believe in the duality of Christ as both god and living flesh; this paralleled the medieval beliefs that viewed life as a struggle over good vs. evil, light vs. darkness, and so on. This outlook further extended into the idea that humans must also possess a dual nature, and that life was a constant struggle to ensure that the good side triumphed. Even the simplest of everyday creatures were thought to have dual natures and special or mystical powers. Medieval people believed that all animals—real or otherwise—had certain powers and proclivities, both positive and otherwise. Likewise, human qualities were often ascribed to animals—that is, the animals were anthropomorphized. This resulted in serious misunderstandings between humans and animals, and sometimes in a great deal of misplaced fear, as seen in the assumed "evil" relationship between cats and Witches. In 1474, a medieval chicken was tried and sentenced to death for allegedly laying a basilisk's egg, while in 1394, a pig was tried and hung for sacrilege. Its crime? Munching on some communion wafers.[1]

During medieval times, people rarely kept animals as cuddly pets; usually they were either part of the food chain—as in the cow, which gave milk, produced more little cows, and was eventually slaughtered for meat—or they presented hazards or dangers that had to be surmounted, such as a pack of wolves, or a much-feared dragon. The idea of keeping domestic animals was a romantic notion, and mostly limited to the wealthy, who could afford to keep the proverbial bird in the gilded cage. If an animal was kept regularly as a house pet by common folk, it was most likely to be a cat, which was self-sufficient and could earn its keep by mousing or ratting.

Animals filled important roles in everyday medieval life, providing food and assisting with heavy labor. Sometimes they were acknowledged in outward displays of public appreciation. In the Middle Ages, it was common to pay homage to saints and church figures by posting their images along a church's roofline. At the Laon Cathedral in France, bulls had held the task of pulling the construction materials to the hilltop building site. In return, the grateful populace placed a row of sculpted bulls atop the cathedral's tower as it was built, giving the bulls equal billing with the local saints.

Traveling Menageries and Bestiaries

Stonemasons found a constant source of inspiration in nature, and used their studies of local flora and fauna to craft detailed sketchbooks. For animals that weren't found locally, the stonemason's knowledge came from traveling menageries and bestiaries.

The traveling menagerie became a kind of mobile zoo that went from town to town. In the 17th and 18th centuries, the only chance most people had to see live wild animals was when a traveling menagerie came to town, an event that caused great excitement. The idea of the menagerie dates back to classical times, where Roman Emperors (and later, European Royalty) kept menageries for both entertainment and prestige. Famed menageries included those of Emperor Frederick II and King Louis the IX. The menagerie was the forerunner of today's modern circus. It also gave artists and stonecutters a chance to view and study animals that were not native to their home lands, which they otherwise would never have seen.

Bestiaries were illustrated medieval books of animal lore that described the nature and habits of animals (fantastical and real) and attached moral and religious meanings, including parallels to Christ, the Devil, and the virtues and vices. Most bestiaries derived from the 4th-century Greek work *Physiologus*, literally "the natural philosopher," thought to have been compiled at Alexandria around the second century by a Christian ascetic. The work included discussions of almost 50 creatures, plants, and stones from classical mythology and Christian tradition.

The animal symbolism portrayed in bestiaries informed the fables, parables, and allegories that influenced medieval intellectual life. Many of the symbolic conclusions drew their origins from second and third century Eastern literature, particularly forms of Asian and Egyptian animal worship. In both Romanesque and Gothic art, the standard forms were largely based on material from bestiaries. By the 12th and 13th centuries, these ideas had become both popular and refined, evolving into written codes for interpreting all types of medieval animal symbolism. The rise of bestiaries and their peak of public interest mirrored the rise of gargoyles, with many gargoyles subsequently becoming a three-dimensional rendition of the bestiaries themselves.

Conceptualized cover from a medieval bestiary.

The following list mentions some of the best-known historical bestiaries (sorted chronologically):

- The *Libri moralium* (or *Moralium libri*) was created by Pope St. Gregory I (also known as Gregory the Great), around the early fifth century. Later bestiaries obtained a lot of valuable material from this work.

- The *Etymologiae* of Isidore of Seville, written between 615–630 C.E., represented his attempt to create an encyclopedia of all knowledge. The work proved invaluable to later bestiary compilers, as the *Etymologiae* not only recorded facts but also traced and assigned meanings through word histories.

- The *Speculum Naturale* ("Mirror of Nature") was written in the early to mid-11th century in France by Vincent of Beauvais, a Dominican friar. The work, comprising 32 books and 3,718 chapters, summarized the science and natural history known to western Europe toward the middle of the 13th century, as well as including the author's own remarks.

- The medieval *Physiologus*, known as a natural history of the Middle Ages, was credited to Bishop Theobald, who probably created it around 1125. This *Physiologus* provided a basis for virtually all of the other medieval bestiaries.

- The *Bestiaire* was written by Philippe de Thaun, an Anglo-Norman poet. His first book, *Livre des Creatures* ("Lives of Creatures"), was probably written around 1119. In addition to describing creatures, he also delved into the calendar, planets, Zodiac, and night sky, particularly in terms of mystical significance. Shortly after 1121, Philippe wrote his *Bestiaire*, 3,194 lines of verse in Anglo-Norman dialect. The work is the oldest of the French bestiaries, with only three existing extant manuscripts.

- The *Aberdeen Bestiary* was written and illuminated in England around 1200. This bestiary may have represented a *chef d'oeurve*— a culminating "chief work"—of an apprentice. It is considered to be one the best representations of a medieval bestiary, particularly because it includes notes, sketches, marginalia, and other evidence explaining its design. The entire collection has been digitized, and the contents and illustrations are available online.

- The *Liber de natura rerum* of Thomas of Cantimpré was written between 1230–1245. Thomas was a medieval writer, preacher, and theologian. His *Liber* was a vast encyclopedic compilation of

the natural history knowledge of his time, including anthro-
pology, zoology, botany, mineralogy, astronomy, astrology, and
meteorology.

⊚ The *Bestiaire d'Amour* ("Bestiary of Love"), suggesting the work
as a labor of love by Richard de Fournival was written in the 14th
century. Modern scholars suggest that this work represents the
bestiary at the height of its form.

Although bestiaries will always be important for their explanation of medieval forms, modern interpretation of medieval symbology is a tricky thing. The
tendency toward dualism in the Middle Ages makes interpretation even stickier,
for even the noblest of animals carried unflattering double meanings. Nonetheless, bestiaries give us a glimpse into the workings of the medieval mind, and
provide evidence that medieval artists seemed much more interested in symbolic
or fantastic sculpture than in portraying realism. Of the estimated 250–350
bestiaries thought to have been created in the Middle Ages, about 50 exist today.

The Christian Bible, particularly the Old Testament, provided another source
of information about animals, both real and imaginary. The Old Testament featured repeated instances of animal symbolism, and regards real and imaginary
animals with equal importance. The animal symbolism of the Old Testament
dictated the way that animals were depicted in Christian art and established
recurrent images linking animals with specific behaviors and tendencies. Thus, a
flock of lambs or sheep came to represent a congregation of believers, doves
represented hope, and the serpent stood for evil, downfall, and so on.

In medieval times, zoomorphic gargoyles were usually modeled on local
animals familiar to the stonemason, and certain animals appeared repeatedly
because of strong symbolic meanings. In the best example of this, the lore
describing dogs and lions as loyal guardians made them the most frequently
used animals in western European gargoyle sculpture. In another instance of
symbolic reference, exotic animals, such as monkeys or dragons, were used to
depict travels or invoke the presence of a place, whether real or imaginary.

Animals, Humor, and the Seven Deadly Sins

When used in gargoyle sculpture, animals often made satiric commentary
on religion, public behavior, or other touchy topics (for example, the wily,

devouring fox becoming a priest and preaching to a gullible congregation). In Christian tradition, the seven deadly sins were pride, covetousness, lust, anger, gluttony, envy, and sloth. In medieval sculpture and art, each sin was assigned to a specific animal, and the animals then became symbols of the designated misbehavior. The lion was equated with the sin of pride—hence the term, "pride of lions." Covetousness (greed) was associated with the wolf, lust with the pig, anger with the wild boar, gluttony with the bear, envy with the serpent, and sloth with the donkey (Table 1).

Deadly Sin	Representative Animal	Representative Human Aspects
Pride	Lion	Head
Covetousness/ Greed	Wolf	Hands
Lust	Pig	Genitalia
Anger	Wild Boar	Heart
Gluttony	Bear	Mouth and stomach
Envy	Serpent	Eyes
Sloth	Monkey	Feet and buttocks

Animals in Gargoyle Sculpture

Lions

Lions, the so-called kings of beasts, were the most depicted animals throughout medieval art, and the most common animal gargoyle model that was not native to Western Europe. Much lore surrounded the lion. Bestiaries claimed that lionesses gave birth to dead cubs, and that the cubs were resurrected and returned to life three days later—a clear parable to Jesus' reanimation after crucifixion. Pilgrims viewed the story of "Daniel in the Lion's Den" as a symbol of the dangers that God puts in their paths. Another story claimed that when a lion was ill, it would eat a monkey to regain its strength; because monkeys were associated with evil and corrupt behavior, the symbol of good literally consuming evil seemed clear. Said to erase its tracks with its tail—a skill akin to Christ's ability to evade the devil—the lion was associated with vigilant, valiant, regal, and powerful behavior; both the Greeks and Romans frequently used lions as sculptural motifs in the waterspouts and gutter work of their homes and buildings, capitalizing on the lion's protective strength. The lion's vigilance was further supported by the belief that they slept with their eyes open.

Throughout ancient times, the lion was linked to the sun, possibly because of power, and also because of the close resemblance to the sun's golden color. The image of the lion's golden mane, which surrounded its face like a solar wreath was also a close similarity. The akeru—the two-headed supernatural lion of Egyptian mythology—guarded the gates of sunrise and sunset, as well as the passage to the Underworld that ran between them and the sun's movement overhead.

Lions were thought to be good family members. They were loyal to their mates, and to humans who aided them. This is depicted in the legend of St. Jerome when he removed a thorn from a lion's paw. They were even-tempered, not prone to excess (gluttony), and generous. Often used to depict kings of Sumeria, Assyria, and Persia, the royal tradition expanded when the lion came to represent Christ, King of Judea and eventually symbolized the church's authority over its subjects. Over time, the lion became a standard part of heraldry, and was widely used in depicting coats of arms.

Leonine adulation changed in the later Middle Ages, when the lion also became the symbol of pride. If a lion was shown to be holding a lamb, it could be interpreted as protecting the lamb, in which case it was a Christian symbol; this could also be seen as threatening the innocent, in which it was considered Pagan—and evil.

Cats other than lions appeared infrequently in gargoyles and grotesques, materializing most often in French churches and cathedrals, such as the Reims Cathedral. Ancient Egyptians believed cats to be sacred, and worshipped the goddess Bast, who is depicted as a cat. The Greeks drew a connection between Bast and one of the most important Greek goddesses, Artemis, also known as Diana. In the Middle Ages, the name Diana became synonymous with Witchcraft, and the cat was swept along, guilty by association. To medieval people, cats were dark, dangerous creatures associated with vain behavior. Because of their nocturnal nature, stealth, and ability to see in the dark, cats became intertwined with Satanism and Witchcraft, and when cat heads were used in gargoyles or related sculptures, they often expressed demonic form and expression. The cat frequently appeared as a Witch's "familiar"—a kind of companion spirit. During the peak of the Witchcraft craze in Europe, suspected Witches were burned with their cats.

Cat gargoyle from Reims Catheral.

These superstitions and fears continue in modern times. Black cats are associated with Halloween, which some Christian groups continue to regard as a satanic holiday. Folklore suggests that a black cat crossing one's path brings bad luck, and that a cat should never be allowed to sleep with a human, for fear of the cat stealing the human's breath.

Dogs

In terms of animals native to Western Europe, dogs were the animals most commonly depicted in gargoyle sculpture. In mythology, dogs often guarded or protected the dead on their journey to the otherworld, and frequently guarded the otherworld itself. The three-headed Cerberus stood watch over the entrance to Hades, while the jackal-headed Anubis was the ruler of the Egyptian Underworld. In ancient cultures, dogs also served as goddess companions; known for loyalty and fidelity to their master, and for being reliable guardians, the term "watchdog" became an honorable term. The word "fido," a colloquial term for "dog," comes from the Latin *fidus*, which means "I trust." The United States Marines' motto, *Semper fidelis,* or simply, *Semper fi*—always faithful or always trustworthy—is a reference to this same origin.

In medieval times, dogs often as shepherds, a position befitting their wisdom and reasoning ability. In bestiaries, a dog's ability to recognize its own name served as evidence of its intelligence. When dogs were portrayed in gargoyle sculpture, they were detailed and expressive, no doubt an outward sign of the affection with which they were regarded. Dogs certainly weren't deemed perfect, though. Their nearly continuous hunger and their tendency to invade kitchens and trash piles to steal food, showed their vulnerability to the Devil's temptations.

Wolves

People feared wolves, the canine's wild progenitor; yet they also revered wolves as fierce, intelligent hunters, and respected their cooperative and protective nature as pack animals. Wolves became a positive metaphor for the priest who gathers his people and fights off danger, which in medieval times always meant the Devil. Female wolves were honored as symbols of maternal devotion.

Cows

Cows, with their benevolent expressions, sound mothering instincts, and bountiful udders were regarded in medieval times as powerful goddess symbols. Much of this belief was linked to the giving of milk, a symbol of life so powerful that it led to the domestication of cattle, gave its name to the celestial Milky Way, and came to suggest paradise as a land flowing with milk and honey.

Bulls

Bulls—the focal objects of the Roman cults of Mithras and Attis—played a central role in the baptism-like ceremonies for initiates, which had them bathed in a bull's blood as its throat was cut. Bulls were linked to the goddess Kali ("the destroyer") and to the Druidic oak god. For people of the Middle Ages, the bull or the ox (a castrated bull), was vital to the daily activities, such as moving stones, logs, and other materials that people otherwise would have been unable to manage.

Birds

Eagles served as symbols of strength and power, and frequently appeared in art, sculpture, and heraldry. Legends suggested that the eagle could slay dragons, and said that the eagle renewed its vigor by staring directly into the sun;

hence the eagle was often painted with a glint of light emanating from one eye. This, along with the bird's acute vision, gave rise to the idea of looking at things with "an eagle eye." Eagles became the frequent symbol of St. John the evangelist, and sometimes of the resurrected Christ. But similar to everything else in the Middle Ages, the eagle also had negative meanings as well. Because of their direct gaze and their tendency to look into the distance instead of what was close by, eagles were sometimes considered arrogant.

The meaning of other birds in gargoyles and grotesques is less consistent. Doves usually represented the Holy Spirit, peacocks represented eternal life, and the sparrow was linked to the soul. Pelicans, who fed their young from a pouch, were thought to sacrifice for their children, and were often used as a metaphor for Christ. Because birds soared through the skies and nested in high places, they would seem to be obvious gargoyle symbols; yet many have been regarded with a less-than-positive eye. In medieval times, people viewed the pigeon and partridge as lustful and indiscriminately homosexual, while corvids (jays, crows, ravens, and magpies) were ill regarded for eating the eggs and young of other birds, and a rooster's crow was sometimes considered the Devil's call. The use of birds in gargoyle sculpture was haphazard, and their representations were not always anatomically accurate, with beaks, feathers, crests, and talons exchanged between birds or even used as decorations or additions to non-avian subjects.

Goats

The goat was somewhat unique in that it was seen as having two distinct sides. On the positive side, its home in green pastures was said to equate it closely with Christ, and in return, the goat was thought to share Christ's omniscience—a quality supported in physical terms by the goat's acute vision. Wild goats found sure footing on steep slopes and knew instinctively where to find food and which foods were safe to eat, again qualities that seemed godly.

In contrast, male goats often symbolized sexual desire and lust. In his

Goat gargoyle from Reims Cathedral.

Book of Beasts, a translation of a 12th century bestiary, T.H. White said, "The nature of goats is so extremely hot that a stone of [diamond], which neither fire nor iron implement can alter, is dissolved merely by the blood of one of these creatures."[2] Goats were synonymous with the horned god Cerrunos or even with Satan. In pre-Christian times, Pagan Shamans and priests often worn horned headpieces or helms as part of their rituals, and it's probably no coincidence that when Christianity began usurping the old Pagan traditions, those same horns became representative of its most feared symbol, Satan. The goat's horns, tail, and cloven hooves were also common demonic and satanic tropes. In this way, the Pagan religions became visually linked to darkness, evil, and animalistic behavior.

Ram

A long-standing symbol of male power and sexual energy, the ram served as a common sacrificial animal in ancient festivals. According to medieval bestiaries, the ram symbolized a priest leading his Christian flock. The ram's heavy head, thick horns, and ability to butt their way around obstacles made them made them similar to the apostles, who also forced their way through spiritual challenges. The horns, hooves, and testicles were often used as fertility charms.

Pigs

Infrequently depicted in medieval art or sculpture, the well-padded pig—which enjoyed food with great gusto—provided an emblem of gluttony and overindulgence. On the other hand, the pig was also the symbol of St. Anthony, who overcame his own struggles to become known as a protector of animals; this led to the term "tantony pig" for the favorite or runt of the litter. The term is still used today; tantony pigs are allowed to roam free, following whoever is gracious enough to feed them, but quick to shift loyalties when a better offer comes along. The term is used less-flatteringly to describe a person who shows similar short-term loyalty.

Wild boars, pigs of the ancient world, were thought to be alert, fierce, intelligent warriors. For those reasons, boars were among the most powerful of sacrificial objects and became known as sacred animals of Celtic Britain. Today, we know that all kinds of pigs are among the most intelligent of mammals.

Donkeys

Medieval folk admired donkeys for their patience, strength, and ability to work hard for long periods. In Christian iconography, the donkey was most notable for carrying Mary to the stable of Jesus' birthplace. However, donkeys (also called asses, which only later became a derogatory term) were thought to be stupid, slow, and stubborn by medieval folk.

Legend said that the onager, an Asian wild ass native to northern Iran, had the ability to recognize the Vernal (Spring) Equinox. The Autumn and Vernal Equinoxes are the times or dates, occurring twice each year, when the sun crosses the celestial equator, and when day and night are of equal length. The word "Equinox" comes from the Latin *aequinoctium*, from *aequi-* "equal" + *nox, noct-* "night." In the northern hemisphere, the Vernal Equinox occurs in late March, marking the beginning of spring in the northern hemisphere and the beginning of fall in the southern hemisphere; in the southern hemisphere, these seasons are reversed, with spring beginning in September and autumn in March. Bestiaries claimed that the onager would bray aloud one time at the height of each hour, 12 times before the turning of the Equinox and 12 times after. In this way, the onager demonstrated the equal length of night and day at the time of the Equinox. This wasn't necessarily a good thing, though—by demonstrating that he was far too clever for an ordinary beast, the onager once again made people turn their thoughts to Satan, who shrieked and brayed as he counted souls lost to the Christian God.

Fox

Medieval folk viewed the fox as deceitful, cunning, crafty, and symbolic of death. The totem form of the god Dionysus was a fox. Immortalized in medieval folklore as the trickster "Red Renaud" or "Old Red Raynard," the fox embodied cleverness and spoke in a human voice as he lured victims in to become his next meal.

Rabbits

Central to mythology worldwide, rabbits were associated with the moon. In traditional Goddess cultures, rabbits served as important totem animals, and eating them was widely prohibited. A Scottish superstition held that eating rabbit was tantamount to eating one's grandmother. Rabbits were used as divining creatures by the Greeks, and also referred to by the Iceni Queen Boadicea, who correctly predicted victory from the direction of a darting rabbit.

Because the hare could sleep with its eyes open, the Romans equated it with vigilance and believed that rabbits watched over everything—just as the moon appears to. In European folklore, the phases of the moon could be seen in the eyes of rabbits. Worldwide, rabbits or hares coexist with the moon as sacred symbols of vitality, fertility, and the life force. In contrast, rabbits are also associated with tricksters, shapeshifters, and longevity.

Bats

Not yet understanding the physics of echolocation—the way that bats use sonar to find their way through the darkness—medieval people feared the flying mammals for their ability to navigate the dark with apparent magickal ease. The fear led to the portrayal of bats as harbingers of darkness, chaos, evil, vampirism, and shapeshifting. Bats quickly became identified with demons, leading to the old belief that human souls took the form of bats during sleep, allowing the soul to leave the body and forage in the dark night air. Because of these associations, bats were viewed as powerful creatures and were often nailed to the doors of homes as a way to repel demons. The process continued into the carving of bat grotesques, many of which adorned church and cathedral walls.

Elephants

Many cultures worshipped elephants. In India, they symbolized sexual energy and were personified by the elephant god Ganesh; Ganesh was later demonized by medieval Christianity, becoming the elephant-headed demon Behemoth—a term still used to describe anything that is monstrous and beastly. But the elephant was also seen standing among the forces of God and sometimes represented Adam. Legends say that the male elephant wouldn't mate until given a mandrake root by a female elephant; the mandrake symbolized the apple in medieval times, hence the parallel to Adam and Eve.[3]

Frogs

To the ancient Greeks, frogs symbolized procreation, birth, and regeneration. In the Middle Ages, the use of frogs in gargoyle sculptures came to be a medieval symbol of the Devil and of temptation, as well as suggesting lewdness.

Monkeys

Monkeys, who medieval folk viewed as unacceptably human, both in appearance and behavior, were thought to show what happens when the laws of nature were usurped—that is, when nature went awry. This transgression of natural, Godly law linked monkeys to the Devil and to everything that mocked or usurped the Christian God. Thus, the monkey itself became a symbol of sin.

Although regarded by medieval folk as being stupid and witless, monkeys are very intelligent. In modern times, the nonhuman primates have been shown to be one of five species of animals capable of reason (the others are humans, dolphins, rats, and some canines). But in the Middle Ages, monkeys represented the baser side of human nature and suggested the fall of mankind. Their intelligence became cunning, their self-awareness vanity, and their interest in one another lust. The monkey was often included in medieval artwork detailing temptation and the fall of Eden.

Rhinos

Bestiary authors frequently confused the rhinocerous and the unicorn, a good example of the fine line between real and imagined animals. The horns of the rhinoceros, when removed and ground into powder—were used to treat disease, cure poisonings, and remedy male impotence. Legend said that the rhinoceros could only be caught and tamed by a virginal girl.

Serpents

In ancient times, serpents were associated with goddesses and with both giving life and with wisdom; a vast snake guarded the Celtic Yggdrasil, and the serpent Ladon watched over Hera's apple tree in the garden of the Hesperides. Because of their association with Adam, Eve, and the fall of Eden, the medieval Christian church viewed serpents as one focus of the constant struggle between good and evil. Thanks to regular shedding of their skin, snakes were believed to be immortal and suspected of being dragon kin. When the snake held its tail in its mouth, forming a ring, it became Ouroboros, an Earth dragon associated with immortality.

Animal Monstrosities

Creatures that didn't correspond to the groupings of normal genus, families, and/or species fell into the category of "animal monstrosities. Some were chimeras, while others simply represented exaggeration, superstition, or misinterpretation of existing creatures, such as the platypus, sloth, or armadillo. This also included marveling at the process of metamorphosis, such as a tadpole becoming a frog, or a chrysalis morphing into a delicate butterfly. Many of the monstrosities and chimeras no doubt resulted from artists with a sense of humor, who simply mixed and matched parts to create a desired effect.

The *parandrus* or parander was a monstrosity described in bestiaries as being about the size of an ox and having ibex footprints, a stag head with full, branching antlers, and the fur of a bear. Chameleon-like, the parandrus could change its coloring to blend into the background. For medieval folk, this illustrated what happened when real and mythical natures of animals were confused and jumbled together.

The *antlion*, or mirmecoleon, had the hindquarters and back limbs of an ant and the torso, head, and forelimbs of a lion. Janetta Benton suggests that this creature resulted from literal misinterpretation of written sources on the insect *myrmeleon*, the name deriving from the Greek *myrmex* (ant) and *leon* (lion)[4]. The modern insectoid antlion is an insect resembling a dragonfly, with predatory larvae that construct conical earthen pits into which insects prey, wander, and fall.

At least one scholar has presented evidence suggesting that gargoyles might have been inspired by the pre-Christian discoveries of the skeletal remains of prehistoric dinosaurs and other fossils in central Asia.[5] Apparently, ancient Greeks and Romans collected and displayed bones and fossils, and may have believed them to be remnants of a mythic race of beasts. In particular, the skeletal structure of the protoceratops is quite similar to that of a mythic griffin. Protoceratops lived 65 million years ago; they were 8 feet long and had a beak and a bony ridge on the back that could have been misinterpreted as part of the wing structure.

Dragons

A few gargoyles were modeled after magickal creatures, and dragons were the most common of these. The word "dragon" is said to either come from the Greek *drakōn,* "serpent," from the Latin *draco* (also "serpent"), or from the Sanskrit *dric,* "to see," the latter a reference to the dragon's mythical ability to destroy with a simple glance. The typical dragon of medieval imagination looked similar to a giant reptile with a long tail, taloned legs, a scaly snout, sharp teeth, flaring nostrils, and membranous, leathery wings.

In European traditions, dragons breathed fire and tended to symbolize chaos or evil. In contrast, in the Far East the dragon was usually a beneficent symbol, associated with water, creativity, fertility, and the heavens. In the Middle Ages, dragon images were always evil, and usually were intended to symbolize the Devil, his demons, or sin. The Bible referred to dragons as serpents and compared them to the Devil. The Book of Revelations featured a menacing dragon with seven crowned heads and 10 horns; Revelations 20:2 spells out the dragon-as-Devil relationship with, "the dragon, that old serpent, which is the devil." When medieval tombs or headstones featured dragon images, they were usually placed at the foot or bottom of the stone, representing the evil that the deceased had overcome during his or her own life.

In all cultures, dragons came to symbolize struggle or conquest, giving rise to the legend of the dragonslayer. Stories developed of saints who conquered dragons. St. George was often pictured standing on a dragon, a representation of good triumphing over evil; indeed, in medieval art and sculpture, a serpent or dragon shown curled around the feet of a knight or clerical figure was a reliable symbol of the victory of God over the Devil. St. Michael was also

St. George the Dragonslayer

known to engage in combat with dragons and serpents. These depictions gave voice to the never-ending struggle between good and evil, and between Christianity and Paganism.

Psychologist Carl Jung saw the dragon as representing the darkness or shadow that resides within all humans. Perhaps the dragonslayer might then stand for the constant human struggle to overcome that darkness. St. George and St. Michael were so revered for their dragonslaying that they were immortalized in oaths of knighthood. The knights-to-be kept watch through the dark hours, guarding their weapons and armor in the local church. The next morning, the king or lord knighted them; as the knight-to-be knelt, the king grasped a sword, touched it to the new knight's head, neck, and shoulders, and administered an oath that was similar to this:

In the name of God, St. Michael, and St. George, I give you the right to bear arms and the power to mete justice!

Medieval bestiaries clearly identified dragons as akin to the Devil. The crown-like crest ridge on a dragon's head and back established it as royalty, and Satan was often referred to as the Prince of Darkness. Both dragon and Devil were associated with fire, and both were thought to have magickal strength in their tails, which they used to coerce and strangle their victims. The dragon's and Devil's wings symbolized their fallen angel status. The Northern English called dragons "lairdly wurms," literally, "lordly worms," something that had crawled up out of the dirt and now sought unholy dominion. Two-legged dragons—wyverns— resulted from a sacrilegious union between basilisk and dragon.

The wyvern, a two-legged dragon.

While universally portrayed in the Middle Ages as both frightening and ugly, dragons were also respected for the level of power they commanded. The dragon became perhaps the most powerful medieval metaphor of that which was simultaneously striking and malevolent.

Chimeras

A variety of animal chimeras appeared in gargoyle sculpture, including the basilisk, a huge serpent-like creature. Medieval people believed that dragons and basilisks were related. Differing bits of lore suggested that basilisks came to be when a snake's egg was brooded by a chicken (or vice-versa), or by the satanic mating of venomous toads and roosters.

Basilisks were believed to be capable of petrifying and killing living beings with a single gaze. Variations suggested that their breath was also lethal, and that their tail left a wake of poisonous venom as they crawled along the ground. Artists and sculptors often pictured the basilisk with a three-pronged tail or with a crown on its head. During the 15th century, syphilis spread through Europe in a plague believed to have been caused by basilisk venom. In the following traditional poem,[6] the monster is killed by seeing its own reflection in a mirror:

To eye of basilisk that
e'er with venom slew,
returns the looking-glass
the beast's death-bringing gaze;
so to themselves returns
the evil-sinners do.
And what more fitting
Than its poison end
Their days?

One of the most common chimeras, the griffin—with a lion's body and the head and wings of a large bird, often an eagle—was common in gargoyle sculpture and usually symbolized courage and bravery. Traditional guardians of the sun, the golden apples of immortality (kept by the Norse mother goddess Idun), and the stars, griffins were often depicted guarding treasure or precious objects.

The centaur, a popular chimera.

The other popular chimera, the centaur, had the head, arms, and torso of a man and the body and legs of a horse. It may have been created in response to the surprising appearance of the first men ride horses. Often portrayed either as virile and sexualized or as armed and engaged in combat, people believed that centaurs had magickal powers, as well as knowledge of lore, shapeshifting, and divination.

The harpy had a woman's head and body and a bird's wings and claws; alternatively, it was depicted as a bird of prey with a woman's face. Harpies may have developed as a mythic incarnation of the Cretan funerary princesses, who wore feathered costumes and plucked harps while tending the dead.[7]

The mermaid had the head and trunk of a woman and the tail of a fish, while mermen had a man's upper body. Usually depicted as a beautiful woman with long flowing golden hair, the mermaid tradition was linked to Aphrodite. India had its own mermaid variation in Nagas, with a human upper body and that of a water serpent below. The mythic siren was often portrayed as a bi-tailed mermaid, with each hand holding a tail.

A harpy.

The satyr, a man with a horse's ears and tail, showed up in Roman representations as a man with a goat's ears, tail, legs, and horns. The satyr was a Pagan embodiment of nature, wildness, sex, and fecundity. Christians used horned deities, such as the satyr and Cerrunos, as models for demonic figures.

The sphinx, a winged monster of Thebes with a woman's head and a lion's body, symbolized the sun god Harmackhis from ancient Egypt. Harmackhis' sacred bird was the phoenix, and most sources agree that the sphinx's wings probably represented phoenix wings.

The unicorn, a horse with a long horn growing from its forehead, sometimes displayed a goat's beard and maybe cloven hooves. Similar to its modern relative the rhinoceros, the unicorn—and its horn—was equated with the ability to treat disease and cure poisoning and impotence. In the book *Harry Potter and the Sorcerer's Stone*, the unicorn was notable for its

The mermaid, an undersea chimera.

The satyr: Rome's embodiment of nature.

purity, and its blood could confer immortality, albeit at a terrible price to one's immortal soul. So-called unicorn horns displayed throughout Western Europe in the Middle Ages were probably those of narwhals, horned marine creatures of the walrus family that lived in the cold, northernmost seas. Apparently, medieval people didn't consider the discrepancy between a 6-foot-long narwhal horn and the slight build of the horse-like unicorn. A similar feat of public foolery was seen in the selling of "griffin eggs," with people failing to grasp the idea that something with the hind end of a lion probably wouldn't lay eggs!

Biting, Pouncing, and Grimacing

The unicorn.

Another recurrent motif in medieval times was that of an animal or beast shown consuming a human head, or sometimes one or more human limbs. Biting creatures in general may have referenced the church's literal devouring of the old religions and traditions. If the animal was significantly larger than the human, the work also suggested the human fear of giants.

Sculptors typically placed animal gargoyles into a dynamic posture. An eagle might be posed holding onto a building's edge by their claws, with wings outstretched as if they planned to fly away. A lion might be shown crouched, muscles gathered and ready to spring, or an animal face frozen into a frightening or fierce grimace, with teeth bared.

The Beasts and the Church

While many deity figures, both pre-Christian and Christian, were associated with animals or animal companions, not everyone was a friend of gargoyles. Medieval clergy believed that using animals for imagery or ornamentation in church was simply a form of idol worship. The Catholic church in particular saw animals as soulless beings. In the 12th century, St. Bernard of Clairvaux, a church leader and an advisor to kings and popes, observed animal gargoyles and grotesques and wondered aloud at their suitability:

> *What are these fantastic monsters doing in the cloisters before the eyes of the brothers as they read? What is the meaning of these unclean monkeys, these strange savage lions, and monsters? To what purpose are here placed these creatures, half beast, half man, or these spotted tigers? I see several bodies with one head and several heads with one body. Here is a quadruped with a serpent's head, there a fish with a quadruped's head, then again an animal half horse, half goat...Surely if we do not blush for such absurdities, we should at least regret what we have spent on them.*[8]

Clairvaux's question was a nice bit of pure posturing—if he had really wanted an answer to his question, all he would have needed to do was seek out the nearest stonemason and ask. In reality, his words acknowledged the latest decorative trend (no doubt funded by wealthy patrons) while making the church's opinion clear.

Despite the church's skepticism regarding animals in sacred art and sculpture, beasts became enshrined in arcane and modern iconography worldwide:

- Animals circle above our heads in the heavenly zodiac and constellations, including *Aquila* (the eagle), *Cancer* (the crab), *Canis Major* and *Minor* (the dogs), *Capricorn* (the goat), *Columba* (the dove), *Corvus* (the crow), *Draco* (the dragon), *Hydra* (the sea serpent), *Lepus* (the hare), *Monocerus* (the unicorn), *Serpens* (the snake), and *Taurus* (the bull).

- The Chinese culture follows an animal zodiac, with years occurring in cycles of 12 animal signs, each animal endowed with specific attributes and powers: rat, ox, tiger, rabbit, dragon, snake, horse, sheep, monkey, rooster, dog, and pig.

- The Muslims place 10 animals in the heavens: Abraham's ram, Balaam's ass, Balkis's lapwing, Jonah's whale, Mohammed's Alborak, Moses's ox, Noah's dove, Saleh's camel, Solomon's ant, and the dog of the Seven Sleepers.

- Three of the four Evangelists were sometimes depicted as animal-human chimeras: St. Matthew as a winged man, St. Mark a winged lion, and St. Luke, a winged ox. The evangelist St. John was represented as an eagle.

- In 19th century symbology, the lion would come to represent the continent of Africa, while the buffalo stood for North America, the bull for Europe, and the elephant for Asia.

Try This

Create your own bestiary of real or fantastic beasts. Use an empty notebook, and allow one or two pages for each creature. Make notes about the appearance, size, habits, and meanings of each. Sketch your creatures, or find pictures that you can glue into your bestiary. You may even wish to create and name your own chimeras!

3
The
Humans

Humanoid (anthropomorphic) gargoyles leaned toward the bizarre and exaggerated, with imperfect physical characteristics sometimes mixed with demonic forms. Posture and expression hinted at sinfulness: A gargoyle with a large mouth might reference the sin of gluttony. The style may have reflected the medieval belief that physical ugliness and illness were caused by demons or evil. Specific secular (historical) figures were rarely, if ever, portrayed in medieval gargoyle sculpture. A few grotesques exemplified knights of the realm, or the occasional manor lord, but these were uncommon; in the Middle Ages, human gargoyle subjects tended to retain their anonymity. This is probably one of the ways that modern gargoyles have changed the most, for today's carvings often mimic politicians, academics, or financial magnates.

The Queen's head gargoyle from Westminster Abbey.

Nonetheless, medieval carvers had a good, if sometimes misplaced or irreverent, sense of humor. Although sometimes referred to as "The Dark Ages," the Middle Ages also had its share of festivals, carnivals, and recurring holidays, which provided the citizens with a chance to let their hair down. The annual Feast of Fools on January 1 lasted for several days, celebrating the New Year with feasting, dancing, and a reversal of social positions through a tradition known as the *inversi mundi*, literally, the "upside-down world." During the Feast of Fools, citizens elected their own political and religious leaders and engaged in several days of just about every kind of impropriety, while the *real* church and government officials looked in the other direction. In fact, the church actually sanctioned these celebrations, perhaps seeing them as a healthy way for the populace to let off steam in a "controlled" setting.

Angels, Demons, and Witches

While angels, saints, the Virgin Mary, and Christ were frequent themes in medieval painting, tapestry, and sculpture, they were not popular as gargoyles or grotesques. Few gargoyles emulated saints or angels; however, demonic themes were much more common in gargoyle sculpture. Devils and demons were usually anthropomorphic—standing on two legs and with a human shape. However, they often had tails, horns, wings, beaks in place of noses, and scales or feathers instead of skin.

Historically, there are many demons, but there is only one Devil, and medieval folk called him Satan or Lucifer. The word "devil" comes from the Latin *diaballein*, "to slander," from *dia* "across," and *ballein*, "to throw," which come, in turn, from the Greek *diabolos*, "accuser" or "slanderer." The depiction of a slandering, dishonest creature. In Christian history, the fallen angel Lucifer descends into the Underworld and becomes the creature known as Satan; medieval people used the two terms interchangeably. It was also during medieval times that the iconography of devils and dragons—both widely feared—became fully formed and consistent. The presence of wings on most demon and devil statuary was felt to reference their status as fallen angels. In contrast, the use of wings on humans and non-avian animals tended to have ambiguous meaning.

By the end of the Gothic period, the devil had become less human and even more bestial. In Dante's *Inferno,* written in the early 1300s, Lucifer is described as having leathery, bat-like wings. During art and sculpture from this same period, the Devil's horns became larger, teeth became dripping fangs, ears became sharply pointed, feet grew sharp claws or turned into cloven hooves, heavy beards and eyebrows formed, and the body became heavily muscled, graphically nude, and covered with hair. The tail also became longer and more serpentine. For these reasons, medieval people regarded gargoyles with any combination of these characteristics as demonic.

In medieval times, demons were seen as the devil's subordinates, or groupies. The word comes from the Latin *daemonium* "lesser or evil spirit," and the word came to mean an evil spirit, especially one that possessed a person or acted as a tormentor in hell. Medieval paintings portrayed humans being overwhelmed by groups of gleeful, voracious demons. Images of the Devil, demons, and Hell were chaotic and disorganized, reflecting the medieval concept of Hell as a place of danger and disorder, versus the peaceful, pastoral setting of Heaven.

Witch gargoyles exist, but they're few in number. When older versions are found, they tend to be the stereotypical, maligned witch, with long, pointy noses and lots of warts. Modern Witch gargoyles are more fanciful.

Beauty, Ugliness, and Sin

Medieval folk tended to see the world as black or white, and human nature as either good or evil. People of the Middle Ages believed that beauty was a god-given reflection of inner goodness, while ugliness, physical imperfection, or illness were abnormal and signs of evil, spiritual failure, or demonic possession. Physical imperfections were also linked to the seven deadly sins: defects of the head were due to a sin of pride, while greed was associated with the hands, lust with the genitalia, anger with the heart, gluttony with the mouth and stomach, envy with the eyes, and sloth with the feet and buttocks (see the table in Chapter 1).

In the art of the Middle Ages—most of which was religious in theme—Christ, Mary, saints, and other religious figures were always shown as handsome (or beautiful), while demons or other enemies of Christ appeared as ugly, frightening, and monstrous. The creation of the so-called monstrous races was probably linked to these societal opinions. Displays of emotion followed a similar pattern in medieval times: The ability to guard one's emotions and passions was prized as a mark of religious training and good breeding, while overt displays of emotion were seen as base and corrupt. In medieval paintings, the figures showing the greatest emotion were usually those being flayed alive or cast into Hell.

These explanations may help us understand the gargoyles' exaggerated, demonstrative expressions. Perhaps through observing the gargoyle's anguished faces, medieval people could keep a better grip on their own tensions and fears. Or in contrast, perhaps gargoyles gazed down at the tense, difficult world below them and cried out in their own, frozen anguish.

For working gargoyles (those with a drainpipe function), a wide-open mouth was needed for the discharge of water, and the facial expression took shape around that. Still, the stonecarver could easily have made the gargoyle laugh instead of shriek. The occasional humorous or fanciful gargoyle must have been appreciated by people living in the Dark Ages. Even sculptures that might be considered repulsive or intimidating often possessed a certain impish charm.

The Monstrous Races

People of the Middle Ages recognized the existence of several quasi-human, monstrous races, which were believed to occupy places beyond the known world. The Greeks and Romans were probably the first to describe "human monsters" in the dictionary sense, with the word referring to imaginary creatures that were large, ugly, and/or frightening. The word "monster" comes from the Latin *monstrum,* meaning "portent," and from *monere,* "warn." This references the practice of divination among the Greeks and Romans, who saw anomalous, monstrous humans as a kind of warning from the gods that all was not well.

A number of the monstrous races were first reported by Alexander the Great, the king of Macedon from 336 to 323 B.C.E. and a man who traveled extensively as he conquered Persia, Egypt, Syria, Mesopotamia, Bactria, and the Punjab region. But it was Isidore of Seville who, by the 7th century, used the word *monstrum* in written texts to refer to unusual looking humans. Pliny, Solinus, and Saint Augustine continued the discussion and brought it into wider use, where the idea of monstrous humans was also used to describe those who lived on the fringes of society and deviated from societal norms.

A number of the monstrous races were simply variations on the human theme, while others represented animal-human chimeras. The monstrous races were believed to exist until well into the Middle Ages. All appear in myth and literature, and most occupied the edges of one or more of the *Mappa Mundi*, the "maps of the world" created in the 12th and 13th centuries in Europe. A good number of the monstrous races also found their ways into medieval bestiaries and natural histories, or onto the margins of illuminated manuscripts.

Several 12th- and 13th-century versions of the *Mappa Mundi* still exist. Some of the best known—the World Disk of Hereford Cathedral (c. 1280), Psalter Map (c. 1230), and Ebstorf Map (c. 1275)—show imaginary continents and seas, the edges populated with monstrous races and fabulous plants. It is important to understand that for medieval people, a "world map" was something different from what we think of as a typical map today. Medieval world maps were far from geographically accurate, and were as much about social commentary, classical history, cosmology, and theology as they were about an accurate description of place. The places occupied by monstrous races were thought of as remote, exotic, or otherworldly, and far beyond the realm of normal humanity. These maps give us yet one more bit of insight into the medieval mind, particularly when we find the monstrous races relegated to the edges of the maps, symbolically banished from Christianity, which stood in in the center of the medieval world.

It's likely that many of these "races" represented living humans born with birth defects, such as anencephaly (the absence of a brain) or hirsutism (excessive body hair), or those who had experienced catastrophic disease or injury, such as losing fingers, toes, or a nose to leprosy. They also certainly represented normal physical or social variations, perhaps referencing people who were short, had dark skin, lived on a fish-based diet, or stretched their lower lips with labrets. A few of the monstrous races were real and still exist today, as in Africa's Pygmy people. While none of the monstrous races are intentionally represented in medieval sculpture, their characteristics surfaced on gargoyles in different combinations.

From a moralistic standpoint, the monstrous races were consistent with the negative medieval view of physical imperfection, which was viewed as "ungodly" and an outward sign of sin. They certainly sparked the imagination of those stonecarvers creating gargoyles!

Conceptualized *Mappa Mundi*—a medieval "Map of the World."

The monstrous races include[1]:

- **Abarimon**, who lived in the far or unknown north, and whose feet were turned backwards.

- **Albanians**, who were owl-eyed—that is, they could see better at night. Albanians were born with gray hair that darkened as they aged.

- **Amazons** (literally "without breast"), tall, warlike women who—according to legend—cut or burned off their right breast so they could draw a bow. Alexander the Great was said to have had contact with the Amazons, who lived without men. Over time, they were idealized, seen as heroic warriors, and acknowledged as one of the "noble monsters."

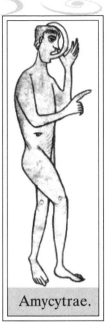

- **Amyctyrae** ("unsociable"), with enormous lips that were large enough to turn up or wrap around the head for use as earmuffs or umbrellas. The Amyctyrae were said to live on raw meat.

- **Androgynii**, hermaphrodites that either had genitalia of both sexes, or genitalia that was neither female nor male. They lived in Africa, and were fertile, generating and birthing their own young.

- **Anthropophagi**, who were cannibals (see Donestra).

- **Antipodes** ("opposite-footed"), with the right and left foot reversed, and who were similar to the Himantopodes.

Amycytrae.

- **Arimaspians** (see Cyclops).

- **Artibatirae**, who walked on all fours, beast-fashion.

- **Astomi** (var. Gangines), were mouthless and existed on the scent of fruits—especially apples—and flowers. They were covered with hair, and susceptible to a quick death if they smelled a foul or strong odor. Pliny located these creatures near the headwaters of the Ganges. In some accounts, the Astomi were all males. Astomi literally means "mouthless."

- **Bat-eared people**, who could hear at frequencies far beyond those of other humans.

- **Bearded ladies**, normal-appearing women with heavily bearded faces, who were said to hunt with dogs in India.

- **Blemmyae**, who had neither heads nor necks; their "faces" were found on their chests. They were recorded as living in the Indian desert. Shakespeare included them and the Androgynii in *Othello*: "The Cannibals that each other eat/The Anthropophagi, and men whose heads/Do grow beneath their shoulders."

Blemmyae, with neither heads nor necks.

🕉 Bragmanni, naked wise men of India who spent their lives in caves. The name was thought to be a variation of the Indian *Brahman*, members of the highest Hindu caste. Brahmans were renowned for their wisdom and insight. They were sometimes combined with the Gymnosophisti.

🕉 **"Conception at age five" people**. A race of women said to conceive children in their fifth or sixth year and who died before age 10.

🕉 **Cornuti**, horned men who were sometimes found in England. They were also called Gegetones (see Gegetones) or simply Horned Men.

🕉 **Cyclops** (var. Cyclopes; literally "round eye" or "wheel eye"), also called Arimaspians, a giant race with a single eye in the center of the forehead. Ogres were thought to be a variation of the Cyclops. Although the most famous literary examples (from Homer's *Odyssey*) lived in Sicily, one-eyed giants were said to live in India as well. The Cyclops' skill in fitting together stone masonry without mortar led to the expression of "cyclopean" masonry. A striking version of the Cyclops is found in Thomas Cantimpré's *Liber de natura rerum*.

🕉 **Cynocephales** (var. Cynocephali; "dog head"), who had human bodies but the heads and voices (barking) of dogs. Said to live in the mountains of India, Cynocephali were carnivorous hunters with huge teeth. They lived in caves, wore skins, were fast runners, and hunted with swords, javelins, and bows. Some legends said they breathed fire.

🕉 **Donestre** (var. Anthropophagi), a fabulous race described by Alexander the Great. The Donestre knew all human languages; they greeted travelers with familiar speech, convinced them that they were kinsmen, and then killed and cannibalized them. The head was reserved, and the Donestre were often depicted drinking from emptied human skulls, or wearing heads and scalps as adornments.

- **Epiphagi**, an Indian race who had no heads; their eyes were on their shoulders and their other facial features were on their chests. They looked much like the Blemmyae except that their eyes were directly on their shoulders and were sometimes bright gold in color.

- **Ethiopians**, tall black men who lived in the Ethiopian mountains. Described in legend by Alexander the Great, their popular name was said to derive from the Greek words *aith* and *ops*, literally, "burnt face."

- **Gangines** (see Astomi).

- **Garamontes**, another Ethiopian race known for intentionally not practicing marriage.

- **Gegetones** (var. Gorgones), men with horns and tails.

- **Giants**, very large and tall people who were normally proportioned and sometimes covered with fur or hair. Alexander the Great contacted—and defeated—them in India. In looking at varying accounts, giants were the tricksters of medieval times, occupying a position that was sometimes dangerous, often capricious, and occasionally even kindly or beneficent.

- **Gorgades**, hairy women who lived in the Gorgades Islands.

- **Gorillae**, hairy women first mentioned by Homer; they may have been a variation of the Gorgades.

- **Gray-eyed race**, who could see best at night.

- **Gymnosophisti**, who stood in fire and stared directly at the sun.

- **Hairy Men and Hairy Women**, who appeared throughout legends of Alexander the Great and Pliny the Elder. Known as river dwellers, they often hung around river fords and interfered with people trying to cross. The women had dog or boar teeth, and many of the men and women had six fingers.

- **Himantopodes** ("strap feet"), a race of the Far East, with elongated, star-like feet.

- **The Hippopodes**, who had a human body with horse's hooves for feet. The Hippopodes were found near the Baltic Sea.

- ◎ **Horned Men** (see Cornuti and Gegetones).
- ◎ **Icthiophagi** ("fish eaters"), lived on or next to rivers and ate fish exclusively.
- ◎ **Macrobii** (see Pandae).
- ◎ **Maritimi** (also called Maritime Ethiopians), who had exceptionally keen sight and were gifted bowmen. They're often shown in texts as having an additional set of eyes directly above their natural ones, and are usually shown holding bows and arrows.
- ◎ **Monocrus** ("one leg"), a variant of the Sciopods.
- ◎ **Monoculi** ("one eye"), a variant of the Cyclops.
- ◎ **Pandae**, a race living in the Indian Mountains. The Pandae bore children only once during their lives. The children were born with white or grey hair that darkened to black as they aged. The Pandae had enormous, elbow-length ears. They were often described as having eight fingers and eight toes.

- ◎ **Panotii** ("all ears" or "everywhere ears"), shy people with enormous ears—often reaching to their feet and large enough to wrap around themselves like a cloak, or even to allow flight.
- ◎ **Pygmies**, who may have been the first monstrous race of record. Mentioned by Homer and Herototus, they were usually dark skinned and had long hair, which they braided to form clothing. They averaged 1 1/2–2 cubits tall and herded proportionately sized cattle. In the later Middles Ages, they were often confused with dwarves.

Some of the monstrous races.

- **Raw Meat Eaters**, a handsome people who lived on a diet of raw meat and honey.

- **Redfooted Men**, who lived near the Brixton Rover (a tributary of the Nile). A variation of giants, they were said to be 24 feet tall, with 12-foot-long thighs. Their markings were striking, with white arms, black ears, red feet, a round head, and a long nose.

- **Sciopods** (var. Sciapods, Skiopodes; literally "shadow foot"), who had a single gigantic foot—big enough to serve as an umbrella when held overhead. A variation had two oversized feet on a single leg. All Sciopods were fast hoppers.

The Musteros, Pigmei, and Sciopedi.

- **Sciritae**, men with flat faces and no noses. They were Northern dwellers and tended to be of small stature.

- **Shining-Eyed Men**, who were normal in appearance, with the exception of brightly gleaming eyes.

- **Speechless Men**, Ethiopian men who did not speak but communicated by gesturing.

- **Straw Drinkers**, another Ethiopian race that was similar to the Astomi. They had no nose or mouth, and breathed, ate, and drank through a single orifice (and often with the aid of a straw).

- **Troglodytes** ("hole creepers" or "hole dweller"), who lived in Ethiopian desert caves and were mute. They were extremely fast runners and good hunters.

- **Wife-Givers**, who shared wives with travelers that stopped among them.

- **Wildmen and Wildwomen**, who were covered with hair or fur and lived in wild, remote areas.

- **Wodwoses** (var: Woodwose, Wodwos, Wodewose, Wudewasa, and ancient Anglo-Saxon Wudu), called "the spirit of the woods," were variations of Wildmen seen in pre-Christian Gaul. Covered with hair, they had long, coarse manes that trailed along they ground as they walked. Although Wodwoses did not speak in human languages, they could understand them. The Wodwose was also suggested as a variation between civilized humans and the chaotic spirits of the untamed woodlands, such as satyrs, the god Pan, incubi, and fauns. Wodwoses appeared frequently in medieval art and particularly in manuscript illustrations and illuminations. In modern terms, Wildmen, Wildwomen, and Wodwoses may have represented early versions of Sasquatch and the Yeti.

4

The Details

In pondering gargoyle symbolism, it's important to consider cultural- and time-specific details. When used in any kind of art, wings, horns, beaks, and grimaces meant different things to different cultures, and even within a given culture, symbols could mean something entirely different when examined in different time periods.

Singles vs. Multiples

Gargoyles rarely appeared alone. Once architects saw how effectively a gargoyle could divert water, they figured if one gargoyle was good, a dozen would be even better. Using several gargoyles to drain a single location divided the flow of water, and because water damage was related to both volume and speed of flow, anything that could reduce both was of great value. Thus, most gargoyles were arranged in lines or groups; only rarely was a single gargoyle found working alone. Sometimes the gargoyles stood in a quasi-military line along a roof edge; other times they were clustered in groupings, looking similar to an aerial community set in stone.

A row of gargoyles at the Notre Dame Cathedral.

None of the gargoyles from the Middle Ages are known to have been identical—each was a unique artistic creation. Even when a group of gargoyles were carved and posed together, each was original, a testimony to the creativity of the stonemasons of the time.

Torso vs. Full Form

Gargoyles may depict only the subject's head, torso, and upper limbs, or may feature the entire body. Gargoyles are often posed so that they appear to be sitting, crawling, or clinging to the building. This dynamic involvement between sculpture and structure adds to the gargoyle's energy and dynamism, and makes the creatures seem much more real.

Italy's doccioni and gigantii—enormous standing humans—are unusual gargoyle forms. Not only are they full-length, standing sculptures, but each one features two creatures (one animal and one human); the water exits through something that the gargoyles are carrying or holding: either another animal or a vessel of some kind.

In bicorporate gargoyles, either zoomorphic or anthropomorphic, two bodies grow from one head.

Nudity and Gender

Many anthropomorphic gargoyles are nude, or nearly nude. This is interesting because nudity was rarely depicted in medieval art, except when necessary for accuracy, as in a crucifixion scene. In the Christian Middle Ages, nudity referenced the fall of Adam and Eve and was a symbol of shame and loss of godly virtue. Thus, many anthropomorphic medieval gargoyles were usually garbed in clothing, jewelry, hats, or armor.

Regardless of the type of gargoyle, virtually all are gender-neutral, that is, sexual organs are usually not depicted and most gargoyles are neither clearly male nor female. This surprised my oldest daughter, who, at age six, stated her feelings by saying if there was such thing as gar-goyles, there should also be gar-boys!

Depictions of sexual interest or activity were uncommon in medieval gargoyles and grotesques. Yet, considering the starchy attitudes of medieval Christianity, sexual references popped up with surprising frequency. Sexually explicit gargoyles were usually tucked well off the beaten path, where few people would have seen them. A few gargoyles depicted women as being held or embraced by monsters or monstrous animals, but without clear sexual intent. However, if a serpent, frog, goat, or monkey was depicted in a gargoyle sculpture with a woman, it is almost certain that sex was being referenced.

In the eyes of medieval clergy, women were regarded as less holy and less perfect than men and were more easily tempted by debauchery. Church teachings were critical of women and established narrow roles within which women could function safely. The depiction of women in questionably sexual attitudes in gargoyle sculpture probably reflects these ambivalent feelings.

Other Details

In anthropomorphic gargoyles, the sculptures were invariably of adults; only rarely did gargoyles feature children or infants. In zoomorphic gargoyles, juvenile and adult animals were usually not distinguished.

Some humanoid gargoyles had bestial characteristics, such as excessive hairiness. A few had animal extremities, tails, hairy palms (a medieval sign for laziness), or were shown transforming into animals. A few anthropomorphic gargoyles had horns, usually indicating demonic transformation. These depictions echoed the animal nature of humans, the soul battle waged throughout medieval times by the church, and the visible outcome of sin. Animal-like qualities were also associated with demonic or monstrous transformation, as in lycanthropy (werewolfism, with the human transforming into a wolf or, rarely, another feral creature), or vampirism (with the human becoming a blood sucking creature of the night). Such transformative gargoyles probably intimidated onlookers by suggesting what might happen to them if they, too, transgressed.

Close Cousins on the Gargoyle Family Tree

Within the gargoyle bestiary, a myriad of other stylized carvings exists, each a close family relative.

Carved Heads

Carved heads are found on structures all over the word, particularly on fountains and on the ramparts of buildings. Carved head imagery may come from the Celts. Known for being fearsome warriors, they frequently cut the heads off their victims and posted the heads on their entry gates, a gory practice later replaced with replica heads carved from stone or wood. Carved heads can be fully dimensional but are usually carved in low relief, similar to portrait style. Most of the medieval carved heads were ornamented with feathers, foliage, or something even scarier, such as the snake hair of the gorgon Medusa. When they incorporated foliage, the heads were thought to reference the intersection of Christianity with the old Pagan religions, as seen in the Green Man.

The Green Man is arguably the most famous carved head motif (see Chapter 14). Some carvings were decorated with rings of stone around their necks, reminiscent of Celtic torcs or neck rings. Others bore flaring nostrils, pointed ears, or tufts of forehead hair, evidence of allegiance to Silenus, an aged woodland deity. Silenus was usually depicted in art as old and having ears like those of a horse.

A Green Man interpretation.

Carved heads on or over doors often bore brass or bronze doorknockers in their mouths. When used in fountains, water might spew from the mouth of the carved head. Other heads incorporated celestial imagery, featuring a sun or moon in addition to the carved face.

Roundels

A roundel is a distinctive, mostly round logo or marking contained within its own circular frame or border. In a roundel, a three-dimensional carving is created, but in such a way as to almost appear as if it is a two-dimensional piece of art. Roundels were often used to frame carved heads, particularly those of the Green Man.

Hagodays

Another kind of carved head was the Hagoday, a head carved in the shape of a human, animal, or in some cases, the sun, with a large knocker or "closing ring" held in the creature's mouth. In medieval times, churches operated under their own laws, often independently of the law of the land, and a lawbreaker in the regular world could seek asylum or sanctuary within the walls of a medieval church. All they had to do was make it to the church walls and clutch the Hagoday's closing

A Hagoday.

ring; once they had done this, they were safe and granted sanctuary under tenets of canonical (church) law. Hagodays were thus also called "sanctuary knockers," and were sometimes cast in bronze.[1]

Janus Heads

A bicephalic or tricephalic carved head—a head with two or three conjoined faces, each looking in a different direction—is sometimes called a Janus head. In Roman mythology, the god Janus was an ancient Italian deity, guardian of doorways and gates, and protector of the state in time of war. Mythology says that the doors to Janus' own temples were kept open in time of war and closed in times of peace. Because someone, somewhere, was at war throughout most of the Middle Ages, the temple doors rarely closed.

The number 3 was sacred to the Celts, and to give an image three faces or heads was to imbue it with power and vision. With its multiple faces and

A Janus head, looking at the past, present, and future.

views, the tricephalic Janus head was able to see into the past, present, and future simultaneously; alternatively, it was able to see what was in front and behind at the same time. This multi-directional gaze, which symbolized vigilance and new beginnings, was what made Janus the guardian of the Gregorian New Year, giving his name to the first month of the year, January. Janus' idealized vigilance reminded people to continually be aware of what surrounded them, and of the peril that resulted when they lost sight of what was happening around them.

Bicephalic Janus heads were sometimes portrayed with one female and one male face, echoing the monstrous Androgynii. Janus' name also led to the descriptor of being "Janus-faced," a label for someone who was two-faced, hypocritical, or deceitful. In the moralistic symbolism of medieval art, the Janus head also reminded humans of their dualistic nature, and of the never-ending battle between forces of good and evil.

Janus heads are often crowned, and are elaborately carved. They are common in the United Kingdom, where they are found on or above the doorway of homes and temples, as well as on fountains, misericords, and roof elements.

Tongue-Pullers and Mouth-Pullers

In tongue-puller sculptures, the subjects are shown with their tongues protruding or with their hands stretching their mouths wide open, respectively. Nondescript images with protruding tongues may reflect heretical or blasphemous behavior—Satan is often shown with tongue sticking out—or they may simply be trying to look rude, or intimidating. One of the world's most famous gargoyles—the gent who sits atop the Cathedral of Notre Dame—

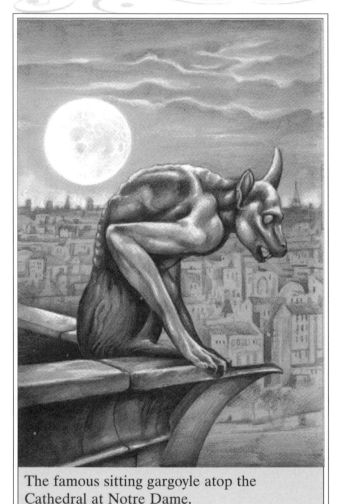

The famous sitting gargoyle atop the Cathedral at Notre Dame.

is a tongue-puller; he also makes frequent appearances in local French advertisements, which may explain why he's sticking his tongue out!

Mouth-pullers may reference the sin of gluttony, via the person trying to stretch his mouth to admit as much food as possible. Sometimes said to represent Christ's torment during the crucifixion, mouth-pullers may reference a fear of giants, or of being consumed by monsters or devils. Mouth-pullers are also seen as sexualized, with the exaggerated mouth and lips representing the female genitalia à la the Sheila-na-gig. A more simple view links them to English customs, where face-pulling competitions were common among country folk. In Japan's popular *Ringu* film series, the victims are found dead, with grotesquely stretched mouths.

Sheila-na-gigs

In the Sheila-na-gig (var. Sheelagh-na-Gig), a clearly female carving, the subject uses her hands to hold open and expose her vagina. "Sheilas" were commonly placed over the doors to churches, perhaps as a reminder to those entering to leave their worldly or base selves at the door before walking into the holy place. The most ancient Sheilas show evidence of having been repeatedly rubbed or caressed over the years, and anthropologists believe that women would rub the carvings as a charm to increase fertility or allow conception, a reference to Goddess-centered worship. The Sheila-na-gig is related to the mouth-puller in that both have sexual connotations.

Ireland has more Sheila-na-gigs than any other country, but the sculptures are also found elsewhere, including guarding many of India's temples. Still, for a woman today to be called a "Sheila" is to suggest that she is highly sexual and of questionable morals.

Hunkypunks

The classic Sheila-na-gig.

"Hunkypunk" is a local (British) term for grotesque carvings found on the sides of buildings, especially churches. The actual origin of the term is unknown, but local definition says that a hunkypunk is an architectural feature with no obvious purpose—something that today might be called an architectural "doodad" or, on Victorian buildings, "gingerbread." Hunkypunks had no obvious function and were purely decorative. In some areas, hunkypunks were short squatting figures, similar to the Sheila-na-gig.

Roof Bosses and Corbels

Grotesques and carved heads also appeared on interior roof bosses—carved projections of stone or wood placed at the intersections of ribs in vaults—and on corbels, projections that jutted out from the wall to support the structures above it. The word corbel comes from the Latin *corvus,* (raven), and is perhaps named because of the way that a corbel resembles a crow's beak.

Roof bosses and corbels were almost always located in out-of-the-way locations, allowing the sculptor more freedom in creating the works, which would not be seen by the church's clergy or parishioners. These small carvings may have represented the artist's signature, much as a painter signs the painting in one corner. A similar tradition is seen in the habits of today's American patternmakers, a modern engineering and tradecraft with artisan roots;

patternmakers often seal a noisemaking "rattler" within the core of a finished pattern. The rattler is the patternmaker's signature and a little joke, in that it makes noises and befuddles foundry workers, while not affecting the pattern's function.

Corbels and roof bosses are among the less visible parts of a building, and those unseen areas became an artistic forum for unsavory, marginalized subjects. In medieval times, corbel sculpture often featured satiric or mocking depictions of people frowned on by the church, such as bondsmen, prostitutes, beggars, and so on. Relegation to these remote locations might have been punishment for people who had sinned or who had worked against the church; in their commemoration on bosses and corbels, those imaged were forced, literally, to support the church.

Column Figures

Column figures consisted of heads carved directly into columns. In some instances, the entire head was featured and in others, only the eyes and a portion of the face could be seen from peepholes in the column. The practice may reference the sanctuary of Acropolis Roquepertuse in France, where niches in the square columns are filled with actual human skulls. In other instances of column figures, the heads were located at the bottom of the columns, as if providing a supporting foundation.

Memento Mori

Memento mori, literally "memories of death," were sculptures made of the skull, upper limbs, and/or torso of persons who died in the Middle Ages, particularly those who died of the Black Death. In a time when a person could literally be well in the morning and dead by suppertime, death was a subject of fear and fascination, and these obsessions continued into the creation of *memento mori*. The sculptures also reflected the medieval fascination with the severed head as an emblem of power.

The Dance of Death, a thematic folk painting in which a spectral figure of Death is shown leading dancers to their own graves, was a common theme in medieval art and probably related to the *memento mori*.[2]

Misericords

Between 1200-1300 C.E., an increase in decorative sculpture and woodworking made grotesques increasingly popular. One of their most interesting expressions was in misericords, small ledge-like projections placed inside choir stalls to provide support to the clergy and choir members, who had to stand through long services. The word comes from the Latin roots for "pity" and "heart," no doubt a reference to the misericord's compassionate function. Small corbels supported the misericords, with the entire apparatus folding flat against the stall when not in use.

Misericords were often decorated with miniature grotesques and carved heads. Their subjects tended to be secular—folk images, animals, mythology, and ribald scenes were common—rather than sacred, an interesting find in that most misericords were located within churches and used specifically by church members and clergy. The mundane carvings may have reflected the misericord's simple, mundane purpose, providing rest and relief to ease fatigue.

Illustrated and Illuminated Manuscripts

Although not technically a kind of gargoyle or grotesque, illustrated and illuminated manuscripts of the Middle Ages contained the same themes and motifs shown in gargoyles and grotesques of the same era. In an illuminated manuscript, colorful ornamentation was added (for example, decorated initials, borders, or highly detailed drawings). Some images were even "animated,"

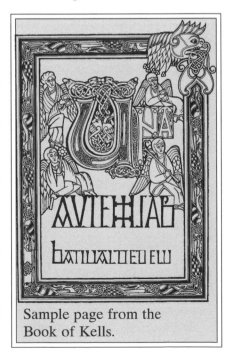

via drawings of tiny monks laboriously pulling lines of inadvertently omitted script toward their insertion points in the text.

Motifs used in illumination were taken from heraldry or religious symbolism. Probably the most famous illuminated manuscript was *The Books of Kells*, a religious manuscript dating to 800 C.E. and currently residing in the Trinity College Library in Dublin, Ireland.

When creating an illuminated manuscript, the text was usually written first. Sheets of vellum (animal hides specially prepared for writing) were cut to size, the page was ruled with a pointed stick, and the scribe then worked with an ink pot and either a sharpened quill feather

Sample page from the Book of Kells.

or a reed pen. Manuscript illumination was a complex and costly process, and thus was usually reserved for special books, especially religious texts. The wealthy often had richly illuminated "Books of Hours" made, holding prayers for various times of the day. Green Men and other types of two-dimensional carved heads made frequent appearances in ancient manuscripts, including the *Book of Kells* and the *Lindisfarne Gospels*.

Try This

1. Imagine you were helping to build a cathedral. Visualize and design your own carved head, roundel, Hagoday, or roof boss sculpture.
2. Look up an image of *The Books of Kells* online. Use pen and paper to practice the techniques that you see in the image. Later on, you may want to use these techniques to decorate a journal.

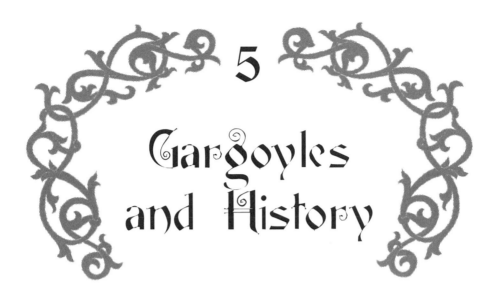

5

Gargoyles and History

In the Middle Ages, men had no great thought which they did not write down in stone.

—Victor Hugo

Who made the first gargoyle? No one really knows, but simple or primitive gargoyles can be traced back at least 4,000 years to ancient Egypt, Rome, and Greece, where terra-cotta waterspouts depicting lions, eagles, and mythological creatures (such as griffins) were common additions to buildings.

But who had the first idea? That question will probably never be answered, but it is likely that someone once noticed rainwater coursing down one side of a roof and flowing over a sculpture, or perhaps changing direction to follow a piece of roof edging that stuck out a little bit. Maybe the water was channeled or directed by the protruding piece, so that it flowed away from the roof in a certain way, or shot out a couple of feet from the building before hitting the ground. In any case, the proverbial light bulb probably flickered on, as it did with Sir Isaac Newton when the apple of the legend fell on his head, leading to thoughts of gravity and physics. It would have been a small step for our innocent passerby to envision the gargoyle as something of useful function, and then to decide that it might as well be decorative, too. What we know as "the gargoyle" came to life as a sculptural form in the medieval period, a time preceded by ages of stone, iron, and bronze, of natives and conquerors, of farmers and fiefdoms and flourishing civilizations. Understanding how these threads of history weave themselves together will help our understanding of the gargoyle's world.

Upper Paleolithic: 40,000–10,000 B.C.E.

Also known as the Old Stone Age (or Ice Age) this period began around 40,000 B.C.E. Human life was sparse and subsistence-based. People lived in caves or built simple dwellings, moving from place to place in accordance with the weather and seasonal hunting and gathering. The lifespan was short, mortality was high, and life was exceedingly difficult.

Neolithic period: 8500–3000 B.C.E.

Literally, "New" (*neo*) and "Stone Age" (*lithic*), the most striking development of this period was the development of farming. This represented a huge step forward, as people who could raise animals and crops no longer had to continually move from place to place to keep ahead of the weather or available food supplies. Neolithic people had an advanced, elegant culture, as typified by highly developed art and exquisite, complex buildings and archaeoastronomical monuments. One of the best examples is the building of Ireland's magnificent Newgrange passage tomb in 3200 B.C.E. The earliest gargoyles were also created during this time.

Bronze Age: 3000–1500 B.C.E.

Sometimes called "The Golden Age," the Bronze Age began in the Near East and southeastern Europe in the late fourth and early third millennium B.C.E. During the Bronze Age, weapons and tools were made of bronze rather than stone, the first European civilizations appeared, and urban life began in China. The day was officially divided into 24 hours, standard weights enjoyed wide, common use in commerce, the Egyptian people perfected

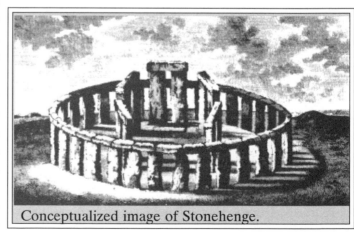

Conceptualized image of Stonehenge.

hieroglyphic script and erected their great pyramids (c. 2500 B.C.E.), and Stonehenge was built in Britain (c. 2800 B.C.E.).

The earliest Bronze Age cities began around 3500 b.c.e. in Mesopotamia, in the so-called "fertile crescent" between the Tigris and Euphrates Rivers. Around this same time, civilizations flourished in ancient Egypt (3500–2000 B.C.E.), as well as around the Mediterranean and throughout western Asia.

The Millennia	
3999–3000 B.C.E.	Fourth millennium B.C.E.
2999–2000 B.C.E.	Third millennium B.C.E.
1999–1000 B.C.E.	Second millennium B.C.E.
999–0 B.C.E.	First millennium B.C.E.
1–1000 C.E.	First millennium C.E.
1001–2000 C.E.	Second millennium C.E.
2001–3000 C.E.	Third (current) millennium C.E.

Iron Age: 1000–1 B.C.E.

Sometimes called the "Classical Era," the Iron Age first appeared north of the Alps and then spread south into Europe. During the Iron Age, weapons and tools came to be made of iron. Ancient Greece flourished during this time, taking shape as a series of "city-states," each controlling the lands within their boundaries; the most powerful city-states were Athens and Sparta. A democratic vote drove city decisions, but only free male citizens voted—no women or slaves were allowed. Known for their beautiful architecture—the Parthenon, for example—the ancient Greeks worshipped a pantheon of gods and goddesses who were believed to live atop Mt. Olympus in northern Greece.

The Roman Empire: 27 B.C.E.–476 C.E.

The Holy Roman Empire, established by Augustus in 27 B.C.E., was later divided by Theodosius in 395 C.E. into the Western (Latin) and Eastern (Greek) Empires. In 410, the Visigoths sacked Rome, and the last emperor of the Western Empire, Romulus Augustus, was ousted in 476, creating what is known as "the fall of the Roman empire." The Eastern Roman Empire, whose capital was Constantinople, lasted until 1453 and then was overrun in an event known historically as "the fall of Constantinople."

Some historians also reference an "Age of Steel" as beginning during this Roman-Christian era around 50 C.E., just as the Roman Empire was taking shape. The Age of Steel persists today, although arguably giving way to an era of plastic and silicon. During the time of the Roman Empire, paper was invented and concrete was perfected as a building medium.

Who were...	
Anglo-Saxons?	Germanic inhabitants of England, from their arrival in the 5th century until their fall during the Battle of Hastings in 1066 C.E.
the Celts?	A branch of the Indo-European family, including Irish, Scot, Gaelic, Welsh, Breton, Manx, Cornish, and several pre-Roman peoples, such as the Gaulish.
the Franks?	A group of west Germanic tribes that entered the late Roman Empire from Germany and the Southern Netherlands and settled in northern Gaul.
the Gauls?	People of an ancient region in Europe that corresponds to modern France, Belgium, the southern Netherlands, southwestern Germany, and northern Italy.
the Goths?	A Germanic people that invaded the Roman Empire from the east between the 3rd and 5th centuries.
the Normans?	People of mixed Frankish and Scandinavian origin who settled in Normandy from about 912 C.E. and became a dominant military power in western Europe and the Mediterranean in the 11th century; in particular, any of the Normans who conquered England in 1066 or their descendants.

Who were...	
the Ostrogoths?	The eastern division of the Goths, who founded a kingdom in Italy.
the Romans?	Citizens of the ancient (Italian) Roman empire.
the Vikings?	Scandinavian seafaring pirates and traders who raided and settled in many parts of northwestern Europe in the Dark Ages.
the Visigoths?	The western division of the Goths, who founded a kingdom in Spain.

The Middle Ages: 500–1500 C.E.

The Middle Ages, also known as the medieval era, is the period of European history that began with the fall of the Roman Empire and ended with the fall of Constantinople (see previous chart). The Middle Ages were characterized by the emergence of separate kingdoms, the growth of cities and trade, the rising power of monarchies, and the flourishing of the Christian (Catholic) church in Europe. It was a time of intense superstition, with nearly constant war and chaotic upheaval. During the early Middle Ages, Vikings plundered and explored Europe and the British Isles. The Germanic inhabitants of England, beginning with their arrival in the 5th century and ending with their fall during the Norman Conquest, were known as the Anglo-Saxons. In 1066, William of Normandy conquered England in the Battle of Hastings.

The earlier part of the Middle Ages is sometimes called the Early Middle Ages or the Dark Ages, while the latter part of the period (1100–1453 C.E.) is often called the High or Late Middle Ages. During the High Middle Ages, the quill pen was developed, eyeglasses were invented, and Oxford University founded. Cathedrals sprung up all over Europe, Gothic architecture appeared, and modern gargoyles reached the height of expression. Cities grew rapidly, decimated by the occasional plague.

The Renaissance: 1300–1500 C.E.

The Renaissance was the period that began slightly before the end of the Middle Ages and concluded around the time of the Protestant reformation.

The word "renaissance" means "rebirth," and the period marked a rejuvenation and flourishing of art, science, and classical learning in Europe. Even today, to say someone is a "renaissance man" (or woman) implies their skill in the classic disciplines of art, poetry, astronomy, philosophy, and foreign languages. The growth of interest in classical models within art and scholarship in Italy in the 15th century is seen as marking the full transition into the Renaissance period and the end of the Middle Ages.

Protestant Reformation: 1500–1600 C.E.

The Protestant Reformation was a 16th century movement aimed at reforming the Catholic Church in Western Europe. Prior to the reformation, the Catholic Church issued indulgences, that is, it allowed people to perform acts of prayer, study, or penance (or sometimes to give money to the church) as a way of paying for their sins, and hopefully speeding their path to heaven. Martin Luther started the Reformation in 1517 when he created his *95 Theses* and nailed them to the door of the Castle Church in Wittenberg. The practice of nailing notices to the door was standard in the local university community, and it got people's attention; in addition, Martin Luther also mailed his *95 Theses* to local religious authorities. The end result was the division and reformation of the Catholic church, and the establishment of several new Protestant religious institutions, notably the Lutheran and Anglican churches. The Anglican church would become the official "Church of England."

During the period of the reformation, the Tudor Age began in Britain, the wristwatch was invented in Germany, Michelangelo finished painting in the Sistine Chapel, and Copernicus defied the Catholic church to prove that Earth orbited the Sun.

The Age of Reason and Enlightenment: 1600–1700 C.E.

The Age of Enlightenment marked a philosophical movement in 18th-century Europe, while the Age of Reason included the 17th and 18th centuries. Both refer to a historical period advocating the use of reason, and supporting each person's ability to make their own reasonable, ethical decisions, independent of church doctrine. The period saw leaps in science, mathematics, astronomy, liberalism, and the arts, and inspired the American and French Revolutions.

A Brief History of Gargoyles

Now, back to our stony friends. We've already noted that simple, primitive gargoyles were found in ancient Egypt, Rome, and Greece. One of the earliest known members of the gargoyle family was a lion mask found in the Acropolis at Athens. The Egyptians and Etruscans used stone waterspouts shaped similar to animals. Gargoyle waterspouts were also found at the ruins of Pompeii, which had been buried by the eruption of Mt. Vesuvius in 79 C.E.

The first grotesque figures probably came from Egypt and were based on Egyptian deities, which combined the heads of animals with the bodies of humans. Two of the best examples of this are the cat-headed goddess Bast and the jackal-headed Anubis. And of course, one of the most famous (and gigantic!) of Egyptian chimera sculptures is the Great Sphinx, 240 feet (73 meters) long and almost 70 feet tall.

A spouting gargyole from Notre Dame.

After seeing the Great Sphinx, the Greeks began to incorporate grotesques into their own stone sculptures and gutter work. Statues of guardian animals, known as *acroterium*, were often placed on the roof corners over temples or special buildings. The griffin was a common motif for *acroterium*; the tradition springs from Greek mythology, where griffins guarded Scythian gold from the Arimaspians, a race of Cyclops who loved nothing better than to plunder gold and treasure.

Before gargoyles were developed, rainwater simply ran down the rooftops and poured directly onto the streets. The first modern gargoyles appeared around the beginning of the 12th century, and during the High Middle Ages era of Gothic architecture, gargoyles became the standard method of roof drainage. Some of the best-known early gargoyles were those of France's Laon Cathedral, with the famed gargoyles of Paris's Cathedral of Notre Dame following soon after. Gargoyle sculpture reached its peak in the Late Middle Ages, then declined with the introduction of lead drainpipes and downspouts in the 16th century. But even when gargoyles were *de rigeur*, not every waterspout was a carved gargoyle. Quite a few plain drainage pipes and troughs were used, especially in places where they couldn't be easily seen. Conversely, many of the most architecturally striking gargoyles were placed so high on their structures that people of those times would have been unable to see them.

Try This

What happens to the rainwater that hits the roof of your home? Find out how the drainage system works—gutters, downspouts, sewer, drain field, and so on. Where does the water go next? Would it be feasible to install a gargoyle on your roof? Why or why not? Can you find any craftspeople near your home who work in stone or metal gargoyles?

6
Life in the Middle Ages

e've learned that Gargoyles, both in terms of functional application and use as an art form, reached their height of creation and expression in the Middle Ages. But what were the Middle Ages like? Described as a bridge between ancient and modern cultures, the Middle Ages saw the development of a rich European civilization, born of Roman, Celtic, Slav, Germanic, and Norse cultures in a time when the old Pagan traditions were giving way to Christianity, and when warlike kings ruled the land. To better understand the nature of gargoyles and the people who created them, let's take a bit of a detour, stepping back several centuries to explore life in medieval times.

People of the Middle Ages

The medieval era was popularly known as "The Age of Faith," and this tells a lot about what the people thought and how they lived their lives during those times. Above all, medieval people were religious, with a powerful belief in God and the afterlife, and churches and cathedrals were the outward manifestations of their beliefs. Every citizen was expected to contribute toward the creation and beautification of religious buildings, whether through donations of money, goods, or labor. In exchange, people believed that these "good works" would function as indulgences, helping them gain entrance into Heaven.

In addition to their financial support, dutiful Christians were expected to go to church and confession regularly, study their bibles, visit the sick, give money to the poor, make pilgrimages, fast periodically, and honor religious holidays. Evil was both an abstract thought and a concrete reality; the idea of going to Hell was palpable for people in the Middle Ages, and the specter of a fiery, tormented eternity was motive enough to keep them working tirelessly for the church and giving money to fund new buildings.

Life in Medieval Towns and Villages

Medieval life focused on the church. Small towns formed when peasant houses sprung up close to their local Lord, and churches were built within the resulting towns and villages. Cities and larger towns took shape around castles, and a cathedral was quickly added, usually on the highest, most visible point. Where a church was the seat of ordinary clergy, a cathedral was the seat of the local bishop. Cathedral building became a kind of medieval one-upmanship, with each town wanting their cathedral to be the tallest and most spectacular around.

For ordinary people, homes were small wattle and daub dwellings, with beaten earth floors, thatched roofs, and several generations sharing a single cottage. The women of the house cooked meals over a fire circle placed right on the central floor, with some of the smoke escaping through a roof vent. Villagers worked to support their local Lord's land and farms, but also maintained their own gardens and feed animals. Meals were simple pottages of lentils and vegetables, supplemented by bread, herbs, and meat from feed animals—all wild game belonged to the Lord. Wind and water powered textile and grain mills.

The earliest castles were built for wars, housing the local King, Duke, or Lord, and their knights and troops. Early castles were simple wooden affairs, set on a hill and surrounded with fenced walls. Later castles became small villages in their own right, built of stone and surrounded by thick stone "curtain" walls, sometimes by water-filled moats. Kings and nobles built vast households of servants and workers to support the castle's interests. Noblewomen managed the castle's affairs, while the men were off protecting the realm. Food was quite similar to that eaten by the peasants, but there was more of it and more meat on the table. Ale, usually watered down, was the chief drink for all, whether young or old, rich or poor.

Medieval cities were always built near water, allowing ships to move goods from one city to another. In the later Middle Ages, cities and towns were fortified by strong stone walls; the film *Chocolat* features an excellent example of a walled medieval town. Cities were crowded, dirty, and disease-ridden, with trades people, craftsmen, and businessmen plying their wares via on-street businesses. Most city families lived in a single room, and sanitation was mediocre at best. Plagues were a constant threat.

Who Ruled the Land?

While Kings ruled the land in medieval times, the church was almost equally powerful, and disagreements between the King and the reigning pope were frequent and fierce. In an attempt to create a Christian church-state, a joint medieval entity was created combining the *sacerdotium*—a hierarchy of church jobs and positions, held by church officials and clergy—and the *imperium*—a companion group of secular leaders. The process never worked well. The sacred and secular leaders competed with each other and argued incessantly; eventually, each went their separate way. The end result? Not only did the medieval church engage in protracted battles with the forces of Paganism, but also within its own ranks.

While clergy led the earthly church, a canon of saints led the heavenly branch. The saints' main virtue in medieval Europe was their fund-raising ability. "Holy relics," such as bones, hair, or pieces of saints' clothing were thought to have magickal healing powers, and were sold for large sums of money, all of which went to fund church projects and construction. Through these practices, some saints became medieval cult figures. The creation of saints may have been the church's way of emulating the idea of polytheism and thus pacifying the Pagans, who were used to a pantheon of gods. Each saint was said to have certain qualities and to be the patron for certain humans, animals, and places. The resemblance to the old Pagan gods was meant to reassure, while simultaneously gathering the locals together under one roof and asking them to revere and worship a single Christian god. In the 9th century, the church began a golden age of saint-making, not only canonizing those who were truly qualified, but sometimes creating fictional life stories that made saints out of imaginary heroes. A number of the best-known Pagan deities, including Diana, Artemis, and Aphrodite, were also canonized.

While the churches themselves may have been beautiful, they were anything but comfortable to their parishioners. Churches had no pews—the people stood throughout the often hours-long services. On the other hand, the spacious, open interior of churches and cathedrals provided sanctuary for people and their animals during times of war and siege. The church doors would open, and people would drive in their chickens, cows, and pigs.

Knights were the soldiers, and defenders, of the land. Aristocratic boys were sent away from home at around age seven or eight to be fostered as pages (serving boys) in a noble household. Pages were introduced to the knightly arts; if they did well, they become squires in their early teens, sent into the field to serve their Lord and undergo additional training. After a few years, they could be knighted, after which they began a lifetime of service to the realm. Being a knight was far from a romantic job: a large number died in action, while others were sent to foreign lands on quests and crusades, many never seeing their families again.

School

During the Middle Ages, education was designed to prepare children to take up their adult roles or occupations. For girls at all levels of society, this meant preparing to become a wife, raise children, and run a household. For boys, it might mean learning to farm, entering a trade or apprenticeship, or, for young aristocrats, either being fostered and trained for knight service or entering a formal monastic school.

School curriculums followed the Roman model of the Seven Liberal Arts. These were divided into the *Trivium*—grammar, rhetoric, and logic—and the *Quadrivium*—arithmetic, geometry, astronomy, and music. The *Trivium* had to be mastered and completed before the *Quadrivium* could be started. Pupils wrote with styluses on wax tablets, and later, after the quill was invented, used parchment, quill, and ink.

Public schools and universities gradually replaced monastic and nunnery schools. Students in the public institutions studied a common curriculum that mirrored the *Trivium* and *Quadrivium* through the study of philosophy, grammar, linguistics, logic, mathematics, music, and astronomy. Schools devoted to the study of law and medicine also sprung up around this time.

The Calendar

The calendar was in a state of confusion throughout much of the Middle Ages and well into the 16th century, with disagreement about when each new year began and how each year should be structured. Two completely separate calendars existed in the Middle Ages: the liturgical calendar of the Christian (Roman) church, and the pre-Christian, agricultural, and seasonal-based calendar of the people. The Roman civil year began on January 1, but even those who followed this calendar couldn't agree on the model. Many believed that the time of the Christian Passion and Resurrection should properly mark the start of the New Year, but adherence was sporadic. In Venice, March 1 the beginning of the New Year. In Pisa, the year began from the date of the Annunciation, presumed to be March 25 preceding 1 B.C.E., while in Florence, years of the Incarnation were dated from March 25 preceding 2 B.C.E. Still, other sources place the beginning of the church's new year at Christmas. In pre-medieval Pagan Scotland and Britain, the seasonal New Year commenced on Samhain, a holiday spanning October 31 and November 1.

Gies and Gies noted the following in their book, *Life in a Medieval City*: "In a treatise on medieval timekeeping[1] Reginald L. Poole imagines a traveler setting out from Venice on March 1, 1245, the first day of the Venetian year; finding himself in 1244 when he reached Florence; and after a short stay going on to Pisa, where he would enter the year 1246. Continuing westward, he would return to 1245 when he entered Provence, and upon arriving in France before Easter (April 16) he would once again be in 1244."

To make things even weirder, the Julian calendar was used in England between the 11th and 16th centuries, organized either by historical year or, from the Norman conquest, by regnal year (that is, according to the dates of reign of the current monarch). As the Middle Ages progressed, the confusion deepened when the church attempted to Christianize (and absorb) the existing canon of seasonal and Pagan holidays.

It's easy to see why people gave up trying to track the year, and instead simply followed the month or season, or trusted the church to let them know of the next feast or Saint's day in advance!

Timekeeping

Henry de Vick invented the first mechanical clock in 1360, but clocks were large, expensive, and unavailable to most people. The wristwatch wasn't invented until the late 1700s. Seasonal changes, animal migrations, and heavenly movements helped track larger spans of time, while people kept daily time with sundials, hourglasses, metered candles, and clepsydras. Similar to the sandglass (hourglass), the clepsydra was a timepiece in which water dripped slowly through a small aperture and drove a mechanized timekeeper. Clepsydras were the medieval ancestors of modern clocks.

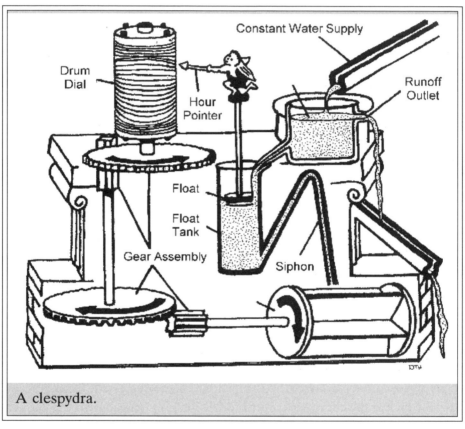

A clespydra.

In addition to actual time-keeping problems, documents were rare; most people in the Middle Ages couldn't read or write, and the printing press had not yet been invented. Medieval scholars, especially monks, kept detailed and dated chronicles; but the local rulers often demanded changes in those documents, restructuring history to look as they wanted it to. Poets, minstrels, and bards functioned similar to griots, composing poems and songs that captured famous events and heroic acts.

Just for Fun

While it may have been tough to live during the Middle Ages, the people had fun, too. Fairs, festivals, and carnivals popped up throughout the year. On holy days, members of the local craft guilds and mummers danced and put on mystery plays in the streets, with musicians adding to the festivities. Towns held sports competitions, horse races, and wrestling matches. Taverns sponsored chess tournaments and card games, local knights hosted elaborate tournament games, and carnivals and menageries added magick to the daily routine.

It is into this milieu that the gargoyles made their appearance, their presence perhaps a play on medieval life itself, and on the overarching presence of the church.

Try This

Today, a small number of environmentally aware folks build dwellings of "cob," a modern variation of wattle and daub. Do some research on cob building. Recreate the process to create a small structure, such as a small table, bench, or plant stand in your garden.

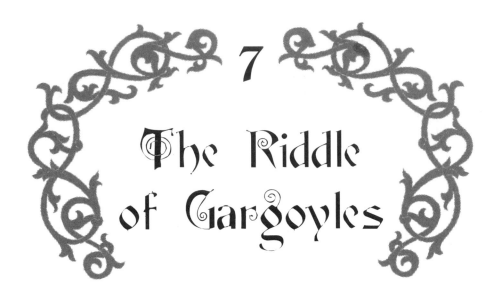

7

The Riddle
of Gargoyles

Ever watching,
Never seeing;
Always commanding
Without decreeing;
It works in the dark,
But rests in the sun;
It swallows all,
But digests none.
A riddle! You say—but not at all:
It's the gargoyle on the church's wall.

—*The Riddle of the Watcher*
by Elizabeth Barrette

The idea of gutters and drainpipes providing structural protection is nothing new—these functions were carried out by wood, ceramic, terra-cotta, and even metal downspouts in antiquity. It is the ornamental nature of gargoyles that is striking. After all, a simple drainpipe would have served the same function as an ornately carved gargoyle. Why, then, were gargoyles so carefully made? What purpose did they serve? Why did people labor to create them?

Unfortunately for us, nothing exists to provide a definitive answer to this question. History suggests a number of possible explanations, but in the end there are only the gargoyles themselves, and the constant repetition of their themes and forms throughout the Gothic period. Medieval art was full of ambiguity and layers of meaning, particularly in religious symbolism. What appeared obvious to an onlooker might have nothing at all to do with the meanings attached by the original designer. But whatever the purposes of gargoyle design, it is certain that their decision was intentional. Stone carving in the Middle Ages was too time consuming and too expensive to have been haphazard, coincidental, or merely decorative, and every image created in those times was created out of reason and for a specific purpose.

Architectural Function

Although gargoyles have a long list of hypothetical duties, the architectural function is the only one that is absolutely clear: By protruding from the building's rooflines and parapets and directing water off of the lead roofs and away from the building's foundation, gargoyles kept water off of the masonry mortar and prevented their buildings from disintegrating. A fully functioning gargoyle with an unimpeded channel could gargle out several gallons of water per second during a rainstorm. (Best not be standing underneath one when that happens!) Some medieval gargoyles have been outfitted in recent times with lead pipes that protrude from their mouths, allowing the stream of water to be spat even farther from the building, and, via Bernoulli's principle, with more force.

We know that grotesques had no architectural function—they were purely ornamental. The popularity of grotesques declined after 1350, though they were still created in the 1400s, particularly as woodcarvings. But what about the non-functional aspects of gargoyles? Before we go further, let's note that gargoyles came with an assumption of permanence. They were made of stone, after all. In the pre-printing press era, when most of the public was illiterate and little was written down, words were the main way of tracking public thought and, as we know, words are fraught with not only misunderstanding and disinfection, but are also short-lived. But stone? When a medieval stonemason installed a gargoyle or grotesque, he intended it to endure, an unchangeable message set in rock. Let's consider some of the possible meanings of those messages.

Vision of the Christian God's Power

By studying gargoyles, we learn about the medieval church and society. In the Middle Ages, the Christian God was in charge of the universe, and the placement of gargoyles on the outsides of churches and cathedrals, with contrasting scenes of the Bible and statues of Jesus, Mary, and the Saints on the inside, was thought to represent the Christian God's power as well as the struggle between good and evil. By making gargoyles part of the Godly world, and maintaining control over their allegedly dangerous attributes, God was once again standing at the helm.

Francis Bligh Bond, an English architectural historian, had an interesting take on the location of grotesques and gargoyles sited on or within the church. He suggested that they were a symbol of the church's ability to overtake evil, change it to good, and put it into service for the benefit of the church.[1] Mounting gargoyles on the church's exterior also became a testament to the power of the Christian church: The gargoyles obviously served the church, but only through the grace of the church were they allowed to do so, while also being spared eternal damnation.

Gargoyles may also have been a reminder to Christians of the evils that always lurked in the shadows, ready to overpower good and cast the unfortunate perpetrators into sin, a Hellish state depicted in paintings and carvings of fire and torment. Yet another popular interpretation suggested that gargoyles were souls of the eternally condemned. Intercepted on the way to Hell, they were turned to stone, forbidden to enter the church, and doomed to lurk on the roof edges where they might remind others of the price of sin. A similar explanation was that gargoyles represented actual sins or manifestations of chaos that had been turned to stone. Whatever the details, the sculptures seemed designed to, literally, scare the Hell out of their beholders!

A few gargoyles may have sprung from the pages of the Bible. The following passage, Psalm XXII, is used to support this possibility:

> *Many bulls encompass me, strong bulls of Bashan surround me; they open wide their mouths at me like a ravening and roaring lion. I am poured out like water ... my heart is become like wax, it is melted in the midst of my bowels.*[2]

Insurance Through a State of Grace

During the Middle Ages, the church was central to, and, in fact, controlled, people's lives. The concept of a fiery, literal Armageddon was omnipresent, and people worked hard to try and insure a place in Heaven. For the wealthy, this meant donating gold—and lots of it. For those who couldn't afford that kind of tithe, the next best offering was one of personal creativity, whether helping build, furnish, or adorn the church. However, working on a church or cathedral was a special honor not accorded to all; such work implied a state of grace and goodness, and was only available to skilled craftsman who were in a state of grace. These craftsmen designed and sculpted the church's gargoyles and grotesques, and because all acts of creation were thought to express the glory of God, gargoyles were venerated as being godly.

Religious Instruction

In the Middle Ages, most people could not read and write, and churches relied on visual images to teach scriptures and biblical stories. These images included paintings, frescos, stained glass, statuary, and gargoyles, which could be "read" and understood by an illiterate population. The church became its own stony sermon. Much of this art, most commissioned by patrons, was created within strict guidelines to fulfill its purpose.

Another common teaching medium was the *Biblia Pauperum*, literally the "Bible of the Poor." Appearing in the Late Middle Ages, these picture Bibles used large graphic images and brief bits of text to teach bible history and lessons. In some instances, the figures in the images spoke the words that appeared on scrolls above their heads, placing the *Biblia* among the progenitors of today's modern graphic novels and comic strips. Most of the *Biblia Pauperum* were printed on vellum, but woodcut versions eventually appeared. In an odd twist of irony, the *Biblia* were quite expensive—definitely out of reach of the illiterate poor people for whom they were intended. However, much in the same way that the bestiaries were sources of animal information, the *Biblia* provided models for adding biblical images to churches and cathedrals. Many of the stained glass windows and carvings of the Mid- and Late Middle Ages, including gargoyles and grotesques, appear to have their origins in illuminated Bibles such as these.

Francois Villon, a French writer in the late 1400s, offered the following poem:

I am a woman old, poor, and ignorant,
who has never learned to read.
In my parish church I see
a painted Paradise with harps and lutes
and a Hell where the damned are boiled:
one frightens me-the other gives me joy and happiness.
Let me have that joy, high Goddess,
to whom all sinners in the end must come,
filled with faith, without idleness or pretense.
In this faith I wish to live and die. [3]

Veneration of Pre-Christian Symbols

Gargoyles may be symbols, intentional or otherwise, of two important pieces of pre-Christian symbology. First, the cult of sacred springs and wells: By virtue of the water flowing through them and issuing from their mouths, gargoyles may have referenced ancient water symbolism. And second, the cult of the severed human or animal head, which the gargoyle certainly evoked! (See Chapter 14 for additional details on both cults.)

Artistic Function

Placement of gargoyles on the outside of a building created intentional contrast with the beauty inside the building, particularly in churches and cathedrals. The coarse, often ugly appearance of gargoyles may also have been a reminder of the superficiality of beauty. Surely you've heard the expression, "Beauty is only stone deep."

There remains the question, though, of why so many gargoyles were exquisitely detailed and ornate, even though they were often placed high on a building where most people could not see them. One possible explanation can be found in the old axiom, "art for art's sake." Another, perhaps more likely theory is, because the building and its art were dedicated to God, putting the art high above the ground put it closer to God, where it might venerate and be appreciated by Him. The same was true of stained glass, another art form that reached its peak during the Gothic architectural period; a number of stained glass windows were placed high in cathedral towers and turrets, and the colors and detailing of these were every bit as exquisite as those at street level. These works of art were almost certainly offerings to the Christian God, dedicated to his watchful eye in hopes of courting heavenly favors. No matter how much time, expense, or sweat was involved, nothing was too much for the medieval glorification and praise of God.

Vestiges of Paganism

Gargoyles may have represented the last remnants of Paganism at a time when the old ways were usurped by the Christian churches. By incorporating familiar Pagan images, such as Celtic gods, the Green Man, and bicephalic heads within churches and cathedrals, church officials encouraged the populace to intermingle the two spiritual traditions in their mind, supposedly easing their acceptance of the new religion and smoothing the transition from the old ways to the new. We can see this in Pope Gregory's instructions to St. Augustine, regarding the conversion of the Pagans to Christianity:

> *Destroy the idol. Purify the temples with holy water. Set relics there, and let them become temples of the true God. The people will have no need to change their place of concourse, and, where of old they were wont to sacrifice cattle to demons, thither let them continue to resort on the day of the saint to where the Church is dedicated, and slay their beasts, no longer as a sacrifice but for social meal in honor of Him whom they now worship.*

In these ways, Pope Gregory led the integration of pre-Christian and Pagan practices and symbols into the Christian church, and enticed the heathens into accepting Christianity.

Protection

The idea of giving protective function to physical items threads throughout the history of art and architecture. Sometimes called "horrific antefixes," these include totemic pieces, guardian statues, the dragon prows of Viking longboats, the figureheads of sailing ships, crown jewels, masks, and even heraldry. Likewise, gargoyles may have provided personal protection to people, homes, and public structures in the Middle Ages, at a time when God was at hand, but evil wasn't far away. Evil could also be invited in by choice—as shown in Adam and Eve's downfall—and by demonic temptation. Anything that helped ward off evil was a good thing, and because mid-air was believed to be the realm of demons, gargoyles were positioned high on the building walls, ready to leap and protect the passersby below.

Guardians of Churches and Buildings

In another kind of protective function, gargoyles might have been intended to intimidate and scare away demons and evildoers. Medieval people believed that keeping away evil spirits required something even more frightening, and if the gargoyles were hideous enough, it was thought they would be effective at scaring off threatening creatures. Thus, gargoyles were portrayed with their mouths frozen into horrible grimaces, or carved into perpetual screams. The idea of demons scaring off other demons, especially smaller demons of less consequence, was well within the belief system of medieval minds, that is, my demon can beat up your demon!

A common medieval belief said that gargoyles came alive at night, and offered their protection while people slept and were at their most vul-

The "Refuse to Listen" gargoyle, from the Washington National Cathedral.

nerable. Winged gargoyles were thought to be particularly helpful as they could fly about and protect the entire village as well as the focal church.

Defense Against Enemies

A large number of gargoyles are carved with mouths wide open and tongues protruding. The open mouth and show of teeth works as a threatening gesture, reminding people of their vulnerability by creating a monster that seems to say, "I am going to eat you!"

There may be a connection between gargoyles and the worship of the human head in the old Celtic religions, who staked severed heads around their encampments as an implied threat to enemies. Or perhaps the gargoyles were meant to confuse or perplex their potential enemies. An old adage says that the more complex the plumbing, the more difficult it will be for water to get through. Could the same be true for evil spirits and demons, confronted by a tangled warren of gargoyles and grotesques?

And while we're on the subject of plumbing, one tongue-in-cheek medieval suggestion said that relegating gargoyles to the drainpipes and gutters of the church labeled them as sinners and sentenced them to serve the literal bowels of the church they'd sinned against.

Humor

Medieval times are recognized as a difficult, dark time in which to live. Nonetheless, people in the Middle Ages possessed a sardonic, often mocking sense of humor. This was shown in their spirit of the carnival—festivals where the people donned elaborate costumes and took part in activities that were decidedly Otherworldly, poking fun at everything from authority to sexual activity to the Lords of the land to devils and even to death itself. This dark whimsy can be seen in the more fanciful gargoyles, which might appear as sweet-faced animals, humans in ribald or goofy situations, or even inspired caricatures of local clergy or political figures. A few gargoyles tended to the scatological, as seen in the occasional defecating sculpture. Could some gargoyles simply have been a source of popular entertainment? Whatever the explanation, these odd creatures still exist today, the sacred and the profane crouched side by side atop the roofs and parapets.

Human Interest and Fascination

Humans have long been fascinated by the strange, the obscure, the macabre, and the unknown. Who's to say that part of this same fascination didn't inspire the medieval stonemasons who created gargoyles? What better way to give life to ghost stories or nightmares than to embed them in stone and winch them up to perch high on a stone wall, where they might continue to enliven the imaginations of passersby?

Human fears

Gargoyles might have been the expression of peoples' subconscious fears, embodying a dimension of medieval society. People of the Middle Ages lived amidst chaos, and had little control over their own lives. Not only did God control their world, but lesser forces in the universe also had a hand in their lives, and gargoyles gave shape to a host of unspoken fears. The link between gargoyles and fear took an overt turn at the Cathedral of Saint John in Den Bosch, in the Netherlands, where a monstrous gargoyle appears to leap toward a group of people who cling to one of the flying buttresses, leaning back to avoid entanglement with the creature.

Gargoyles may have represented the suppressed fears and superstitions of medieval humans, providing a way to embody the terrifying in a way that was harmless. As time passed and life became more secure, gargoyles lost their fearsome appearances and became more comical and whimsical.

Magick

Although medieval humans were a devout group, and disinclined to practice magick, we could argue that gargoyles dripped with it. Their stony nature, lofty elevation, passionate expressions, and water-channeling pastimes evoked the Four Elements of Earth, Air, Fire, and Water, respectively. Their visage and demeanor, created with the gifted hands of the stonemason, imbued them with magical purpose, and possibly with qualities that allowed them to become charm, talisman, or even egregore, while also performing near constant warding actions. It's the old axiom… if a tree falls in the woods, and no one is there to hear it, does it make a sound? Well, of course it does! Sound happens, whether or not anyone is there to hear it. And it is almost certain that wherever gargoyles were placed atop walls or roofs or doors, magick happened, whether or not it was intended.

Medieval Architecture

In the shadows of tall buildings
of fallen angels on the ceilings
oily feathers in bronze and concrete
faded colors, pieces left incomplete.

—*Cathedrals*
Lyrics by *Jump Little Children*[1]

ay the word "gargoyle" and you work a neat little bit of magick, instantly invoking the world of Gothic architecture. Gargoyles and all things Gothic were as good as synonymous in medieval times. The term "Gothic" derived from the Goths, a Germanic tribe or group of invaders and conquerors. Thus, Gothic art was originally thought of as barbarian art. But the Gothic period, which took off in northern France in the 12th or 13th century and slowly spread throughout Europe, would one day be recognized as one of richest and more imaginative architectural styles in history.

Before we look at Gothic architecture, it's worth studying the styles that came before and after. They're all intertwined, and the journey will help us understand the gargoyle on yet another level.

Neolithic Architecture

Neolithic or "stone age" architecture includes the earliest known structures designed and built by humans. Neolithic builders used mud bricks, wattle, and daub to construct houses and villages. Many of the buildings were plastered and painted with scenes of humans and animals. The Neoliths also used stone to create elaborate stone tombs, particularly in Ireland, where thousands still exist. Their patience is proven by archaeoastronomical observatories such as Newgrange and Stonehenge, where decades of observation would have been necessary to track the alignments of heavenly bodies before beginning construction. Most stone construction was unmortared; the corbelled ceiling of the Newgrange passage tomb was so effectively engineered that the inner tomb remained dry for more than 5,000 years.

Ancient Egyptian Architecture

Wood was scarce in the Egyptian desert, and the two main building materials were unbaked mud brick (the building material of the people), and quarried stone—reserved for important structures, such as tombs, palaces, temples, and fortress walls.

Most of ancient Egypt's everyday town architecture was lost to Nile River floods. What remains are the great Egyptian monuments, such as the pyramids at Giza, the temple of Abu Simbel, and the Great Sphinx. Characterized by massive constructions, thick walls with few openings, geometric structures, columns and piers, and symbolic motifs, buildings were of post and lintel constructions, with flat roofs supported by the walls and columns. Hieroglyphs and pictorial carvings festooned both inner and outer walls.

Ancient Greek Architecture

Classic Greek architecture is exemplified by its public buildings and temples, such as the Parthenon, the Hephaesteum at Athens, and the sanctuaries at Agrigentum. Most buildings were rectangular and made from limestone or tufa, with marble used in decoration. Framed on two or more sides by rows of columns, the buildings were roofed with timber beams overlaid with terracotta tiles. A chubby triangular pediment at the end of each building provided a focus for sculpture and decoration. In temples, the altar space was usually open to the air, while other parts of the temple provided storage space for offerings left by worshippers.

Greeks understood the principles of the masonry arch but made little use of it, and they did not put domes on their buildings—these elaborations were left to the Romans.

Ancient Roman Architecture

The Romans modified classical Greek and Etruscan architecture to create their own unique architectural style. Roman buildings emphasized arches and domes, and used innovative materials such as brick, concrete, and brick-faced concrete. Stronger than stone, concrete was easily adapted to all kinds of uses and quickly became the Romans' primary building material. Extraordinary constructions followed, including elaborate buildings, bridges, roads, aqueducts, and public baths with intricate water systems. Even today, Romans are credited with not only perfecting the use of concrete but with creating a kind of durable concrete that has never been surpassed.

The mosaic was an important design contribution of the ancient Romans. Created of colorful stone chips set into cement, mosaics were popular additions to all surfaces of Roman buildings.

Romanesque Architecture

Romanesque (Norman) art and architecture borrowed features from Roman architecture. Romanesque architecture was around between 400-1200 C.E. and characterized by round or pointed arches, massive barrel vaults, and cruciform piers (a square or rectangular pillar) supporting the vaults. Vaulting was a new concept, and Romanesque buildings used thick walls to support the heavy vaults and roofs, as well as for insurance against weather and invading hordes. Narrow windows let in light without weakening the walls' weight-bearing abilities. Because of the small windows, Romanesque buildings were quite dark inside.

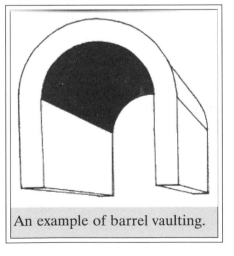
An example of barrel vaulting.

Decoration and ornamentation were felt to be very important in Romanesque buildings, and were often used as visual learning devices, allowing Bible stories and history to unfold before churchgoers. The earliest ornamentation was done with paintings; the first carved stones appeared in English churches around 900 C.E. Since Romanesque churches were so dark, detailed ornate artwork could not be easily appreciated; the larger scale of statues and carvings were much easier to see. Artwork of this period tended to be frightening, grotesque, or monstrous.

Gothic Architecture

Gothic architecture, present from 1100-1500 C.E., represented a huge structural leap over previous styles. The pointed arch and ribbed vault allowed builders to create high ceilings and tall spires that emphasized height. Thanks to the ribbed vaults and the use of external flying buttresses to support load-bearing walls the walls were thinner than those in Romanesque buildings and could feature large windows, allowing light to pour into the structure. The addition of spires, gabled roofs, slender columns, tall lancet windows, and a wealth of sculptural detail, including gargoyles, led to huge, gorgeous buildings that were full of light, ushering in a brilliant period of stained glass artistry. Stained glass would reach its peak of expression during the Gothic period, with the available window space creating an ideal canvas for the multicolored windows.

Besides stained glass, Gothic churches and cathedrals capitalized on the available light by decorating with statues, paintings, tapestries, and carvings. Artwork leaned toward grace and realism, although the frighten-

Chartres Cathedral; the insert shows how flying buttresses support the outer walls.

ing images from the Romanesque period remained as well. During this time, roof bosses developed as another locus for art and sculpture. Molded and carved arts on corbels and molding became common. A great deal of woodcarving was done during the Gothic period; unfortunately, most of it was lost during the Reformation. The overall effect of Gothic architecture was of huge, tall, spectacular buildings aimed at glorifying God. And it was an effect people loved; most of France's 93 cathedrals were constructed in the Middle Ages, and most were in the Gothic style.

The typical Gothic cathedral was and still is laid out via a cruciform floor plan, that is one that looks like a huge cross. The "foot" of the cross is the nave—the place where the congregation sits. The crosspiece or arms of the cross are known as the transept. The "head" of the cross is the apse, the most sacred part of the cathedral. The altar may be placed at the point where the nave, transept, and apse meet, or may be located within the apse. Gothic churches and cathedrals were usually sited so that the apse was in the east—in accordance with the rising sun—a practice that continues today.

Renaissance Architecture

On the heels of the Gothic period came the first hints of a new cultural movement that came to be known as the Renaissance, literally the "rebirth." Beginning in Italy, the movement spread quickly throughout Europe. So-named because it brought back certain elements of Classical Greek and Roman thought and culture, the Renaissance also revived Roman architecture, including its symmetry, proportions, and geometrical perfection. The period marked the official end of the Gothic movement and of the high period of gargoyles and grotesques. Classic examples of Renaissance architecture include St. Peter's Basilica in Rome and the Louvre in Paris.

The Evolution of Gargoyles

At the outset of the Gothic period, when the utility of gargoyles was first established, the sculptures tended to be coarse and crudely carved, and most were zoomorphic as well as short and stubby. Features were commonly exaggerated, and the appendages oddly proportioned.

Toward the end of the 13th century, the art and architecture of the Gothic period was clearly more refined and detailed than the Romanesque art of the

An example of
ribbed vaulting.

preceding era. However, the gargoyles continued to mimic the Roman interest in monstrous, frightening forms. Gargoyles had become more complex, and anthropomorphic figures had surpassed animals as subjects for gargoyle sculpture. Many of the sculptures had sternly religious connotations.

During the 13th and 14th centuries, gargoyles because increasingly exaggerated, with a tendency toward caricatures and a developing sense of satiric humor. Gargoyles also became longer, more slender, and more finely detailed. By the height of the 14th and 15th centuries, gargoyles had evolved into fully realized works of arts over which sculptors would labor for long periods, perfecting their work. The gargoyle's facial expressions became more expressive and less demonic during this period, and humorous creatures continued to surface, often showing exaggerated poses or expressions. In the late Gothic period, secular subjects were increasingly used as gargoyles and grotesques.

The use of gargoyles persisted into the 16th century in Europe, but fell from favor with the advent of lead drainpipes and closed drain systems. Nevertheless, limited numbers of gargoyles were still fashioned in the later Baroque, Art Nouveaux, and Art Deco periods.

9

The Stone Trades and Guilds

In the Early or Low Middle Ages, the church controlled the subject and content of art. During the Second Council of Nicaea in 787 C.E., the Decree of the Fathers stated, "The composition of religious imagery is not [to be] left to the initiative of the artists, but is formed upon principles laid down by the Catholic Church and [its] religious tradition."[1]

Such doctrines were slowly relaxed over the centuries, and much of what we know about medieval artisans and craftsmen comes to us from records and manuscripts kept by monks. For example, in the manuscript, *On Diverse Arts*, written by the monk Theophilus—a man skilled in the arts and crafts, particularly metalwork—we can study details of the forge and furnaces of metal workers, kilns used for creating stained glass, and the mixing of colors for painting. Another famous monkish text, the *Album* of Villars de Honnecourt, relates details of stone carving and architecture, as in his sketches of flying buttresses, vaulting, and supporting arch ribs.[2]

History suggests that Gothic stonemasons had a great deal of choice in selecting and depicting their gargoyle subjects. However, open expression of personal style and artistic innovation was not necessarily encouraged. As artisans working within a guild system, stonemasons were expected to posses certain skills and to be able to work within standard representative forms. Similarly, artists and designers were told what was required and how to depict it. Artisans worked from model books and often copied each other's work. Despite this, each medieval gargoyle was unique. The stonecarver might exaggerate certain details of a gargoyle to aid visibility, and often gave attention to illustrating its undersurface, as that might be the only portion visible from the ground.

Gargoyles inside of churches and cathedrals or in places of direct visibility were bound by stricter guidelines than those outdoors or in hard-to-see locations. The sculptor working on a small piece high up near the cathedral ceiling had "preventative obscurity," allowing him to exercise a degree of personal creativity that he couldn't have explored in an eye-level carving on the church's main floor. This was also true of the two-dimensional "sculptures" found in illustrated or illuminated manuscripts. The main content in the center of the page tended to adhere to traditional forms and guidelines; but once the illuminator moved into the liminal border surrounding the page, the usual restrictive rules were less evident.

The Medieval Workforce

In medieval times, societal and work roles were tightly controlled. Within a township, the main divisions of labor included politicians, financiers, businesspeople, merchants, professionals, everyday craftsmen, and town/artisan craftsmen. Politicians were citizens elected by the populace to run cities and large towns. Financiers coined money and ran the banks, while business people provided boarding houses, stables, markets, and other day-to-day needs. Merchants sold or traded goods produced by others; they were generally among the wealthiest people in town, particularly if engaged in trade outside of the city limits. Professionals included lawyers, physicians, alchemists, herbalists, and apothecaries.

The everyday craftsmen, such as potters, cobblers, smithies, farriers, butchers, and knife grinders, made simple, utilitarian objects, while town or artisan craftsmen—stained glass workers, carpenters, tapestry weavers, jewelers, glass blowers, and stonemasons—created works that were as much about aesthetics as function. The various crafts were organized into membership-only guilds, and the guilds not only held a monopoly on their products within their towns, but also kept tight control of trade and prices.

In the Early Middle Ages, it was the monks who had the necessary mathematics and engineering background with which to design and decorate new buildings. As the trade and artisan guilds took hold and flourished, these tasks moved into the hands of craftsmen.

Apprentices

Crafts endured because of the apprenticeship process. Boys were typically apprenticed to a master craftsman at around ages 10 to 12, and for most trades they served an apprenticeship of four to 12 years; apprentice periods of five to seven years were the most common. In general, the more complex the craft, the longer the apprenticeship lasted: A weaver's apprentice might finish in three or four years, while a goldsmith's apprentice might require 10 years or more. Apprenticeships were not available to girls; they were expected to learn how to run a household and prepare for marriage.

Apprentices led difficult lives. As much servants as they were students, apprentices could be forced to perform chores not only for their master but also for the master's wife. How well they were treated depended solely on their master, and boys prayed that their master would be a kind one. The requirement to attend school, usually part-time, further added to their workload.

Most apprentices were bound by five agreements. First, they signed a pledge of loyalty to their home guild. Second, by the conclusion of their apprentice period, they agreed to produce a "masterpiece," the specifics of which were mandated by the guild, that showed their mastery of the craft. Third, they had to prove that they had the resources needed to take up the craft independently; this might involve property, money, tools, or other means of preparation. Fourth, they swore to uphold the customs and traditions of the craft. Finally, the graduated apprentice had to pay a summative fee to their guild, upon which they became a full member of the guild's "corporation," with all of the rights thereof. Most apprentices, when finishing their training, sponsored a traditional celebration or feast for their fellow craftsmen.[3]

For the young man who entered an apprenticeship, the learning of a skilled trade and admission into a craft guild was a ticket to guaranteed success. Once his apprenticeship was finished, the young man earned the title of "journeyman"; he then took his skills and tools, left the place of his apprenticeship, and literally journeyed from town to town, studying with other master craftsmen and further expanding his knowledge. Given time and practice, the journeyman might qualify as a master craftsman (or master builder) and take on his own apprentices. Master guildsmen were widely traveled, and highly sought out for their unique skills.

There were alternate routes into the craft of masonry. While boys of upper social status might become apprentices, those of lower economic position might start in a direct labor position, such as quarry work. If the youth showed aptitude toward a certain skill, he might then become the servant or yeoman of a trained stonemason.

The Fraternity

For stonemasons, their guild was both a professional organization and a place of fraternal brotherhood. Guilds in medieval times had both public (commercial) and private (internal) functions. The guild's commercial arm managed its relationship with the community, its provision of goods and services, contracts formed with builders, and so on. The internal arm focused on the structure and conditions of apprenticeships, the qualifications for journeyman status, membership dues and privileges, and the obligations of members to the guild.[4]

All guilds were registered with the city as crafts and/or trades. In 1268 C.E., the city of Paris registered 120 crafts and trades. In 1292, the city's tax list had grown to 130 crafts and trades, including these:[5]

366 shoemakers	58 water carriers
214 furriers	56 wine sellers
199 maidservants	54 hatmakers
197 tailors	51 saddlers
151 barbers	51 chicken butchers
131 jewelers	45 purse makers
130 restaurateurs	43 laundresses
121 rag dealers	43 oil merchants
106 pastry cooks	42 meat butchers
104 stone masons	42 porters
95 carpenters	41 fish merchants
86 weavers	37 beer sellers
71 chandlers	36 buckle makers
70 mercers	36 plasterers
70 coopers	35 spice merchants
62 bakers	34 blacksmiths
58 scabbard makers	33 painters

29 physicians

28 roofers

27 locksmiths

26 bathers

26 ropemakers

24 copyists

24 harness makers

24 innkeepers

24 rugmakers

24 sculptors

24 tanners

23 bleachers

22 cutlers

22 hay merchants

21 glovemakers

21 (each) woodcarvers and woodsellers

From a commercial standpoint, guilds had a tremendous stake in their own survival. Through interactions with the public, they ensured that their members had access to the best jobs. Their members swore oaths of fealty, promising allegiance to the guild and its tenets—a promise to "guard the guild"—and also to their craft, for secrets of the process were closely guarded by master craftsmen of all kinds. Oaths were "sworn on the relics," literally, with hands held on or over the craftsman's tools.

The guild's masters elected a slate of officers, who swore additional oaths and promised an additional level of participation. Officers were in charge of overseeing what we would today call quality control. Every product created by the guild and every job completed by the guild was subject to rigorous standards of excellence. Guildsmen made frequent inspections of workers and their materials, both in the guild proper and on the various job sites, verifying that quality was consistent and that no shortcuts had been taken. In this way, the guild became an organization of power and respect, and ensured its own continuing future. The truth in this is seen in today's modern times, as many of the world's existing craftsman guilds are still connected by lineage to centuries-old progenitors.

Guilds also maintained tight control over their own internal processes. Each master was allowed to take on one or two apprentices at a time, agreeing to provide them with food, lodging, clothing, and medical care. Apprentices also received a stipend, which grew as the apprentice became more experienced. Masters had great freedom in choosing apprentices, and often selected relatives, keeping the crafts in the family. In addition to apprenticeships, guilds provided benevolent services to their members, sending gifts to honor weddings and baptisms, visiting members when ill, or providing food or financial support during times of need.

Similar to all guildsmen, journeyman stonemasons had a specific gesture to indicate their craft and rank, akin to having a secret handshake. When meeting one another, they would hold one hand to their throat, with the thumb and palm creating a right angle and making the *signe á l'ordre du compagnon,* literally, "the sign of the order of the companions," or in this case, "the sign of the order of journeymen."

In medieval France, there existed a society of artisans known as *les compagnons du tour de France.*[6] Each French *compagnon,* or journeyman, would make a "tour" around France, journeying from one master to another for one year. At the end of that time, he presented himself with a chef d'oeurve and demonstrated what he had learned. If his craftsmanship was deemed worthy, he was given the title of master craftsman in his field, and would then have been able to take apprentices and teach them. While on tour, compagnons learned trade secrets that they were not allowed to divulge. Not only did this lend an air of brotherhood and fraternity to the order, but it also ensured their job security, for by keeping their secrets, the guilds ensured that they were the only ones who could perform certain crafts, make certain designs, and so on.

The compagnons always signed their work as members of their order. This brings us back to the right angle symbolism, for the right-angle tool, or square, was used by stonemasons in their work and was also used in the rituals performed when the artisan was first accepted as a compagnon. The right-angle sign was given between guild members as a sign of greeting and as a symbolic guarantee that the person you were speaking with was "safe," that is, that the two of you could discuss trade secrets. These traditions remain active today.

Most of the trades and crafts had patron saints, for example, St. Catherine was the patron of wheelwrights and St. Eligius for smiths, metal workers, and craftsmen. The patron saint of masons, St. Blaise, is also a patron of throat and mouth diseases, and a few gargoyles holds their hands to their throats in a similar gesture. Is the link between Masonic gesture and throat-gargling gargoyles a mere coincidence? Or might this be another of the symbolic codes that wend through medieval art, a code that has multiple layers of textured meanings that we still know little about?

In medieval times, the term freemason was another word for stonemason, and probably referred to the trained mason who was free to travel from place to place, selecting his own work as he went. The term may have also referenced masons who were able to work in "freestone," a fine-grained sandstone or limestone rock that could be cut easily in any direction and was used for delicate ornamental details. Another possible point of origin for the term freemason comes from Irish custom, where a skilled craftsman "of unfree race" (that is, a slave or indentured servant) became a free man by virtue of his craft.[7] However, "freedom" was something of a nebulous term in the Middle Ages. Virtually everyone and everything—except, perhaps, the Church—was under the king's rule. If the king decided that a new church or cathedral must be built, everyone available was pressed into service. If the king was traveling the countryside and deigned to stop at a village overnight, all work stopped while the entire populace prepared for the visit. The penalty for refusing the king's orders was tantamount to committing treason, and could lead to imprisonment, or even death.

Fortunately, stonemasons were desperately needed and well-respected in Gothic times, and were able to select from a long list of job opportunities. Because of their status, local governments found it almost impossible to impose regulations on stonemasons in the same way that they regulated other guild members. Stonemasons were ringleaders in attempting to raise wages and improve working conditions, laying groundwork for future labor unions. Guilds decided who to admit for membership and who to reject, often making the standards for a guild worthy "masterpiece" so intricate and difficult that non-local applicants could not qualify. When a new piece was commissioned and completed, the mason paid a mandatory fee to the guild's "craft court," and also provided a celebratory banquet for existing members. Many of these fraternal requirements priced guild membership out of the range of possibility for new members.

Try This

Think about a hobby, craft, or skill that you're good at. Imagine now that you're the master, and must teach the skill to an apprentice. Design an imaginary apprenticeship. How many months or years of study will it take your apprentice to master the skill?

10

Building the Cathedral

Nothing doing in the workyard, for the moment I'm out of money.
—From the ledger of a 14th century cathedral project

The church stood squarely in the center of the medieval world, and in order to ensure their place in heaven, people plunged into church building—a process that could take decades, or even centuries. The wealthy contributed gold or sponsored artisan works, while the lower class helped with the heavy labor. Only skilled architects and craftsmen were allowed to work on the actual beautification of the cathedral, including the creation of gargoyles and grotesques.

Building the great churches and cathedrals in Europe was no small feat. Today, even with modern tools, vast cranes, and available technology, it can take decades to finish a large office building; in the middle ages, a cathedral's construction spanned generations. The Cathedral of St. John the Divine in New York City broke ground more than a century ago and still isn't complete.

In the Middle Ages, new buildings took form under the supervision of master builders: wooden structures were directed by a master carpenter, and stone buildings by a master mason. Few written building plans survive; most of those that do were written on parchment, which was so precious that it was repeatedly used and reused. Work always began with the laying of the cornerstone, a stone that formed the base of the most visible corner of the building, joining two walls. Cornerstones were often inscribed with names and dates.

The laying of the cornerstone came with much ceremony, and marked the official start of the construction process.

A rich mélange of workers helped create new structures. Animals, such as horses and oxen, moved the heaviest materials to the work site. Diggers leveled the ground, mixed and carried mortar (a substance composed of lime, water, and sand), carried stones to and from the masons' workshop lodges, and dug and set foundations. Lime-burners mixed slurries. Tool carriers moved tools from place to place, hod-bearers carried open troughs of bricks and other small building materials, and pulley-workers erected and operated the elaborate pulley systems, essential for moving materials upwards as the cathedral grew taller. In most constructions, a skeleton of heavy timbering was built first, and the vaulting finished around the frame.

Hewers milled logs into workable boards, while layers built foundations and wallers erected walls, finishing the interiors with a plaster surface. Marblers laid decorative features, paviors created floors, and artisans planned and executed decorations in paint, stone, tapestry, and sculpture.

Masons did their work in buildings called lodges, which were large, temporary structures erected on the work sites, and whenever a new church or cathedral was begun, a lodge was built alongside. Besides using the lodge as a workshop, masons ate and rested in their lodges during the day, retiring to separate accommodations by night. Lodges became a temporary outpost of the stonemason's guild. The local stonemason chapter drew up guidelines for lodge operation, and the senior-most master mason on site swore to adhere to the local regulations and to assume responsibility for the project, including monitoring progress and reporting problems or substandard work. Master masons and master carpenters served as foremen on all building projects.

Tools of the Trade

Stonemasons in Gothic times used more or less the same tools that they use today: wooden mallets, iron hammers, chisels, files, and calipers. Pneumatic hammers were introduced between 1885–1890, and replaced much of the work done with mallet and hammer. Carbide-tipped tools appeared in the mid-1900s, yielding a harder, longer-lasting tooling surface. Chisels, largely unchanged with time, fall into three groups: points for roughing out the stone, tooth chisels (claw tools) for shaping, contouring, and modeling, and flat chisels for fine finishing details. Within each chisel group come variations; for example, gouges and miter tools are all variations of the flat chisel. Stone workers dressed in heavy protective clothing and wore heavy leather gloves and a traditional apron of leather or chamois ("shammy").

Beginnings of the Gargoyle

Each gargoyle began with a clay or plaster model. Master stonemasons often used their apprentices or fellow carvers as models for carvings, which meant that gargoyles and grotesques picked up such unique human characteristics such as nosebleeds, warts, and missing teeth.

The stonecutter's tools.

Once the model was made, work began on a large stone block. First the general shape would be etched with pen or pencil and calipers. Calipers allowed the use of triangulation to enlarge or reduce a model image or to produce a mirror copy. The stone was roughed out, and the detail work done. Most details were cut large to allow viewing from a distance as people in the Middle Ages didn't have binoculars or telephoto lenses. Strong relief carving added shadow and contrast. As a final step, the stonecarver worked over the sculpture with a fine chisel, creating an abraded surface that helped the stone oxidize, cure, and harden, a process that could take a dozen or more years.

The stone carver.

Most medieval gargoyles were made of limestone. Red sandstone, which was soft, easy to carve, and took a cut well, was often used for indoor carvings, where it would not be quickly affected by the environment. Masons sometimes used marble for gargoyles, but it was denser and harder to work with than limestone. Stones were cut from quarries in huge blocks. Today, a typical quarried block weighs 15 to 20 tons before transfer to a stone mill, where diamond-edged saws cut it into smaller blocks.

A few gargoyles were made of metal, with lead and copper gargoyles popular from the 16th and 17th centuries onward. Although terra cotta gargoyles are reported from pre- and early medieval times, none survived. Because of its brittleness, brick was never used for gargoyles.

Because medieval schools were attached to churches and monasteries, it stands to reason that the Seven Arts, the *Trivium* and *Quadrivium*, found voice in the structure and decorations of churches. Most medieval people had little or no schooling, but subjects from history, the Heavens, music, and even the Bible were familiar to everyone, and could easily find their way onto the church walls in a way that made them accessible to all.

Similar to most statuary, gargoyles were almost always carved on the ground—either in the open or in the lodge—and then mounted on the walls at a specific point. The actual gargoyle sculpture represented only the leading end of a large stone block, most of which was concealed within the building's walls. The unseen part of the block acted as a counterbalance, stabilizing the entire structure and holding the showy, gargoyled end in position. The finished gargoyles, each weighing several hundred pounds, were winched into position; scaffolds were not used in the Middle Ages. Gargoyles were most often positioned on the cathedral's towers, but also appeared on the roof, walls, or façade.

Most medieval gargoyles were carved *en bloc*, that is, in a single piece of stone. A few were carved in halves, which were lifted into place and then assembled. Although sizes varied, most were carved from stone blocks measuring 4–5 feet long and 2–3 feet wide. Occasionally, gargoyles were carved in place, high on the building's walls; this usually happened if the walls had gone up before the gargoyle blocks were finished. Construction was time and labor intensive, and once the walls started to inch up, they waited for nothing (other than the king, perhaps). Sculptors provided last minute touch-ups to sculptures that were already in place. Builders positioned gargoyles so they projected forward and away from the building for several feet, allowing them to spew rainwater as far as possible from the building's walls. Some directed water to another tier of roofs below, which then fed the water into yet another set of gargoyles, and so forth.

While terra-cotta gargoyles appeared in antiquity, they weren't part of medieval gargoylery. A few have been made in modern times—notably on New York's Woolworth Building. Making a figure out of terra-cotta began with a model, which was used to make a plaster mold. Clay was pressed into the hardened plaster mold. Once the clay began to harden, the plaster was carefully peeled away, allowing the clay to dry. The piece was then treated with sealants and fired before being mounted on the building.

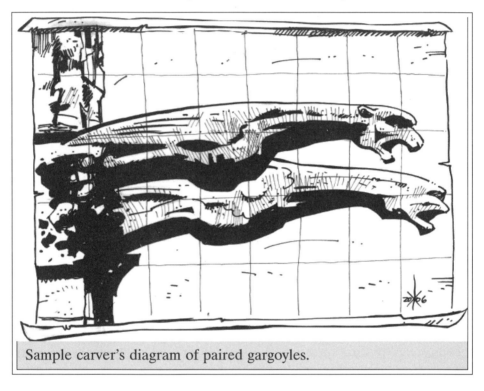

Sample carver's diagram of paired gargoyles.

In Medieval times, bright colors of paint-festooned statues and carvings in churches—bright red and green were favorites. Unfortunately, outdoor paint has a short lifespan under the best conditions, and in their exposed locations, gargoyles needed repainting every few years. It is no surprise that painted examples don't survive today. A few gargoyles were gilded (covered with a thin layer of gold leaf), in which case nearly as much money was spent on the gilding and painting as on the carving. This degree of artistic luxury suggests that gilded gargoyles were considered treasures. In later (and prudish) Victorian times, all traces of the "unseemly" paint and gilding were removed, returning the sculptures to bare stone.

Gargoyles in Peril

If gargoyles can be said to "work" for their buildings, their employment as water workers has always made erosion their chief occupational hazard. Because of their function and their exposed position, gargoyles are vulnerable to all kinds of erosion, decay, and damage. Rain gradually wears away stone and mortar. Acid rain, caused by airborne chemicals, dissolves the minerals in stone and concrete and speeds their disintegration. Limestone sculptures are especially vulnerable—even gargoyles carved within the past century are already showing damage from acid rain, which also discolors the stones. The open rain channels of older gargoyles fill in with dirt, leaves, and other airborne detritus over time, encouraging the growth of plants and moss and causing additional damage. Birds have found gargoyle troughs to make excellent nests. People add to the problems by tossing coins into accessible gargoyles, their wishes only speeding up the damage.

The advent of "progress" marked the death for knell for gargoyles. Cast iron was invented in the late 1700s and quickly replaced lead and stone as the drainage material of choice. Existing gargoyles kept right on spouting water alongside the brand new drainage systems, but unfortunately, no one really wanted water splattering down from above when the modern systems kept things neat and tidy. Many gargoyles were subsequently dismantled and taken down. Others were plugged with concrete; as the concrete froze and shrunk in the cold winters and heated and expanded in the hot summer sun, the gargoyles cracked and disintegrated.

The life expectancy of an exposed limestone gargoyle is around 100 years; after that time, weathering and erosion begin to make the stone "unreadable." A number of gargoyles that exist today have undergone repair, restoration, or refurbishing, many in 19th-century Victorian times. Caring for gargoyles is an act of love, for they require constant maintenance: by the time one is restored, its neighbor needs attention. Most of today's largest churches and cathedrals have resident stonemasons whose sole and constant responsibility is the monitoring and maintenance of the building's rocky denizens. England's Oxford University is home to one of today's busiest, most continuous gargoyle restoration efforts, with the resident gargoyles and grotesques constantly undergoing repair or replacement. Gargoyle recovery projects are in place all around the world, and stonemasons continue to create new gargoyles and grotesques for ornamental purposes, and for the pure love of doing it.

Try This

Experiment with the carving process. A bar of soap makes an easy starting medium—it is easy to shape and you can use the results in your bathtub, so cleanup is easy! You could also try paraffin, which can be found in your local grocery. Paraffin is extremely flammable, so melt it slowly over low heat in a double boiler. Color it by adding pieces of crayon to the melting wax. Once fully melted, pour into a clean, empty waxed milk carton and allow it to cool and harden. The next day, peel away the carton. Carve with plastic picnic knives or a small pocketknife. Add details with toothpicks.

If you enjoy carving, you may want to contact hobby or lapidary shops for soapstone—a soft rock that is easy for beginners to work with. You'll need actual carving tools for this, and be sure to wear eye protection. You could also try your hand at carving wood—most craft stores sell basswood for this purpose.

Go on a scavenger hunt in your home location. For one week, see how many gargoyles, grotesques, and miscellaneous carvings you can identify, classify, and date. (See Appendix B for the template.)

11

Modern Incarnations

Whether in medieval or modern times, people have always embraced gargoyles, seemingly fascinated with their eerie, arcane appearance. In return, gargoyles have surfaced in a good number of modern incarnations. Today it's easy to find gargoyles filling all sorts of new roles, including:

- Cartoon characters.
- Stained glass windows.
- Recurrent motifs in Internet fantasy literature.
- Garden statuary.
- Working downspouts.
- Statuary for shelf or computer.
- Jewelry.
- Incense holders.
- Dollhouse accessories.
- Bookends.
- Indoor fountains.
- Stuffed animals.
- T-shirts.
- Coin banks.
- And…of course…still working as gargoyles!

Gargoyles in Fiction

Gargoyles and their architectural homes haunted the corners of medieval and Victorian era writing. In Rabelais' *Gargantua and Panatagruel,* the rowdy giant Gargantua's antics include stealing the bells of Notre Dame cathedral to hang around his horse's neck. In contemporary fiction, gargoyles are usually depicted as winged humanoids with demonic features, including horns, tails, talons, and beaks. Gargoyles as a monstrous race have been featured in several works of fantasy fiction, such as Terry Pratchett's *Discworld* series. See also:

- *Geis of the Gargoyle*, by Piers Anthony
- *In the Shadow of the Gargoyle*, edited by Nancy Kilpatrick and Thomas S. Roche
- *Rats and Gargoyles*, by Mary Gentle
- *St. Patrick's Gargoyle*, by Katherine Kurtz
- *The Corpse Said No* (*A Gargoyle mystery*), by Barbara Frost

Gargoyles in Television

Gargoyles pop up when least expected, particularly in old horror films, but even in modern movies and television, including *Spider-Man: The New Animated Series, X-Files,* and *Tales from the Darkside: The Movie.* Following are a few of the gargoyle's better-known forays into television.

Gargoyles animated series

1994–1997, rated TV-Y7

Production Company: Walt Disney Feature Animation

Produced by Greg Weisman and Frank Paur

Time: 22 minutes (each episode)

The medieval Scottish castle of Wyvern is home to a band of gargoyles. Stone statues by day, they come alive at night, protecting the castle from hordes of invading Vikings. That is, until a traitor casts a spell that causes them to sleep in stone 24 hours a day. However, 1,000 years later, a rich magnate buys the castle and its gargoyles, moves it to New York, and reassembles it in a way that breaks the spell, causing the gargoyles to awaken in the 20th century.

The series is fun to watch, with first-rate animation that also spawned a set of paperback books. Much of the series is quite accurate, including the time period, the nature of the castle, and the gargoyles themselves, who take zoomorphic and chimeric forms. In an interesting side theme, the gargoyles at first have no names.

"How do you tell each other apart?" a human asks.

"We look different," responds a gargoyle.

"But what do you call each other?" the human asks again.

At this, the gargoyle looks puzzled. "Friend," he replies.

Gargoyles made for television movie

1972, not rated

Production Company: Tomorrow Entertainment, Inc.

Directed by Bill Norton

Time: 1 hour 14 minutes

Originally airing as a made-for-television movie of the week, the story features a researcher, Cornel Wilde, playing an anthropologist/demonologist who, with his adult daughter (Jennifer Salt), travels to the Arizona desert to investigate the discovery of an unusual skeleton. When the pair tries to remove the skeleton for study, they're pursued by a number of creatures—living gargoyles—who have taken up residence in nearby caves. What ensues is mostly a moral battle. The gargoyles are portrayed as creatures that want only to survive and be left alone; unfortunately, they have been hunted over the centuries by humans, who kill the gargoyles out of fear. Now the stakes are higher, for the gargoyles' 500-year old eggs are about to hatch. The gargoyles feel protective and the humans, as always, are operating under the, I'd-better-kill-you-before-you-kill-me line of thought. The film is an example of B movies at their peak. The effects, which look cheesy now (gargoyles in rubber suits?), won an Emmy for special effects in 1972. With much of the filming done in Carlsbad Caverns National Park in New Mexico, the movie is fun to watch, at least once.

Gargoyles in Film

Gargoyle: Wings of Darkness film

2004, rated R

Production Company: Lions Gate

Produced by Lisa Hansen and Neil Elman

Time: 1 hour, 37 minutes

A CIA operative (Michael Paré) and his partner venture into Bucharest, Romania to deal with an international kidnapping plot and end up dealing with an angry gargoyle. Rated R for gore, the film is reasonably campy, but entertaining. The special effects are decent and the setting—complete with actual castles and cathedrals—is stunning.

Gargoyles: Guardians of the Gate documentary

1995, not rated

Production Company: New River Media

Produced by Jonah Goldberg

Time: 52 minutes

This documentary investigates the history of medieval gargoyles. Several experts are featured, each sharing their opinion as to why gargoyles were created and their cultural significance. The film concludes in modern times, with an examination of modern stonecarvers, buildings, and their gargoyles. The greatest value of this documentary is the wonderful photography, which shows gargoyles from different heights, angles, and perspectives. Another excellent sequence introduces a modern stonecarver, who talks about his work in restoring old gargoyles and creating new ones.

The Harry Potter series

While the films aren't specifically about gargoyles, Hogwarts Castle—the center of Harry Potter's world—is home to functioning gargoyles. Watch the exterior scenes in *Harry Potter and the Goblet of Fire*,[1] and see how many you can catch!

The Hunchback of Notre Dame

Victor Hugo wrote the famous novel, *The Hunchback of Notre Dame,* in 1831 at age 27. The story's hero, Quasimodo, was a deformed bell-ringer who both lived in and haunted the Cathedral of Notre Dame, gargoyle-style. In 1923, the story was made into a silent film. Filmed on site and costing $1.25 million to produce—more than 20 times the average film budget at the time—the project drew attention to the Cathedral of Notre Dame and eventually led to a major restoration project. Ironically, restoration isn't always kind to old art and architecture, especially in times past, and much of Notre Dame's original art and gargoyle sculpture were lost during the "improvements."

Decades later, Disney's WDFA created an animated adaptation of *The Hunchback of Notre Dame* that featured dancing gargoyle sidekicks.

Notre Dame: Witness to History documentary

1996, not rated

Production Company: New River Media

Produced by Jonah Goldberg

Time: 56 minutes

This documentary focuses on the Notre Dame Cathedral in Paris. It includes information about gargoyles and medieval art and architecture, but it does an even better job at illuminating the history of the times. If you want to know the politics and uprisings of medieval France (and Europe), this little film does a brilliant job. Note: This film is packaged with *Gargoyles: Guardians of the Gate* as a DVD "extra."

The Stone Carvers: Master Craftsmen of Washington National Cathedral documentary

1985, not rated

Production Company: PBS Video

Produced by Paul Wagner and Marjorie Hunt

Time: 29 minutes

A portrait of the Italian American artisans who carved the gargoyles and statues of the Washington Cathedral, particularly emphasizing their occupational lore and traditions. Academy Award winner for Best Short Documentary.

Washington National Cathedral documentary

1984, not rated

Production Company: PBS Video

Produced by Marjorie Hunt

Time: 60 minutes

The story of the creation of the Washington National Cathedral, and its art and architecture.

Gargoyles in Card and Role-Playing Games

The card game *Magic: the Gathering,* features several gargoyle-themed cards, including the Abbey, Darksteel, Granite, Ivory, Kjeldoran, Leering, Nullstone, Opal, and Wakestone Gargoyles, each with their own magickal attributes and powers. The *Dungeons & Dragons* fantasy role-playing game features gargoyles as chaotic, evil creatures, usually portrayed as winged humanoids with tails and horns. "Sandstone" and "Marble" Gargoyle cards also appear in the *Harry Potter Trading Card Game.*

Gargoyles in Gaming

By Anna Fox

Apart from the numerous computer and board games based on the popular Disney series, gargoyles have been featured in many role-playing (RPGs) and computer games. The bulk of this discussion will focus on graphic rather than text-based games, although numerous text-based RPGs exist both online and in book form.

Computer games, especially of the fantasy and adventure genre, are populated with mythical creatures and characters. Every type of creature from every culture features in one game or another, and gargoyles are no exception.

Sometimes their presence is subtle: They may be depicted as part of the scenery, either traditionally on buildings or more creatively as part of the décor, such as the Gargoyle Traps used in *Diablo.* In some games, your character or creatures may be turned to stone for a time by an opponent, and although we don't call these stone statues gargoyles, we can see the myth in the background.

More often, their presence is obvious, such the Stone and Obsidian Gargoyles that can be recruited into your armies in *Heroes of Might and Magic,* being able to use a gargoyle as your main character (that is, you *are* a gargoyle while you play a game, such as in the Disney games based on the popular *Gargoyles* animated series), or having to defeat a gargoyle (or an entire horde of them) as part of your quest.

In the popular online adventure game *World of Warcraft* (known to fans as WoW), a Stoneskine Gargoyle is one of the more powerful monsters you can battle, because of his incredible ability to regenerate. Other WoW monsters include the Rockwing Gargoyle and Putrid Gargoyle.

A few games provide a totally different take on gargoyles. In the *Ultima* series of games, gargoyles were an older and wiser race of creatures than humans, who once inhabited a parallel world, the destruction of which caused their migration to the human world, called Britannia. There were two races of gargoyles winged, who were the wise rulers of their society, and wingless, who were mentally and physically inferior to the winged gargoyles, but were cared for in their egalitarian society. Having settled in Britannia, however, they became subjects of prejudice and oppression.

An example of a text-based online RPG that puts a different spin on gargoyles is *BatMUD*. The gargoyles in this game were created as slaves by mages and later inhabited by pieces of a demon spirit, thus freeing many from slavery. However, some chose to remain as guardians to humans. *BatMUD* is free to play—see the Resources for information.

Of course no mention of RPGs would be complete without a word on the well-known *Dungeons and Dragons* series, where stone gargoyles tend to live in caves or old castle ruins, and they can be indistinguishable from stone until they ambush and devour adventurers.

Try This

Use whatever creative process you prefer to design your own gargoyle or grotesque. Consider drawing, painting, sculpture, carving, collage, fabric, and so on. You might even make something functional, such as a kite. Or, if writing is your forte, create a story or poem.

12
Gargoyles Today

The Gothic sun set behind the colossal press at Mainz.

—Victor Hugo

By the 15th century, the Gothic era was coming to a close, and the heyday of Gothic art, architecture, and gargoyles was fading into the sunset. The reason?

The printing press.

Even before the printing press, medieval Europe was increasingly bookish. The Paris tax tables of 1292 show eight bookstores, 17 bookbinders, 13 illuminators, and 24 copyists open for business. By 1325, these numbers had quadrupled. During the same time period, the library of the French Sorbonne—the seat of the faculties of science and literature of the University of Paris and a scholarly hub—grew from 1,000 volumes to nearly 1,700.[1]

Movable type (allowing the arrangement of individual letters or characters to form words) was invented in China between 1041 and 1048. The use of movable type to mass-produce printed works—the printing press—had several potential inventors, but is generally credited to Johannes Gutenberg in 1440s Germany. By 1500, at least 40 printing presses were operating in western Europe, granting a new kind of communication that would bring education to the masses, speed communication, and force the Church to find a new way to interact with increasingly literate parishioners who were now learning to think for themselves. Rather than being a precious commodity available to only the wealthiest Europeans, books, newspapers, magazines, broadsides, and other forms of the printed word were now available to everyone.

With the invention of the printing press, history could finally be preserved in a concrete, enduring form. In conjunction with the cultural blossoming inspired by the Renaissance, the printing press ushered in a new way of thinking, and helped pave the way for Europe's Age of Enlightenment. These changes also signaled the beginning of the end of the Gothic period, and the end of gargoyles.

Looking at Gargoyles of the Past

Even today, it is reasonably easy to find original gargoyles clinging to the roofs and walls of churches and cathedrals. A few also survive on castles and other secular buildings, but this is less common, as everyday people in medieval times couldn't afford the extravagance of ornate guttering systems.

Many of today's "medieval" gargoyles have actually been replaced or restored, and this isn't always a good thing, as the underlying structure or meaning of the stone may end up as something quite different than what the medieval creators intended. When looking at "medieval" gargoyles today, it can be almost impossible to tell which are original and which have been recut or replaced. Because few records endure from the Middle Ages, the origin of most gargoyles and grotesques are unknown. Even the names of those who carved many of our gargoyles have already been lost.

To make things even trickier, the dating of extant gargoyles is complicated by a host of factors, most notably erosion and decay. Most medieval gargoyles and grotesques were made of limestone; exposed to the elements and to airborne acid, most have deteriorated. In addition, many gargoyles did not survive the Protestant Reformation in Europe, a time in which the Church's heavy-handed approach destroyed anything considered to be a focus of Pagan worship, including a great deal of art and stonework. Many of the surviving sculptures were destroyed during the two World Wars. Finally, a large number of stonecarvers, whose memories were living catalogs of medieval sculpture, died in the mid-14th century when the Black Death (bubonic plague) killed more than half of London's residents and a large number of people living throughout Europe. Not only were the stone artisans themselves lost, but so was their encyclopedic memory of European gargoyle sculpture.

Finding Gargoyles Today

How can today's gargoyle-hunters tell if the replacements are identical to the originals? How can one determine whether repairs have been made with techniques and methods faithful to those of medieval stonecarvers? How do modern stonemasons really even know what the original looked like, let alone the intent of the original craftsman?

Finding un-bowdlerized gargoyles is difficult. Identifying the type of stone may be useful; most medieval gargoyles were carved out of limestone or marble, while modern replacements are made of regional limestone or granite. Thus, granite sculptures are likely to be recent creations, as are carvings with sharp, fresh edges, looking as if they were wheeled out of the mason's lodge a week earlier. Conversely, an extremely weathered sculpture, especially if softened into little more than a stony "blob," is likely to be original. Finally, original gargoyles tend to function independently, while restored gargoyles are often hooked into gutter systems, often via unsightly, makeshift pipes protruding from their mouths.

New gargoyles and grotesques are still created today, mostly as an act of love or creation rather than of architectural necessity. Some interpret classical medieval forms, while others take on more modern, fanciful themes. The introduction of pneumatic hammers and chisels has made the work easier, although most carvers use the same tools as medieval stonecutters. The advent of the industrial crane, and the ability to easily lift huge blocks of stone into place, has eased the work of placing finished gargoyles. Stone carving, while no longer occupying a central part of society as it did in the Middle Ages, is still practiced by guildsmen and guildswomen, most of whom learn their craft through working apprenticeships. For many, stonemasonry is a family business, passed on through the generations.

Many of today's gargoyles still function as water workers; in most, a hole is predrilled through the stone block before carving begins, and a pipe slid into the hole to provide a reinforced drainage channel. The gargoyle will also last longer, for with the drainage channel on the inside, rather than the surface of the block, it is more difficult for the sculpture to fill with dirt, leaves, bird droppings, and so on.

Centuries after their first appearance, we still enjoy gargoyles, our fearsome companions, those friends in stone. Gargoyles remind us that our world is unpredictable, and that chaos and darkness are right around the corner. Perhaps, in an age when science and technology explain so much of our lives, gargoyles serve by instilling a sense of wonder, inciting our imaginations, and making us giggle or shiver in ways that keep us from turning to stone.

13
Gargoyles and Folklore

I dream the dead into a living presence
and shape dead bones into a new design,
let speak again the ages' buried voices
and so defy the killing power of time.

—Brendan Kennelly

People have always created fantastic art featuring weird and fantastic creatures. These images continue to stir our imaginations, as they stirred the imaginations of the artists who conceived them. Our efforts to understand and explain these works takes us deep into ideas of psychology, culture, symbols, history, religion, and folklore.

One of the best ways of understanding the creations of our fellow humans is through folklore, the unrecorded traditions of a people. In other words, folklore consists of those traditional activities that arise spontaneously among the people, as compared to those that are academic, or scholarly. Folklore includes the form and content of these traditions and the way that they're passed from person to person.

- **Oral folklore** is divided into narrative (that which tells a story: myths, legends, and folktales), non-narrative (riddles and proverbs), and musical (ballads and folksongs) forms.

- ◎ **Customary folklore** involves customs, festivals, or communal celebrations and traditions.

- ◎ **Material folklore** is related to permanent objects or "artifacts," such as food, art, clothing, and the like.

By studying folklore, we learn what exists and persists in culture without the benefit of formal learning, religion, government, or other superstructures. In this way, folklore tells us what people thought was important enough to preserve from one generation to the next, and from one person to another. Nothing in culture is meaningless or random, and every aspect of culture has something to teach us about the people who created or transmitted it, as well as about the place and times to which it is connected. In order to understand folklore, we must consider both the formal and the informal. To understand gargoyles, it is just as important to study the secret lore and traditions of medieval stonecarvers (informal culture) as it is to learn the structure and function of the high Catholic church in the Middle Ages (formal culture). Gargoyles can be linked to a large body of narrative folklore—myths, legends, and folktales.

The Three Types of Narrative Folklore			
	Myth	**Legend**	**Folktale**
Time	Remote past "Before time"	Historic past "Real time"	Vague past "Once upon a time"
Place	Non-recognizable	Historic, defined location	Vague or seemingly familiar location
Players	Supernatural beings	Real people	Real and/or magickal humans and animals
True?	Yes	Yes or No	No, although initially believed to be true
Sacred?	Yes	Yes or No	No
Other	Believed to be true tales of the historic past for the society in which they are told.	Based on traditional motifs. Often reflect folk beliefs, traditions, or religious rites.	The "prose fiction" of folklore

Myths

Myths are a type of narrative folklore that occur in a remote, unidentifiable past ("before time") and in a nonrecognizable place. In the society in which they are told, myths are believed to be truthful accounts of what happened in the remote past. Myths are populated with supernatural beings and are widely recognized as sacred or as part of the creation of a people of civilization.

The Myth of the Gorgon Medusa

In Greek mythology, the Gorgons (from the Greek *gorgos,* or "terrible") were three sisters. Two of the sisters, Sthenno and Euryale, were monstrous immortals with huge teeth, brazen claws, and snakes in place of hair, while Medusa, the third sister, was a beautiful, mortal maiden whose hair was her crowning glory. Poseidon, who resided in the palace of Athena, lusted after Medusa. This so angered Athena that she turned Medusa into a monster and changed her hair into writhing snakes. Medusa became so ugly that anyone who looked directly at her was instantly turned to stone. Because of the curse, Medusa's cavern was soon littered with stone figures of men and animals that tried to sneak a look at her and were petrified by the sight.

Athena later sent Perseus to slay Medusa. Aided by Athena's magickal shield, Hermes' winged shoes, and a "sword of truth," Perseus managed to approach Medusa without looking directly at her. He cut off her head and ended her stony reign of terror.

Note: For a wonderful story about the life of Perseus, including an excellent segment showing the slaying of Medusa, you might want to check out the 1981 fantasy film, *Clash of the Titans.*

The Myth of Cerrunos

Cerrunos, closely related to the Green Man, is a pre-Christian horned god who ruled over the woodlands and animals of Pagan Celtic Europe. He may be related to the horned gods of ancient Greece, or particularly to the satyr, a symbol of lust and abundance. Cerrunos in many legends was interchangeable with the "king stag," a metaphor for the goddess's consort. In the Arthurian legend, young Arthur must bring down the king stag, then assumes the mantle himself; as "king stag," he beds the "virgin huntress," their *hieros gamos* insuring the health and fecundity of the surrounding land.

Cerunnos: Horned God of the woodlands.

The Christian Church later adopted Cerrunos, horns and all, as their symbol of the Devil. In gargoyle iconography, Cerrunos was shown with a combination of heavy horns, furrowed brow, teeth, beard, protruding tongue, and a fearsome expression. He often carried a serpent—a male symbol, and wore a torc—a female symbol.

The Myth of Taranis the Thundered

Taranis, also known as the great rider god of Pagan Celtic Europe, is portrayed in legendary battles with dragons and basilisks. In the stories, Taranis uses his horse to trample and kill the creature, either crushing its body or head.

The Myth of the Futhark Runes

The Futhark (FOO-thark) or "runic" alphabet is named for its first six letters: f, u, th, a (or o), r, and k. Legend says that runic letters were a gift of a Norse goddess, Mother Idun, keeper of the Norse gods' magic apples of immortality. Mother Idun engraved the runic letters on the tongue of her consort, Bragi, allowing him to learn their meanings and making him into the first great poet. The Norse God Odin, thought to perhaps be a masculinized version of Idun, acquired his own knowledge of the runes through sacrifice: He hung himself from the World Tree for nine days and nights, barely escaping with his life and giving up the sight in one eye as part of the process.[1]

The *Hávamál* (stanzas 137–38) describes how Odin received the runes:

I trow I hung on that windy Tree
nine whole days and nights,
stabbed with a spear, offered to Odin,

myself to mine own self given,
high on that Tree of which none hath heard
from what roots it rises to heaven.

None refreshed me ever with food or drink,
I peered right down in the deep;
crying aloud I lifted the Runes
then back I fell from thence.[2]

The Myth of Sucellos

Sucellos, The Mallet God, was a Gaulish deity who was shown holding a mallet and a *patera*, a dish of plenty, with which he fed his people. Sucellos was first and foremost a being associated with fecundity and plenty; legend suggests that his mate was the local earth goddess. He is featured in a pillar in the Copgrove Church in Yorkshire, holding his mallet in one hand and a platter of fruits and foliage aloft with the other. Interestingly, he stands on what is known locally as "The Devil's Stone," another allusion to the relationship between the Celtic Pagans and the new Christian church.

The Myth of the Gargoyle Water Purifiers

An ancient Grecian myth claims that a gargoyle can purify tainted water. Given that many gargoyles served a functional purpose as rainspouts, it was thought that when it rained they purified the water descending from the skies, spitting out clean, clear water that was free of disease or fouling.

There are at least two scientific bases for this. First, it is known that tumbling and aerating water is one way to help leach out toxins. Second, recent science has shown that falling water generates negative ions, and that when people stand near negative ions, they experience a sense of peacefulness and well-being. The effect is best known in terms of waterfalls; but perhaps the heavy flow of water from gargoyles during or right after a rainstorm has the same effect.

Legends

A legend is a type of folklore that occurs in the "real time" of the historic past and in a defined, known location. Legends are based on traditional ideas and reflect folk beliefs, traditions, or religious rites. Legends are mostly populated with real people, are believed to be true by their tellers, and may be either sacred (of a religious nature) or secular (non-religious).

The Legend of La Gargouille

A dragon called La Gargouille, described as having a long, reptilian neck, a slender snout and jaws, heavy brows, and membranous wings, lived in a cave close to the River Seine in France. The dragon had several bad habits, including swallowing ships, causing destruction with its fiery breath, and spouting so much water that it regularly flooded the surrounding countryside.

The residents of nearby Rouen attempted to placate La Gargouille with an annual offering of a live victim; although the dragon preferred virgin maidens, it was usually given a criminal to consume. Over time, the people tired of the arrangement. Somewhere in the period between 520 and 600 C.E., the priest Romanus (or Romain) arrived in Rouen and promised to deal with the dragon if the townspeople would agree to be baptized and build him a church. The people were skeptical at his chances for success, but they agreed nonetheless, anxious for any chance at ridding their town of the dragon scourge.

Equipped with the annual food offering (the criminal) and the items needed for an exorcism (bell, book, candle, and cross), Romanus subdued the dragon by making the sign of the cross and led the now docile beast, tamed with the light of Christianity, back to town on a leash made from his priest's robe.

The townspeople burned the body of La Gargouille at the stake in the center of the town square. However, the head and neck, long-tempered by the heat of the dragon's life-long fiery breath, would not burn. The charred remnants were mounted on the town gate and later moved to the walls of the new church. Legend says that they became the model for gargoyles for centuries to come, while also letting other dragons know that this was a town best avoided!

In memory of Romanus's deed, a stone dragon was placed on the exterior of the Rouen Cathedral, where it can be seen to this day.

Legends of the Green Man

One of the most-often depicted motifs for humanoid grotesques is the Green Man, found in cathedrals and churches all over the world. The Green Man appears on Celtic Pagan sculpture and on 2nd century Roman columns. He is found all over England, Wales, and Scotland, appears in Asia and Africa, and is even present in the great banks and financial houses of Wall Street. Kirtimukha is a Green Man-like image found on Hindu temples in India, and similar images have been identified in Malaysia, Borneo, and Nepal. He is the sole image of legend that appears before the common era and persists through to modern times, where we know him as Robin Hood, as a player in England's Morris Dances and mummer's plays, or as a figure still revered by modern Pagans.

The Green Man's roots may go back to the hunters who painted the caves of Lascaux and Altimira. His history has been verified by anthropologists as dating back at least to Mesopotamia (beginning in the late 4th millennium B.C.E.). Also called Jack of the Green, Puck, Robin Goodfellow, the Old Forest God, the May King, and the Leaf Man, he represents union between the living realms of human and vegetation. In his varying incarnations, he represents the tree spirit, the old forest gods, and the living force of the land. He is credited with personifying the spirit of the oak, a tree sacred to both Celtic and Norse cultures and with descending from the God Pan.

There are at least four kinds of Green Man:

- The foliate head, or simple Green Man, in which the face is surrounded or wreathed in foliage.
- The foliate Green Man, in which the face is made of foliage.
- The spewing, vomiting, or speaking Green Man, in which foliage seems to issue from the mouth.
- The "bloodsucker" head, with branches and greenery coming not only from the mouth but also from eyes, ears, nose, and/or chin.[3]

The foliate head was typically the earliest version of the Green Man, appearing consistently between the 2nd and 12th centuries C.E. At or around the 12th century, the advent of Gothic architecture saw spewing gargoyles on many of the larger European cathedrals, with the bloodsucker varieties following after as a more rare type of Green Man.

These manifestations took on different significances in different times and cultures. For example, in Celtic traditions, branches coming from the mouth or crowning the head of a Green Man were signs of divinity, particularly if the branches were of the sacred oak. But in the Middle Ages, a Green Man wreathed in or spewing grape vines, leaves, and fruit—a "fruitful" Jack-o'-the-Green— was a symbol of debauchery and overindulgence. The foliage of an enwreathed Leaf Man was almost always something local: maple, oak, ash, rose, mulberry, ivy, grapes, nettle, rose, and others. Hawthorne was occasionally used as well;

The Green Man.

considered to a magickal plant and associated with Witches, the flower of the "thorn" usually bloomed around May 1st and was synonymous with Beltane and the coming of summer.

The general circular shape of Leaf Men evokes the magick and mystery of the circle, which represents the eternal cycle of life and the life-giving nature of the sun. The Green Man is often linked to the sun, solar deities, or the sun wheel. Although a few Green Men had bodies, the prototypical version combines a strongly carved head with a wreath of leaves, vines, or other foliage. The "green" label is a reference to his botanical symbolism, while the wreathing of the head is a symbol going back at least as far as the Greeks, where participants in games and contests were rewarded with crowns of laurel.

The Green Man is universally considered to be male, and he is almost always human, although some Green Men have short demonesque horns. A few "Green Animals" exist, including Green Lions, Green Cats, Green Dogs, Green Boars, and Green Serpents. The Green Snake of Appleby spews out greenery that morphs into the snake's tail; hence, the snake appears to be swallowing its own tail, like Ouroboros, the symbol of enduring life.

A Green Man carved with an especially fierce expression and with oak foliage and accords issuing from the mouth was sometimes called a Wodwose. The Wodwose, called "the spirit of the woods," was a variation of the Wildman and may have represented an early Sasquatch figure. Wodwoses appeared on heraldic coats of arms in medieval times, especially in Germany. The creatures were often shown armed with rough, four-lobed clubs. The creature resurfaced in the 1900s when it was used by J.R.R. Tolkien to describe a race of wild men in his fiction, also called *Druedain*.

In pre-Christian times, the Green Man was a Pagan symbol of fertility and rebirth. As such, he appears on ancient monuments and in medieval churches throughout Europe and Britain. Even certain religious orders, such as the Cistercians, once vocal in their opposition to any sort of church ornamentation, eventually featured many Jack-o'-the-Greens in their churches and Abbeys. Rosslyn Chapel, built by William Sinclair in the 15th century, and an important link in the myth and legend surrounding the Holy Grail and the Knights Templar, includes 103 carved Green Man images, and only a single image of Jesus. Templar scholars believe that there may be a connection between the Green Man and the mysteries of the Grail; these theories have yet to be proven.

Green Men may have referenced Silvanus, the Roman god of the wood-lands, and were often shown wearing ornate crowns; this suggested a link between kingship and the fertility of the land, a recurring motif through pre-medieval and medieval times, and an important aspect of Pagan beliefs. Green Men also played an important role in many Pagan celebrations, notably those of Beltane, the May 1 holiday of fertility. It is no surprise that in medieval times, carved images of the Green Man were often used to represent lust or another of the seven deadly sins, particularly when fruitful Green Men were portrayed. Images of Green Men were often part of holiday parades and processions well into Victorian times. One of these celebrations was Rogation Day, the three days before ascension; the holiday was observed by prayer and fasting, and sometimes by processions and blessings over fields and crops.

The Green Man was frequently given protective functions, explaining his oft-placement over entrances or on tympanums via apotropaic carvings, whose design or placement suggests their purpose as magickally warding off evil. At the church of St. Leonards in Linley, Shropshire, United Kingdom, a small, full-bodied Green Man is carved into the tympanum over what is known as the "Devil Door." This version of the church's back door was left open after baptisms, allowing devils to be driven from the church. The door usually faced north, the direction thought by medieval folk to be synonymous with darkness and evil.

Given the Leaf Man's wide penetration through a number of geographically separate countries, his image may represent the surfacing of a primal, archetypal image from Carl Jung's human collective unconscious. In contrast, Green Men may also represent demons, particularly if painted red, or gilded.

In one of his many manifestations as Robin Hood and the Morris Dances of Old England, the Green Man is chiseled in wood and cut into stone even to this day by men and women who no longer know his story but sense that something old, strong, and tremendously important lies behind his leafy mask. One of the earliest English epic poems, "Gawain and The Green Knight" may reference another manifestation of the Green Man as the god that dies and is reborn This powerful theme of death and rebirth runs through all the diverse images and myths of the Green Man, while the color green symbolizes life itself. He also pops up in the Epic of Gilgamesh, with Enkidu and Gilgamesh beheading the Forest Guardian (a version of the Green Man). In his incarnation as a god who dies and is reborn over and over, he shares ties to Dionysus, Osirus, Odun, Tamuz, John Barleycorn, and even Jesus.

The Legendary Bulls of Laon

Bulls were used in medieval times for moving wood, stone, and other construction materials to the building site. In Chapter 2, we talked about how the bulls of Laon were immortalized high atop the Laon cathedral. But there's a charming legend that adds more to the story.

The legends says that as the oxen labored to pull a load of stone up the hill to the site of the Laon Cathedral, one ox fell, exhausted. The wagoner was in despair, for without that space in the yolk filled, that oxen team could not work, and the building would fall behind schedule. Just as the wagoner had almost given up, he was surprised when another ox approached him out of nowhere. The ox offered to be yolked into the team, replacing his fallen comrade.

Once the load of stone had been delivered to the hilltop, the wagoner discovered that the unknown ox had vanished.

In honor of this miracle, and in gratitude to all the horses, oxen, and other beasts whose labors had helped the cathedral reach into the clouds, the stone-mason placed a ring of oxen atop the tower, where they may be seen to this day.

The Legend of the Golem of Prague

About 400 years ago, the European Jewish community was in constant danger of persecution and massacre. Communities would grow and thrive in one location, then, when the locals rose up violently against them, they would be forced to move and start over.

The chief Rabbi of Prague, Rav Loewe, was a scholar of Jewish law and mysticism. The Jews of Prague were under similar threat, and to combat the danger, Rav Loewe created a Golem, a soulless, strong, human-sized being made of clay and mud, and activated by invoking different names of God.

The Golem protected the Jews of Prague until the danger was thought to have passed. The Golem was then deactivated and placed in an attic, the location of the attic being a closely guarded secret. A ban was put on entering the attic so that no one would disturb the retired Golem, and the stairs to the place were shielded, so that no one would stumble onto the hiding place.

Legend suggests that the Golem still exists today, safe in his attic and ready to come out of hiding if needed by his people. Rav Loewe's synagogue, remains the oldest synagogue in Europe.

The Legendary Gargoyles of Notre Dame

The gargoyles of Notre Dame perch on the cathedral walls by the dozens. Staring out over the city, they appear to be on constant watch, and ready to spring into action. According to legend, the gargoyles were chased from the interior of the Cathedral by the Virgin Mary, who then kept them employed as horrifying guardians of the outer walls and towers.

The Legend of the Cerne Giant

This 200-foot-long priapic giant figure was cut into a hillside above the village of Cerne Abbas centuries ago, deeply enough to reveal the white chalk below. His menacing presence, with heavy shoulders and right arm brandishing a heavy club, gives him the attributes of a Celtic god ready to defend his people. In contrast, his other (left) hand is extended and held upwards, in a gesture of benediction. While his creators are unknown, he may be related to the tribal god of the Celtic Durotriges, or could possibly be a presentation of the Irish Pagan god, the Dagda.[4]

Local folklore suggests that the Cerne Giant has powers of fertility, sexuality, and prosperity, and heath-dwellers would often come to bless their union and engage in intercourse within this outline. The Cerne Abbas church honors the giant with four carvings on the church's external walls.

The Legendary Heads of the Celts

The Celtic tribes were known to be fearsome hunters. They believed that the head held divine powers, and that the severed heads of their prey were magickal and could be used to attract good luck, furnish prophecy, enhance fertility, and repel evil. To put these powers to their fullest use, the Celts mounted the heads on poles and placed the poles in standing circles around their homes (the circle being a powerful shape that could invoke a liminal space). The desiccated heads then offered their services as seers and speaking oracles. Such practices coalesced to explain the placement of "dead heads" on buildings and over doorways, where their magickal powers might benefit those within.

Bran, Lomna, Finn MacCumaill, Sir Gawain, and the Green Knight were all involved in The Cult of the Head. The head of Osiris was said to be a divinatory presence at the ancient shrine of Abydos, while the head of Orpheus spoke divinatory poetry and Odin himself relied on the mummified head of an unknown older deity. The Hindu goddess Kali is sometimes shown wearing a necklace or garland of shrunken heads and/or skulls, almost appearing as a kind of rosary. The appearance of skulls in *memento mori* ("remember that you are mortal"), and the use of Golgotha, literally "place of the skull," in the Christian crucifixion myth suggest that even the Christian church understood and supported the powerful image of the severed head. The idea of beheading became a powerful symbol of initiation and rite of passage in medieval times, and the ritual touching of the sword to the head and shoulders during a knighting ceremony was meant to reference the idea of beheading as a heroic act. The severed head became one of the most common motifs of the Gothic period, as shown in roundels, corbel sculptures, Janus heads, Green Men, and other works.

The Legendary Cults of Sacred Springs and Wells

In the Middle Ages, a variety of legend and lore sprung up in association with wells and springs, which were thought to be holy sites and were frequently associated with local saints or with the Virgin Mary. The veneration of springs and wells goes back to antiquity. In Greco-Roman mythology, fountains and springs were inhabited by naiads (nymphs) and minor deities. Certain springs, such as the spring at Delphi, were believed to hold powers of prophecy and divination. The Egyptians worshipped holy wells and springs, as did many Eastern traditions. Indo-European Pagans believed that natural wells and springs, which reached deeply into the Earth, were an aspect of the primordial Earth Mother goddess, and such springs were revered for their healing qualities. The Romans tapped mineral springs and hot springs for healing baths. The legendary healing spring of Avalon/Glastonbury was thought to grant eternal life. These bits and pieces of mythos probably led to modern traditions, such as tossing coins into a fountain for luck, using wells as pilgrimage sites, bathing in holy waters, and the English custom of well-dressing, still practiced today in England's Peak District. The tradition may date to medieval times, when people gave thanks for the purity of certain wells during the period of the Black Death.

Gargoyles in Urban Legend

One of the gargoyles on the Freiburg Munster, the city cathedral in Freiburg, Germany, is an infamous "defecating gargoyle," a human figure holding on to the building with both hands and feet, so that its rear end hangs over the market square. According to local legend, when the structure was being built, the city council kept increasing the demands made on city stonemasons without a corresponding increase in their pay. The masons responded by carving this particular sculpture, set to perpetually "moon" the city council.

A Parisian legend tells of how the gargoyles of Notre Dame come to life at night, leaving their perches to sweep down over Paris and partake of the nightlife.

Folktales

A folktale is a type of folklore that occurs in an imaginary or unreal past and in an imagined or unknown location. Folktales are populated with imaginary people or creatures, are believed to be false by their tellers, and are considered secular.

The Tale of Floucars and the Copper Gargoyles

This story was recorded in the *Roman d'Abladanc* and perhaps written by Richard de Fournival, 13th century bishop of Amiens.

The master Floucars created two gargoyles of copper, and set them over the gate to Amiens. The gargoyles were said to be able to evaluate the motivation and intentions of each person who entered the city. If anyone entered the city with good intentions, they would be allowed safe passage. But if their intentions were malefic, the gargoyles would spit venom on them, a venom so dangerous that the unfortunate intruder would die instantly.

When the Lord of the city came, one of the gargoyles spit down a shower of silver, and the other a shower of gold.[5]

The gargoyles of Floucars.

Part II: Magick and Legend

14

Gargoyles and Magick

For modern magick users, the gargoyle presents a host of opportunities for magickal workings. In the next two chapters, we'll explore the role of the gargoyle in magickal practice, including relationships to elemental correspondences, stone magick, egregores, talismans, spell work, divination, and more.

We begin with an assumption: There is no one true way.

As a practitioner of nature-based magick, and given the always-changing nature of the natural world, I firmly believe that nothing about magick is (excuse the pun) carved in stone. Magick is about art, science, and belief, but most of all, it is a craft that must be studied and practiced. The more you practice, the better you'll get at it.

Those of you reading this book may come from any number of spiritual traditions and styles of magickal practice. Some of you might be completely new to the idea of practicing magick. I think it is critical to make clear that the business of magick is a flexible one. Much depends on your own insights and perceptions, and much of these are only acquired with time and practice. What you read here may differ from what you read in other sources, and that's okay. In my opinion, if you ever pick up a work that says, "This is how you do it, and all of the other ways are wrong," you should calmly drop it into the nearest trash receptacle and try something else.

Magickal Safety

All magick practice must be guided by ethics and safety. The following set of guidelines will help you stay fit and happy as you practice the art and craft of magick. If you're an experienced magick user, these will be old hat; if you're a novice, read (and heed) them carefully.

1. First and foremost, it is patently unethical to cast magick *at* someone, or to use them in a magickal working without their permission.

2. Always practice magick in an optimum state of mind and body. Don't work magic when you're tired, sick, frazzled, or emotionally upset.

3. Most magickal practitioners work with a version of the three-fold law: Magick that you send out into the universe gains energy and returns to you three-fold. Make sure that what you send out is what you want to get back!

4. Trust your common sense and intuition to avoid problems. If you don't feel prepared for a certain magickal working, leave it for another time. While you wait, study and find out more about it.

5. Always prepare yourself before you begin. Cleansing or purification will help you build up a healthy energy charge. This may mean taking a ritual bath and donning clean or ritual clothes; on the simpler end, it could mean simply washing your hands and face before you begin.

6. Acquire and use the appropriate tools for the job.

7. Learn and follow basic practices for your mode of working; this may include casting a circle, grounding and centering, raising your personal shields, clearing your mind of distractions, and so forth.

8. Keep an eye on mundane safety concerns, particularly when using candles, censers, thuribles, or any kind of flame. Never leave a candle or flame unattended. Be careful that the sleeves of your robes or clothing don't hang into a flame and catch on fire

as you work. Likewise, be sure that nothing is hanging over the flame that might be ignited. Always have a fire extinguisher nearby.

9. Don't push yourself too hard. Don't tackle more than one new kind of practice at a time, and stop working if you get a headache or other symptoms of magickal strain.

10. Take care of yourself by having something to eat and drink after your session.

11. Read as widely as possible and talk to other people about your magickal studies. Don't take all information for granted: Crosscheck your references for accuracy, and sample materials from different traditions.

12. Make regular use of a magickal journal, Grimoire, or Book of Shadows. Keep journal entries, and note the procedures, materials, and outcomes of your magickal workings. Over time, these entries will show your progress, and help you build on your successes.

13. The best way to study magick is with an experienced mentor or a respected magickal school. Think of this kind of in-person study as your own apprenticeship in magick. If you study and practice alone as a "solitary" make sure that you're using solid sources. See the Resources section for more information.

14. Have fun!

Quill and Scroll

Writing is a kind of symbolic language—it is the way of using symbols—alphabets, markings, and so on—to stand in for or represent words. Until writing was invented, all communication was oral, and knowledge and history spanned the generations through words and song. While most common medieval folk were illiterate, the Middle Ages saw the creation of fantastic bestiaries, herbal formularies, and glorious illustrated manuscripts, most the products of monastic scholars, and all created with quill and ink on parchment paper, augmented with richly detailed illustrations.

Scrolls, rolls of paper that were wrapped around sticks or dowels, were used by ancient civilizations long before the first book was invented. The handwritten codex (book) dates from the Middle Ages. A great improvement over the scroll, the codex could be opened flat at any page, allowing easier reading and also allowing writing on both sides of the page. The codex also made it easier to organize documents in a library because it had a stable spine on which the book's title could be written, allowing easy retrieval when the books were arranged upright on shelves.

Quill and ink.

Historic evidence suggests that as soon as there were materials to write on, people began keeping journals. Journals served an important role in history and exploration. When ships sailed the oceans, their ship's log or captain's log was their most valuable possession and the log-keeper the most valuable crewmember, second only to the captain. The log allowed monarchs and scientists to evaluate the details of the journey later on; without the journal, much of the journey's importance would have been lost. A good example can be seen in the journals kept by Lewis and Clark on their cross-continent exploration. Even today their journals continue to yield important details to historians and scholars.

In the same way that an explorer's journal marked and recorded their adventures, you can use a magickal journal to track your studies of gargoyles and related magick. Through it, you will be able to chart your discoveries, successes, important dates, fieldwork, and insights, including those "ah-ha moments" so dear to the hearts of magickal practitioners.

Calligraphy

Calligraphy (Greek for "beauty" + "writing") is the art of decorative writing, and a particular style of calligraphy is described as a "hand." In medieval times, calligraphy was used to illustrate and illuminate important manuscripts. Today, as handwritten forms of communication have given way to e-mail, word processors, and text messaging, calligraphy has increasingly been reserved for special occasions and events.

Calligraphy, a skill that is only mastered with practice and time, is also a wonderful challenge for the magickal practitioner, and a nice way to beautify your journal keeping. It's possible to buy how-to books and kits that teach the basics of manuscript illumination and/or calligraphy. Community schools and colleges may offer classes. If you're lucky enough to have a group from the Society of Creative Anachronism nearby, you might also find a teacher of calligraphy within their ranks.

Magickal Alphabets

Magickal alphabets differ from mundane alphabets in two important ways: First, they are special alphabets, rather than those used in everyday life; and second, each letter represents and transmits a fully-developed symbolic force.[1]

There are a number of magickal alphabets, and it can be a lot of fun to learn to write with them. Once you've mastered the letters, you can use the alphabets to inscribe scrolls for spells, to write spells and ritual into your own Book of Shadows, to burn inscriptions onto a wand or stave, or even inscribe a set of stone runes.

Because of their roots and use in the Middle Ages, two alphabets are particularly apt for our discussions of gargoyles.

Futhark

The Futhark alphabet is probably the best-known ancient writing system and may have been derived from Latin. Runic writings have been found throughout northern Europe; most date to the Early Gothic period, c. 1000 C.E., but the earliest known full set of 24 runes dates to 400 C.E., found on the Kylver Stone in Gotland, a Swedish island-province.

Theban

The Theban alphabet is a medieval writing system that may have been developed as a way

Roman	Futhark	Theban
A		
B		
C		
D		
E		
F		
G		
H		
I		
J		
K		
L		
M		
N		
O		
P		
Q		
R		
S		
T		
U		
V		
W		
X		
Y		
Z		
Th		
Ng		
Ei		

to encode Latin. It is sometimes called *Honorarian*, in honor of its supposed creator, Honorious III (var. "Honorius the Theban"), who probably authored the *Liber Juratus* (the "Sworn Book of Honorios"), a text of medieval magick. Theban is widely used today by modern magickal practitioners and is sometimes referred to as "The Witch's Alphabet."

The Elements

Just about every kind of magickal practice is linked to the Elements. But what do I mean when I use the word, "Elements"? Those of you who are new to magick are in for a surprise.

Everything in the Universe is composed of matter, energy, or a combination of the two. All material things, those that are made of matter, can exist in any of four known states: solid, liquid, gas, and plasma. With the addition or subtraction of energy by various means (such as adding or reducing heat or pressure) matter can transition from one state to another. We usually think of water, for instance, in its liquid state. But when energy (in the form of heat) is removed from water, it can be frozen solid into ice. If heat energy is added to water, it boils into gaseous vapor. Its component atoms of hydrogen and oxygen can even be ionized (stripped of electrons) to become fiery plasma, as we see in the *aurora borealis* and *aurora astralis*, the northern and southern lights.

Although modern chemists have adopted the word "elements" to refer to the 100-plus different kinds of known chemical elements, that was not the original meaning or intention of this term. The Elements, as understood by the ancients, were the basic states of matter. Credited to the 5th century Sicilian philosopher Empedocles, the concept of four (or five) elements as the basis of all life and being in the universe became an essential teaching of Aristotle and the Pythagorean mysteries of ancient Greece. This system has since figured prominently in the magicks of all Western systems, from Middle Eastern, Egyptian, Grecian, Roman, Hermetical, and alchemical to modern occultism, Paganism, and wizardry. It is the most widely used conceptual model in the world, and is also the foundation of the tarot, astrology, the seasonal wheel, and the magick circle.

Simply stated, the four classical Elements, also known as the cardinal Elements, are Earth, Air, Fire, and Water. As with everything in the Universe, each Element is filled with the nonphysical essence of the divine, which magick users call Spirit. Just as each person is a unique manifestation of the divine, so is every rock, every tree, every mountain, and every river. Because of this, Spirit is often considered to be the fifth Element, and it is all around us, echoing traditions that poke against the thresholds of modern quantum physics.

The elements are also inextricably interrelated. The first four—Earth, Air, Fire, and Water, are essential to life on Earth as we know it. And the fifth, Spirit, also called Aether, is in many ways the summation of the other four, the absolute expression of both matter and energy in Einstein's terms. Matter cannot be created or destroyed, but mass and energy can interchange, and that may be the best explanation of Spirit that we have. Some practitioners include two additional Elements: "as above" (which also equates to the future, and to concepts of heaven, paradise, and the afterlife) and "so below" (which links us to the past, and to concepts of chaos and the abyss).

A simple burning candle is the most perfect of all magickal tools, for it contains all four Elements simultaneously. The solid waxen candle itself represents Earth; the liquid melted wax is Water; the gaseous smoke is Air; and the glowing flame is Fire. Look into the flame and you can capture the essence of Spirit.

In terms of the Elements, gargoyles also do it all. They're made of earthly materials (stone!), they're perched high in the air (many also have wings), their impassioned expressiveness connotes fire, and their historic or real function links them to water. And spirit? Their design says it all. Their historic timelessness also references the "as above" and "so below" as well.

Using the Elemental Correspondences

Think of gargoyles, and besides their outward appearance, the next thing that's likely to come to mind is stone. Gargoyles are made of stone. The Earth is also made of stone—it's all around us, under our feet, and even present as microscopic particles in the air we breathe and the water we drink. We humans are even made of stone—sure, we're mostly water, but without the calcium in our bones and teeth, the carbon that brings us to life, and the microelements that fire our cellular metabolism, we'd just be one big puddle.

One of the best and simplest ways to invoke gargoyles in magickal practice is via their elemental associations.

Earth

The Earth Element is solid, reliable, enduring, and makes up our earthly home. Earth is a tangible place that we can see and touch. Nonetheless, it retains its mysteries in tall mountain peaks, landforms, and beautiful underground caves. The Elemental spirit representative of Earth is the gnome, a small creature that lives underground and has encyclopedic knowledge of rocks, gems, minerals, and mining techniques. Gnomes are said to guard Mother Earth's treasures. Secretive and hard to see, gnomes are fond of gems and appreciate small, shiny gifts left near their caves and grottoes. They also aren't averse to a tankard of strong ale now and then!

Correspondences of the Earth Element.

Our bodies are made of the solid minerals and traditional (chemical) elements that form the earth: carbon, calcium, phosphorus, iron, and so on. Every plant or animal, even those animals that are aquatic or avian, has correspondence with, and dependence on the Earth's terrain, whether walking on it, settling into the mud at the bottom of lake or river, growing from it, or nesting on a cliff face or tree branch.

Air

The Air Element has long been referenced as a symbol of the sun, sky, and heavens. It is a realm of mystery, for while we cannot see it, we can see its actions, and feel its effects. Because of this, Air is often equated with spirits, ghosts, and the magickal realm. The Elemental spirit representative of Air is the sylph, a small, ethereal deity that lives among the air, clouds, and wind.

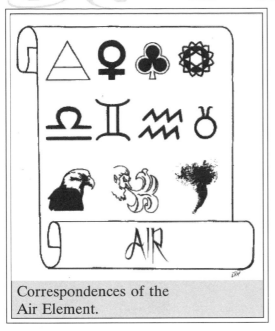

Correspondences of the
Air Element.

Have you ever been standing outside and had a fleeting impression of something unimaginably fast spinning by? That may have been a sylph!

In terms of physical composition, every piece of life on Earth is formed from the atoms and basic elements created from the life and death of stars. Every living creature requires oxygen, (air) for its existence. Whether we breathe air through gills or lungs, we make our own oxygen, the Element critical to the survival of life on Earth.

Fire

The Element of Fire is linked to passion and creation via the so-called spark that powers the fires of life and imagination. Fire's spirit denizen is the salamander, a small lizard-like being that lives among the fire's flames. Watch carefully the next time you stare into a campfire, and perhaps you'll see one.

With regards to Fire, all living organisms are powered by cellular reactions. These processes are fueled by the ATP cycle, which converts molecular substrates into energy at the cellular level in what is arguably

Correspondences of the
Fire Element.

an Elemental furnace. The engine for cellular energy is the mitochondria, the cell's furnace and powerhouse, where all energy production occurs.

Water

The Element of Water is associated with the ocean, the cauldron of life on Earth. Water is seen as divine in many traditions, with wells and springs revered as holy ground. The reverence for water is one of the reasons that baptism, immersion in holy waters, is such an important symbol in many religions. The spirit representative of Water is the Undine, a small entity inhabiting a lake, stream, river, or sea. Undines prefer to frolic among the waves, which references the origin of their name as meaning "of the wave." Undines are often pictured in mythological and magickal

Correspondences of the Water Element

works as small, mermaid-like beings. Next time you're at the ocean, try to spot Undines in the foam of breaking waves.

All living creatures are composed of large amounts of water. Without water, humans would be little more than a handful of powdered minerals, as would other living organisms. At the molecular level, water is absolutely essential for the chemical reactions that power our bodies and keep us alive. The water (hydrological) cycle also gives life to and cleanses the Earth.

Spirit

Spirit (var. Aether, Akasha, the "here and now") is the life force itself, or perhaps the "art force" of life. It is what makes us interact with the mundane and magickal worlds, what makes us wonder, appreciate, and feel. The sprite, which has forms in all of the Elements, is often cited as the representative of Spirit.

Spirit represents the most Elemental form of energy. At the level of quantum physics, the atoms that form matter are broken into progressively smaller subatomic particles, which ultimately are explainable only in terms of the energy they emit or utilize. At this level, everything on the Earth—rocks, humans, water, clouds, birds, and so on—possesses the same atomic structure and the same inherent energy. Obi-Wan Kenobi was right: the Force is all around us.

Whichever elements you include in your own magickal workings, think of them as batteries—storehouses of energy that we can call on and tap into as needed. When we create magick, we give back our own energy, replenishing the Elemental store and maintaining the always-important balance. In the following table, you'll find a chart of Elemental correspondences—use these as you begin your magickal workings.

A Simple Table of Elemental Correspondences					
	Earth	**Air**	**Fire**	**Water**	**Spirit**
Compass	North	East	South	West	Center
Elemental	Gnome	Sylph	Salamander	Undine	Sprite
Powers	Health, wealth, real-world needs, protection	Wisdom and logic	Passion, engery, ambition	Emotion psychic qualities	Awareness, consciousness
Physical rulership	Mountain caves, stones, growing things	Winds, storms, whirlwinds	Flames, sun, lightening, geothermal features, volcanoes	Seas, rivers, lakes, tides, rain, and snow	The heavens, astral planes, other dimensions
Season	Winter	Spring	Summer	Autumn	New Year
Time of Day	Nighttime	Daybreak	Noon	Sunset	Midnight

	Earth	Air	Fire	Water	Spirit
Stone	Metamorphic, rock: marble, gneiss	Air-filled rock: pumice, vesicular basalt	Igneous rock: basalt, obsidian, granite	Sedimentary rock: limestone, sandstone, petrified rock	Magickal stones
Gar-goyle	Simple human or animal gargoyle	Winged gargoyle	Demonic gargoyle	Functioning gargoyle with trough Water creature	Chimeric or monster-ous gargoyle
Gem	Agate, turquoise, garnet, quartz	Sapphire amethyst	Diamond ruby, topaz	Agate bloodstone, pearl, opal	Diamond
Metal	Lead	Mercury aluminum	Gold, iron	Silver	Platinum
Altar tools	Panticle	Wand, Incense	Candles, athame	Chalice, cauldron	Patron figures
Incense	Sage, sweet-grass, patchouli	Wormwood, cedar	Dragon's blood, frankin-cense	Ambergris, sandalwood	Natural scents especially juniper
Color	Green	Yellow	Red	Blue	White
Planet	Saturn, Venus	Jupiter, Sun	Sun, Mars, Jupiter	Moon, Mercury, Venus, Saturn	Stars
Mundane animals	Land dwellers	Air dwellers	Desert dwellers	Water dwellers	Mythical realm dwellers

	Earth	Air	Fire	Water	Spirit
Magickal animals	Unicorns, centaurs	Griffins, harpies	Dragons, phoenixes	Merfolk, water	Spirit animals serpents

Altarcraft

Most magick users have at least one personal altar or shrine in their homes; nature-oriented folks may also have an outdoor altar. Your altar is a magickal focus—it gives you a place to pause every day and reflect, meditate, celebrate, or carry out magickal workings. It may be entirely freeform, encompassing whatever materials you feel are important and meaningful. But there are several components that are found on most magickal altars, including:

An altar cloth: This provides a clean, magickally clear surface on which to place magickal objects and do magickal workings. I like to vary the color and pattern of my altar cloth according to the season, or sometimes to the kinds of workings I'm doing. Be creative—for example, a stone working might include an altar surface of sand, sandpaper, or slate.

A simple altar.

A representation of the Four Directions and elements: A classic way to do this is with a stone (Earth/North), a feather (Air/East), a candle or bit of incense (Fire/South), and a small bowl of water (Water/West).

A chalice or bowl: This may simply be filled with water: spring water, moon water, or rainwater.

An athame (AH-thuh-may): This is a double-bladed knife that is used symbolically in magickal workings, but is *not* used for actually cutting. The blade is often inscribed with magickal characters. A wand may be substituted.

An athame.

Candles and candleholders: These are wonderful additions to any altar, allowing you to add size, shape, color, texture, and scent to your magick.

A panticle: This usually consists of a round or square piece of wood, tile, or pottery with a pentagram or other symbols inscribed on it. The panticle serves as your altar's central focus or "work area."

A panticle.

A thurible: This is a fireproof vessel for burning incense or powdered herbs. Your thurible could be a fireproof bowl, a small iron cauldron, an abalone shell, and so on.

Deity figures or representations: Some people use symbolic representations of male and female; others use photographs, or actual statues of specific goddesses and gods. As you begin acquiring gargoyle figures, you might also use them.

Other objects and materials as desired: Salt, herbs, smudges, incense and holder, seeds, flowers, small lights, stones and gems, and so on.

Spellwork

Writing at the conclusion of the Middle Ages, the poet Robert Herrick (1591–1674) offered this spell for carrying out an exorcism:

Holy Water come and bring:
Cast in salt, for seasoning:
Set the brush for sprinkling.
Bring ye sacred spittle hither
Meale and it now mix together.
Add a little oyle to either.

Give the tapers here their light:
Ring the saints-bell to affright
Far from hence the evil sprite.[2]

Herrick's poem was about exorcism, a spell using holy relics and magickal actions to rid a space of demons. Isn't it fascinating that with only a slightly different slant, today's modern spellcasters use similar processes to create positive magickal workings?

Herrick's poem references traditional spell components: Holy Water, salt, asperging, bread or cakes, oil, candles, a bell, and interaction with the spirit world. Modern spellcrafters use all of the techniques, but with obviously different intent.

There are three main ways of creating spellcraft:

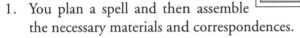

Candle magick.

1. You plan a spell and then assemble the necessary materials and correspondences.

2. You find yourself in possession of a set of materials and/or correspondences, and they magickally come together to create an idea for a spontaneous spell.

3. As a learning task, your study of specific materials or correspondences leads you to create a spell that uses them as a central feature.

For the purposes of this learning experience, we're going to focus on the third approach. You've learned about the world of gargoyles and their stony backgrounds. Now, as a magick user, it is time to consider how you might add the essence of gargoyles and stone to your magickal practice.

As you've read through this book, you've seen gargoyles expressed in terms of magickal qualities and correspondences, including:

- Earth, Air, Fire, Water, and Spirit.
- "As above," "so below," and "here and now."
- Stone: limestone, marble, clay.
- All sorts of animal correspondences.
- Gothic qualities: dualism, veiled meanings.
- Qualities: guardianship, strength, terror, humor, protection, and so on.

Let's develop these correspondences into actual spells.

Spellcraft 101

The following is a *very* simple overview of spellcraft. If this piques your interest, I suggest that you consult the Bibliography to identify resources for more in-depth magickal study and education.

Basic guidelines for the spell user:

1. Always purify yourself before enacting a spell, with the idea that you must create sacred space within yourself and your surroundings before bringing magick into that space. Some or all of these ideas may be used:

   ◎ Shower, bathe, or simply wash hands and/face (frankincense soap is ideal for purification); dry with a clean towel and put on fresh clothing.

   ◎ Meditate.

   ◎ Put on magickal jewelry or regalia.

2. Think of ways to purify the area. If working indoors, turn off the television, radio, phone, and so on. Keep cellular phones away from your magick—microwaves and magick don't mix! Open the windows to allow nature to enter the ritual space. Make sure that you will be undisturbed throughout the working.

   Smudging is one kind of purification. To do this, you'll need a fireproof dish or thurible and a smudge stick (or loose dried herbs). If using herbs, pile them loosely in the dish, light them, then snuff them quickly with a snuffer or spoon; if using a smudge stick, light one end and then snuff it by tamping it in the thurible. Both herbs and smudge will continue to smoke slightly. Hold the smudge up in front of you and use your free hand (or a feather) to waft the cleansing smoke over you. Walk deosil (clockwise) around the room, allowing the smoke to purify the entire space.

3. Making magick is a lot like cooking. Make sure you have all ingredients prepared and at hand before beginning the work. If working from a written text or spell, read it through before starting and make sure you understand the steps.

4. Ground and center before and after doing spellwork.

5. Spells may be done on your altar or virtually anywhere. If working off-altar, use a clean altar cloth underneath your workings. A freshly

washed tablecloth, towel, or placemat can serve.

6. Conduct all fire work, such as incense, candles, smudging, using safe practices.

7. In general, any movements, such as walking, smudging, string, and so on, should be done deosil (clockwise) if your spell is trying to attract or increase energy, and widdershins (counterclock-wise) if you are trying to deflect or decrease energy.

Tools for spellworking.

8. When you're finished, spell materials should be handled and/or disposed of respectfully, using the Elements. Candles should always be put out with a snuffer or with wet fingertips, but never blown out. A teaspoon makes a good makeshift snuffer. Smudges may be snuffed in sand or loose soil, then replaced in the thurible to cool. Used herbs, salt, smudges, and so on can be buried in the earth, cast into the wind, burned in fire, or strewn onto a body of water (stream, lake, river, sea). Note: There's nothing wrong with reusing materials that are still fresh, such as candles, herbs, stones, or part of a smudge stick. Even the best magick-user doesn't like to waste anything.

9. "Cakes and ale" (sometimes called cakes and wine) are a part of most ritual work and some spells. The term refers to a small amount of food or drink that are consumed during or after the working. If cakes and ale aren't a part of your magick, make sure to have a bite to eat after the work is finished, to replenish your strength.

10. Magickal tradition says that the spellcasters should not talk about their spell until its outcome is clear; doing so diminishes the power of the working. Some magick users also do not write about the spell for the same period of time. I take the middle ground—I always make notes immediately (otherwise, I forget the details), but I don't discuss magickal workings until I understand how the results have played out.

Timing Your Spellwork

Life on Earth is full of cycles, as the sun, moon, and seasons turn and spin around us in a never-ceasing spiral of life. By placing your magick in synchrony with these cycles, you will increase its power and the likelihood of success.

The Hours of the Day

Dawn: A time for new beginnings, fresh starts, and rebirth. The morning dew is often collected for use in charms and potions.

Morning: A good time for establishing patterns, for preparing potions that will have lasting actions, for gathering herbs and flowers, and for doing magick that needs time to work.

Noon: A time of balance, with the sun directly overhead and at peak power. This is the time to work spells requiring a male correspondence or honoring a male deity.

Afternoon: A time of quiet. In many societies, this is the time to take a nap, or siesta. Afternoon is a good time to relax, meditate, study, plan, and work divination.

Dusk: A time of great power, as the sun's energies ebb and give way to those of the moon. This is a good time to do work that reaches into other planes or dimensions, or that attempts to contact other beings. Spells involving protection, vigil, and guardianship are appropriate for this time.

Night: The moons, stars, and planets hold sway during the darkness of night. Many practitioners conduct rituals and do spell work during the night-time hours, especially that which involves waning or ebbing actions.

Midnight: Like noon, this is another time of balance, with the sun at its greatest ebb and the heavenly bodies at their maximum power. Midnight is often called "the witching hour." This is the time to work spells requiring a female correspondence or honoring a female deity.

The Days of the Week

Monday is the "Moon's Day," and a good time for spells with a feminine or birth aspect.

Tuesday is "Tyr's Day." This day is under the rule of Mars, and is a good day for spells involving strength, courage, and power.

Wednesday is "Woden's Day" (or Odin's Day). Ruled by Mercury, Wednesday is an apt time to do spells involving wisdom, creativity, and divination.

Thursday is "Thor's Day." Thursday is ruled by Jupiter, and is a good opportunity for magick involving money, luck, and success.

Friday is "Freya's Day," ruled by Venus. Spells for love, romance, friendship, and beauty are best done on Friday.

Saturday is "Saturn's Day," and is ruled by the planet Saturn. Work your spells for protection, structure, and resolution on Saturday.

Sunday is the "Sun's Day." Ruled by the sun, this is a good day for masculine spells and those involving peace, harmony, and divine power.

The Cycling of the Seasons

Spring: Fertility, birth, new beginnings, fresh starts, initiations, youth.

Summer: Growth, gathering, richness, adulthood, peak energy.

Autumn: Harvest, fading, ebbing, old age.

Winter: Sleep, low energy, death (symbolic).

The Moon

If the moon is powerful enough to move the oceans, doesn't it stand to reason that it affects people and magick as well? Lunar magick is complex enough to need its own library of books. But in general, when you do a working that requires strength, growth, abundance, or gathering power, work during the time between the dark (new) moon and full moon, when then moon is symbolically "growing" in size and power, that is, when it is waxing. If you're working with fading, banishing, eliminating, or dispersing, work between the full and dark moon, when the moon's size and power are ebbing, that is, when it is waning. The full moon is felt to represent the height of lunar influence, and is a time of great power. As for the new moon, many practitioners don't work magick when the moon's face is dark and hidden.

Colors

Colors can be useful in magick, adding their magickal correspondences to candles, altar cloths, stones, and more.

Using Color in Magick	
Color	**Correspondences**
Black	Night, dark arts, hex work, absence, banishing and repelling, discord.
Blue	Healing, protection, emotions, protection, opposition to the evil eye.
Brown	Nature, Earth, creatures, grounding and centering, stability.
Gold	Wealth, spells associated with the sun and male energies.
Gray	Knowledge, wisdom, fairness, judgment, respect.
Green	Healing, natural world, prosperity, luck, spells for increasing.
Orange	Intensity, passion, attraction, health.
Pink	Love, romance, attraction, friendship, honor.
Purple	Success, authority, royalty, wealth, ambition, power.
Red	Power, dominance, love, sex, passion, fertility, heat, fire, energy, blood.
Silver	Psychic gifts, divination, spells associated with the moon and female energies.
Violet	Perception, intuition, psychic powers.
White	Unity, purity, sincerity, spells associated with the moon
Yellow	Mental work, prosperity, growth, vigor, plenty.

Charms and Talismans

Different magick users have differing ideas of what constitutes a charm and what constitutes a talisman. After a lot of study and personal experience, I have developed my own definitions:

A charm is similar to a miniature spell. It combines intention and components to create something that is "set in place" to send magick out into the world, creating an effect. A charm's energy reaches outwards, extending away from the charmcaster. Most work for a specific time period, as they usually have a starting and stopping point.

Example: You've been having a nightmare about being chased by a gargoyle. On a Saturday night (for protection and resolution), you cut an 8-inch circle of yellow fabric (for mental work); on it, you place a small opal (a psychic stone) and a pinch of dried chamomile (for calm). You tie the bundle up, hobo style, with a piece of silver embroidery floss (for psychic intuition). You then put it under your bed pillow. Before turning in for the night, you speak aloud your wish for a peaceful, calm night's sleep. In working through these steps, you have created a charm that will help you sleep and should control the nightmares.

A talisman is an object (stone, metal, shell, and so on) that either is embodied with naturally occurring magick or is intentionally charged with magick. Talismans might be thought of as acting as a sort of "storage battery" for energy, or as actually drawing energy inwards, toward the talisman's wearer or bearer. Talismans are often linked to a specific deity, or to a branch of Elemental energy. They are typically worn or carried by the person seeking the magickal effect; magickal jewelry, medicine bags, and amulets are talismans. Most talismans work indefinitely.

Example: A stone that appears in your path, offering itself to you, can become a powerful talisman. Pick the stone up, offer it thanks, take it home, and set it on your altar in a dish of salt, allowing it to cleanse itself and to fill with Earthly energies. On the next full moon, hold the stone aloft, allowing it to similarly fill the lunar energies. You now own a powerful talisman—keep it with you for best results.

Egregores

An egregore (var. egrigor) is a thought form that is created by will, invocation, and visualization. It works best as a group effect, the more people that manifest the form, the more likely it is to, literally, take on life. For many people, gargoyles not only seem alive but full of power and energy. It stands to reason that they might take on life as the focus of an egregore.

(And by the way, probably the best-known egregore in the world is Santa Claus, in all of his visages!)

A Case for Cuthbert

By Estara T'Shirai

At the Grey School, the Defense Against the Dark Arts Club has been working on developing a sort of mascot and protector for the school: a purple gargoyle named Cuthbert. A gargoyle is an excellent shape for such a protector, with wings for getting around quickly, hands for detailed work, and claws for defense. And their history in art is centered around them guarding the outsides of churches and other important buildings.

When he's finished, Cuthbert will be what many call an egregore. Now, what exactly an egregore is and how it is formed is a matter for debate. The most common view, which comes from the ceremonialist framework, is that an egregore is created entirely by the wizard. You create a detailed image of what you would want in an astral servant, and you feed energy into that image to give it life. At that time, you define its duties very carefully, so as not to allow the egregore any free will, and you choose the times of both its birth and its death. (Most people who use this method say that the date of death must actually be set at the time you create the egregore.) It has essentially no will or purpose except what you give it. Recent books use the term "familiar," which has also meant a helping animal or spirit, with this same meaning.

My own view of this process has always been slightly different, perhaps because the idea of an unthinking slave whose life and death are in my hands doesn't appeal to me. When I "create" an astral servant, what I actually do is to clearly imagine what job I have for it and what form it would best take, just as others would do. However, what I am doing is similar to sending out a want ad. In "creating" Cuthbert, for example, I would actually be offering a contract to any spirit that was willing to take on the astral shape of a gargoyle and perform the tasks I needed done. When a spirit fitting the bill arrived, I would offer it the contract and do the appropriate things on my end to allow that spirit to manifest on the terms we'd agreed upon.

Ultimately, the difference may be one of semantics: We may be dealing with two different ways of looking at the same actual process. But I think it makes sense to work with the theory that resonates better with you.

Whichever theory you prefer—egregore as construct, or as a job offered to an unemployed spirit—you need to provide certain things. First is, of course, choosing exactly what job the egregore is to perform. If there is no work, there is no point to having an egregore hanging around, because bored spirits, whether natural or artificial, tend to end up causing trouble. There are all sorts of jobs that can be given to an egregore, with "guard dog" type duties and going out to fetch information being two of the most common.

Second, you need some sort of physical vessel to represent your link to the egregore. This should not be thought of as the spirit's literal body or a prison, but as the anchor that allows the spirit to manifest in the physical world, and a sort of nest for it to rest in when it is not doing its job. Although there is a history of housing spirits in simple containers such as jars, this being the origin of the Arabian "magic lamp" with a genie inside, for example, because many people today like the vessel to actually resemble the type of spirit that lives in it. Since there are many places where one can buy a wide variety of gargoyle statues and images, this isn't very difficult in our case. Note, also, that if an egregore is going to be shared by a group, it can have more than one vessel. This just provides it more touch points with the physical world. (Ensouled deity statues, such as the ones used in Egypt and still are today in India, work by this concept.) For each vessel, there should be a ritual in which the vessel is blessed by techniques appropriate to your style, and the egregore is invited to use it. Some people cement this link by placing special symbols representing the egregore on or in the vessel, or using special herbal mixes. You might try simply writing the egregore's name and the date on which you created it/ started the contract in the vessel.

Should the time come when you and the egregore are going to part ways, at the time of its "death," if you are using a construct for example, it would be best to destroy or at least thoroughly cleanse and de-energize the vessel it used.

Third, you need to keep regular contact with the egregore and give it energy in some way. If you are working by the construct theory, the egregore is your creation, completely dependent on you for its existence. So, if you don't feed it, it must either starve or break off in search of other sources of energy, in which case it may choose something inappropriate and troublesome. If your egregore is a hired hand, regular contact and offerings help cement your relationship and motivate your spirit to continue to work faithfully for you, rather than trolling around for better offers or doing a less-than-optimal job at its assignments. How often you will check in with the egregore and what you will use to "feed" it should be worked out before you actually create/summon it. You should then consider this to be your minimum obligation: having an egregore is a responsibility, not unlike having a pet or a child, and you must be ready to do your part to take care of it for as long as it stays with you.

Latin Words for Your Gargoyle Spellcraft

Latin is one of the languages known as "old speech," and it is frequently used as a magickal language in ritual and spellcraft, where its antiquity adds power to the workings. Table 7 features Latin words that may be useful for your gargoyle workings.

Latin for Spellcraft

Nouns			Verbs	
Air (sky)	*Caelum*		Banish	*Pellere*
Animal	*Animal*		Build	*Aedifico*
Art	*Ars*		Carve	*Caelo*
Earth	*Terra*		Cast	*Iacere*
Fellowship	*Societas*		Conjure	*Elicere*
Fire	*Ignis*		Decrease	*Decrescere*
Gargoyle	*Caelature*		Design	*Describo*
Magic(k)	*Magicus*		Divine	*Auguror*
Man	*Homo*		Fly	*Volare*
Night	*Nocte*		Foresee	*Provideo*
Power	*Potestas*		Foretell	*Praedico*
Spell	*Carmen*		Increase	*Increscere*
Spirit	*Animus*		Possess	*Habeo*
Stone	*Lapis*		Practice	*Exerceo*
Time	*Tempus*		Protect	*Defendere*
Water	*Aqua*		Search	*Quaero*
Will	*Volentas*		Serve	*Servio*
Wizard	*Magus*		Study	*Studeo*
Woman	*Femina*		Transform	*Transmutere*

Spellwork Featuring "Gargoylish" Correspondences or Actions

It's time! Let's try putting everything together and working with spells that invoke the nature, presence, or symbolic meanings of gargoyles and their stony relatives.

A Spell That Imparts Tenacity, Permanence, or the Idea of Something That Endures Over Time

Materials:

- A stone or rock.
- A gargoyle figurine (optional).
- A wristwatch or other time device.
- A small bowl of sand.
- A small bowl or chalice of water.
- A candle (brown or gray).

Light the candle. Say,
Sands of time, Water, and Fire.
Fist and might of mother Earth.
Stones formed of her loving power.
May I, too, have the strength of stone.
May its birth energies sustain me.
May my spirit stand strong
Through the millennia.

Contemplate the forces symbolized in the fire, water, and sand before you. Now hold the charged stone in your hand and feel the energy move through your body. Keep the stone, which has become a working talisman, on your altar, or carry it with you in a pocket or medicine bag.

Best done: morning, Tuesday or Saturday, spring or summer, waxing or full moon.

A Spell That Imparts Strength and Protection

Take a walk in a natural area in which you feel relaxed and protected. While you walk, pick up a number of small stones. At the conclusion of your walk, but before you return home, hold the stones in your hand. Hold your hand up in front of your face, and open it flat, so that you can clearly see and appreciate the nature of the stones. Now, close your hand into a fist. As you do, imagine the energies of the stones spilling from between your fingers. Imagine the strength of these stones; though tiny, they have endured for centuries, perhaps even millennia. Consider stones as gargoyles, keeping watch from high atop their cathedrals. Imagine this strength and protection coursing through you, and keeping you safe.

After arriving home, carry the stones (or at least one of them) with you at all times for protection. The stones may be used in different ways or different locations. You might carry one in a pocket, leave one on your altar, place one over the entry to your home, incorporate one in a talisman, and so on.

Best done: dusk, Tuesday, summer, waxing moon.

A Spell That Imparts Good Fortune

On New Year's morning, go outside right after midnight. Look for the first stone that catches your eye. Take it home, and display it on your altar or in a place of prominence. Offer it thanks whenever you pass by, along with occasional sprinkles of water and salt. Keep the stone throughout the year, and watch your luck and prosperity grow. At the next New Year, find a new stone, and "retire" your previous New Year stone to a place in your *Sanctum Sanctorum* or garden.

Best done: between dawn and noon (especially Wednesday or Thursday), waxing moon.

A Spell in Which Negative Energy or Emotions are Banished

Materials:
- A tall taper candle (black).
- Oil (olive or almond, or essential oil of your choice).
- Matches.
- An abalone shell, or other fireproof container.
- Candle snuffer.

Anoint the candle with the oil, working from top to bottom with long strokes. As you work, talk aloud about those things that you wish to banish. These actions will capture the intention of your banishing into the candle.

When you feel as if you're finished, light the candle. Hold it at an angle, allowing wax to drip onto the rock. As the wax drips, speak again about the obstacles and negativities that you're banishing. Continue this for as long as you wish, then use the snuffer to put out the candle.

Now, bury the stone, symbolically giving a funeral to your overcome obstacles. Do this silently, then, as the last bit of earth is tamped into place, say, *The path is clear. So mote it be.*

Best done: midnight to dawn, Saturday, autumn, waning moon.

A Spell That Invokes or Implies Guardianship, Duty, Vigil, or Protection

Materials:

- ◎ A small gargoyle statue (a photo of a gargoyle or a small stone can be substituted).
- ◎ A full moon evening.

On a full moon evening, as close as possible to the actual point of fullness, go outdoors to a location where you can easily see the moon. Hold your gargoyle up toward the moon in both hands. Say,

Shining moon and starry night,

Watching with protective sight,

Bathe this stone in holy light.

Hold the gargoyle thus for several moments, then say,

Fearsome gargoyle in the sky,

Perched atop the building high,

Guard us well as we pass by.

Bow your head slightly to the moon and to the gargoyle, murmuring the words *thank you, blessed be,* or another acknowledgement. Leave the gargoyle outside or in an open window, in a place where both the full moonlight and night air can bathe it.

In the morning, bring in your gargoyle and install it in a location where it can provide guardianship.

Best done: midnight, Monday, summer, full moon.

A Spell That Creates a "Silent Summons," Invoking a Reminder or a Call to Action When You Gaze Upon It

Materials:

- ◉ A pile of different sized stones. If you want to build a tall cairn, make sure to include large (perhaps cantaloupe-sized) stones. Note also that irregularly shaped stones are easier to stack than round ones.
- ◉ Work gloves.
- ◉ Symbols of the Four Elements [salt (Earth), incense (air and fire), water].

Determine the purpose for your cairn. Are you honoring a sacred location? Creating a place for worship or reflection?

Determine the size—a "yard-sized cairn" would be made of large stones, while a miniature one might be create of river rocks.

Consider timing when building your cairn. Because you are building something literally from the ground up, you'll have the best results if you work in times when the energy is increasing: waxing moons, morning, hours, and so on.

Decide on a base for your cairn: round or square. You may wish to bless to smudge the area before you start.

Build your cairn, starting with a foundation of large stones and using smaller ones as the cairn grows taller. Don't go too high—a foot or two should be fine. The taller the cairn, the less stable it will be and the more likely to fall.

As you build, reflect on (or speak aloud) the purpose of the cairn, thus infusing your own magick into it as you work.

When finished, say:

Just a simple pile of stones,
Built simply from the mother's bones,
Catch my eye as I walk past,
Devotions offered, long to last.

Now, bless the cairn with your Elemental offerings: sprinkle it with salt, waft incense across it, and drizzle it with water.

The creation aspect is finished. The second aspect is ongoing: Whenever you walk by the cairn, stop and meditate, or chat with it. Strengthen or repair it as needed, add tiny stones to fill in the chinks, leave offerings at its base, and so on. The cairn could also be used more formally, as an outdoor altar or as the focus of outdoor worship. Watch where it casts a shadow on the equinoxes and solstices and you'll have your own working archaeoastronomical monument!

Best done: dusk, Saturday, summer, waxing or full moon.

A Spell That Honors the Night's Magick

Materials:

◎ A warm sweater or jacket.

◎ A flashlight.

◎ A chair or blanket.

◎ A bottle of water, tea, or juice.

◎ A 6 inch circle of cloth.

◎ Your favorite dried herbs: chamomile or lavender would work well.

◎ Your favorite essential oil: Lavender or patchouli would work well.

◎ A small bit of thread or string .

The night is a place of magick and enchantment, but too often we fear the night rather than enjoy it. Legend says that gargoyles unfurled their wings and flew by night. You, too, can do this.

Make an herbal sachet. Place a teaspoon or so of dried herbs and a few drops of essential oil on the cloth circle. Gather up the edges, hobo style, and tie the little bag shut with the thread. Slip the bag into your pocket. Just before dusk, find a safe, quiet place where it will be dark once the sun sets. Settle down in your chair or on your blanket. Slip into a quiet meditative state—this can be helped by humming a soft tone to yourself, and by breathing the scent from your herbal sachet. Open yourself to the sounds and feelings of the night. Be aware of the light slowly ebbing away, and the darkness coming to life. Breathe deeply and allow your awareness to open to messages and discoveries coming from around you. Sip from your water bottle now and then. When you're finished, allow your normal consciousness to surface, and return to your home in silence. Maintain darkness if you can, but use your flashlight as needed for safety. Once home, place the sachet under your pillow for safe, sweet dreams.

Best done: night, Tuesday, any season, waxing moon.

A Spell That Honors the Ancient Ones

Materials:

◎ A small gargoyle statue, or other statuary, or photographs of departed ones.

- A candle (silver or violet).
- A plate or saucer.
- Offerings: salt, grain, a piece of bread, a small chalice of red wine or ale, and so on.
- Cakes and ale (especially family favorites).

Place the candle in the saucer. Arrange the statuary or photos next to the plate. Light the candle. Say,

Wise ones of the past,

Honored ancestors,

This simple feast is shared with you.

Add the offerings to the plate. Then, enjoy your own cakes and ale, reflecting on the ancient ones as you do so. Note: You may also wish to set up an ancestor altar as a focus for your working.

Best done: noon or midnight, Wednesday, winter, waxing moon.

A Spell That Blesses Flying Creatures (Including Gargoyles!)

Stand in a safe, open outdoor space. Light your favorite incense, or choose one that corresponds to Air. Say,

Owners of sky, that wing above,

Cast in stone, or feathered dove,

Venture safely, wrapped in love.

Meditate on the safety of winged creatures. Cast your gaze to the air, and let it remain there until you see a flying creature. Then say, "*Safe passage,*" and put out your incense.

Best done: morning to dusk, any season (particularly autumn and winter), any day, any moon.

Mind Magicks

Mind magicks have to do with psychic development, including studies of meditation, dreamwork, telepathy, and others.

Our left brain, in which we experience normal waking consciousness, operates with deductive logic, reasoning from the specific to the general. This is the kind of linear scientific problem-solving thinking made famous by Sherlock Holmes and modern detectives. When people use deductive logic to solve concrete tasks, they are using their left brain.

Our right brain, however, works on inductive logic, reasoning from the general to the specific. The right brain is the center for artistic expression, creativity, and imagination. When people are gifted by the muse to draw, paint, compose music, write poetry, and so on, they are using their right brain.

Both parts of the brain are important in magickal functioning. The left brain helps with study, deductive reasoning, and planning. But the right brain is what creates spiritual and magickal insights, and the right brain may be what allows us to come loose from our corporeal body and enter the magickal realm. Meditation is a kind of mental exercise that helps clear and strengthen the right brain.

The following is what is called a guided meditation. To use it, find a place where you can sit quietly and undisturbed. Have someone read this aloud to you, or read it into a recording device and then play it back. Sit comfortably, with your back straight and your eyes closed.

Gargoyle Meditation for Perspective

By Kalla

Think of something that you have trouble thinking clearly about—something that is too close to your heart to be reasonable about, but that you want to be able to see from the outside. Keep this in your mind. Take a deep breath and relax. Feel connected and comfortable with your body. Breathe in and out. Breathe in and out. Breathe in and out. Open your spirit eyes. Before you is a beautiful mist—the boundary between worlds. Look with your spirit's eyes beyond the mist. Take a step forward and begin to walk through the mist. You feel the soft, cool mist all around your body. You smell the earth and the rain.

You finally emerge from the mist into a vast stone hallway. The hall is made of large, grey stones. Torches line the wall, creating pools of light and shadow on the floor. The smell of incense wafts towards you. Walk forward. Your steps echo off the hard stone. Walk forward, from light to shadow, light to shadow, on and on. You pass closed door after closed door.

Eventually you come to the end of the hall. A hooded man stands at the base of a staircase. He looks up at you with wrinkled eyes.

"Hello there. I was wondering when you'd get here. So you want to see more clearly, with less of your emotions mucking things up. This is the place for that. But are you sure?"

You tell the man that you are sure you want to know.

"All right," he says. "Up these stairs sit the gargoyles. They see everything that goes on. Always above, seeing clearly. They're not a part of the action, so they can see where others falter. Go up and see what can be seen about your situation. But keep in mind that you may not like what you see. And you may not be ready to see at all. Go up, find out."

He moves to the side to let you through to the stairs. Up and up they go, stories and stories into the air. Your legs are on fire and your chest heaves with effort. Finally, after what seems like ages, the stair come to the top and you emerge into the cool night.

The air is crisp and clean. You stand at the top of a large turret. Three gargoyles sit along the edge. One young and small, one big and strong, and one old and wise. Looking down over the side of the turret, you see scenes from throughout your life playing around you. To your left you see the past, ahead the present, and to your right, possible futures. Go to the side that shows what you want to understand. Sit amongst the gargoyles and see with clarity.

The sight of your life fades, and below you is only a sea of grass, waving in the breeze. You have seen all that you can for now and have much to think about. Stand up and thank the gargoyles for what they have shown you and turn back down the staircase.

As you walk downwards you feel different...wiser...clearer.

You get to the bottom of the stair and walk back down the hallway. The torches fade and the mists once again appear before you. You step through them, and their warmth comforts you. You return to your ordinary self, settling comfortably and securely into your body.

Open your eyes.

A Focus for Your Mind Magicks

A gargoyle figure—or simply your favorite rock, stone, crystal, or gem—can be used as an effective meditation aid. The figure will create a visual focus, helping you center and clear your mind. It could also teach you about the nature of being petrified, with quiet and motionlessness used to support deep meditation.

Creating an Ancestor Altar

The ancestor altar is for honoring and remembering one's ancestors, not worshipping them. It can be set up as part of your regular altar/shrine, or it can be assembled in a separate location. Many of us set up ancestor shrines without thinking about it, whenever we arrange pictures of our departed ones, or special photographs, objects, or symbols that they have left us.

In my tradition, there are three kinds of ancestors: those who came before us, those that are with us now, and those that are waiting to be born. Another view suggests the three groups as blood ancestors, ancestors from our spiritual lineage, and ancestors of the land. However, each ancestor should be honored, for each is important.

What do gargoyles have to do with this? We think of gargoyles and grotesques as guardians of the past, and because they are also here with us in the present, gargoyles can be a powerful focus for an ancestor altar.

When setting up an ancestor altar, it is traditional to use a fringed altar cloth. The fringe functions similar to a dreamcatcher and helps connect your consciousness with your ancestor's. Candles and incense are optional, but a nice addition. One way to honor ancestors is with a small a pot of earth on the altar; earth from a quarry or a graveyard is especially powerful. You can honor your spiritual ancestors by adding an object with a symbol of your spiritual path: a pentacle for Wiccans, the Awen for Druids, and so on. Another good option is to add a small plate of the ancestor's favorite food or drink.

Once the altar is set, call to the old ones, inviting them to be present. Note: Never demand that any spectral visitor, even if family, attend your workings! Always invite, or request. Let them know that you have created a sacred space where they will be welcome, safe, and honored. For best results, be sure to invite only those ancestors who come in love and peace, and intend no harm.

Weatherworking

Obtain a small gargoyle or grotesque sculpture. Set it outside in an open area. Now amaze your friends by telling them that your gargoyle is a fully accurate weatherworker! When they express doubt, explain:

- If the gargoyle is hot, it's sunny.
- If the gargoyle is wet, it's raining.
- If the gargoyle is white, it's snowing.

- If leaves are blowing past the gargoyle, it's windy.
- If the gargoyle is spinning about, there's a tornado.
- If the gargoyle's hair is standing on end, watch out for lightning!

(Magick users are known for having a good sense of humor.)

Ritual

A magickal ritual combines spellcraft and ritual actions, the details of which vary among practitioners and magickal belief systems. Instruction in ritual work is beyond the scope of this book; please see the Resources section at the end of this text.

The following is a sample ritual that could be adapted for any form of spiritual practice.

A Gargoyle Protection Ritual

By Kalla

Materials:

- A small statue or image of a gargoyle.
- Dragon's blood oil (buy at a magick or herbal shop).

This ritual is best done during waxing to full moon. Open the circle and call quarters and deities in accordance with your usual practices. Anoint the gargoyle with dragon's blood oil, charging the image with protectiveness. Hold the image in your projecting hand and say:

Guardian stand true, allow nothing intending me or mine harm pass by you. Allow friends and loved ones in, and all the happiness they bring. Stand guard and keep foes out until I say so or the next full moon.

Dismiss deities and quarters and close circle as usual.

After the ritual, place the gargoyle near the front door. The spell must be renewed each full moon.

Note: This ritual may be done with multiple gargoyles so that everyone in the circle has one for their own home. It could also easily be modified to become a spell, rather than a complete ritual.

Try This

Cast yourself back into medieval times by writing magickal alphabets with your own parchment, quill, and ink.

Create a Scroll

Materials:

- Parchment paper (craft and scrapbooking stores).
- Scissors.
- String or thread.
- A wooden spoon or dowel (about 1/2 inch diameter).
- Ribbon (your choice of color).
- Deckling scissors (optional).

Cut the parchment paper to the desired size. (If you choose, create a rough edge with deckling scissors.) Roll the parchment tightly around the wooden spoon handle, secure with string, and allow it to sit overnight. The next day, remove the string and slip the parchment from wooden spoon handle. Tie a decorative ribbon around your scroll and set aside.

Make a Quill

Use a bird feather or buy a quill at a craft store. Use a pocketknife to sharpen the feather tip, then use the quill as a pen, dipping the tip in ink.

Craft Your Own Ink

Materials:

- 1 black tea bag.
- Unsoaped steel wool.
- Vinegar.
- A small saucepan.
- 3 percent hydrogen peroxide.
- Strainer.
- Small bowl.
- Quill (or toothpick).

Place the tea bag in a teacup. Add a 1/3 cup boiling water and let it steep for 15 minutes. Wring the tea bag out and throw it away. Save the tea—it contains tannic acid.

In a small saucepan, warm a 1/4 cup vinegar. Use scissors to snip bits of unsoaped steel wool into the hot vinegar (add as much as you can, but make sure the vinegar continues to cover the steel wool). Heat until the steel wool dissolves and/or forms a colored solution (iron sulfate). Cool. Note: It is very important to be careful when handling any liquids of this nature.

Pour the tea into the small bowl. Strain the iron solution into the tea. This will form black iron tannate. Be very careful: This is indelible and will stain clothes, carpet, or whatever it touches!

Dip a quill into the "ink" and try writing with it. If the ink seems watery, let it sit out for a day or two until enough evaporates to make it slightly thicker.

Store in a tightly capped bottle.

Create Your Own Gargoyle Spells

- A spell that invokes the Elements.
- A spell that creates strength of purpose.
- A spell in which you invoke the ability of clay or stone to be shaped or carved to suit a specific need.
- A spell in which you invoke a wall or structure of stone as an emblem of strength.
- A spell in which a gargoyle dispels fear.
- A spell in which the meanings of an animal or magickal creature are harnessed for specific magickal intent.
- A spell in which a gargoyle creates fear as a means of providing warning.
- A spell in which nightmares are prevented or frightened away.

15

Stone Magick

Stones are the Earth's children, the most visible offspring of Mother Earth, who is also known as Artha, Demeter, Edda, Eortha, Erce, Erda, Ertha, Europa, Gaea, Gaia, Hel, Heortha, Hera, Hretha, Nerthus, Ops, Rhea, Terra, Urd, and Urth in different traditions. Created, demolished, and rebirthed over and over in geological cycles that last millions of years, stones work their magick each and every day. Many aboriginal traditions refer to stone as the skeleton of the great Earth Mother. It's interesting that in no mythology or spiritual practice has Earth ever been referred to with a male pronoun—*she* is always life giving, and always a mother.

Stones are the Earth's truest elder race. Each stone retains traces of ancient memories, making them silent witnesses to millennia of history. But while stones and rocks correspond closely to the Earth Element, they also evoke the other magickal elements as well.

Air

Many stones are ejected through volcanic action into the air, and fill with bubbles and air pockets. Examples include pumice and all sorts of vesicular rock. Stalactites, which hold tight to the ceilings of caves, could also be equated with air, as could spires of rock that rise into the air, such as the needles of Monument Valley in Utah and Arizona. The enormous "crystals" of columnar basalt form when melted rock meets the air and cools into giant multi-sided structures, leaving something that looks similar to a giant honeycomb.

Fire

At one time or another, all stones are shaped by fire, whether through volcanic eruption or by heat and pressure deep below the Earth's surface. Fire and heat can change one form of rock, for example sedimentary limestone, into another: metamorphic marble.

Water

Volcanic rock is cooled by water. Sedimentary rock and petrified wood are formed by nothing less than vast amounts of water and time. In contrast, water and its various forms of rain, snow, and ice are responsible for weathering and eroding rocky surfaces, returning them to the Earth mother's arms so that they may be rebuilt into new stone.

Spirit: Here and Now

Rocks are alive, composed of the same atoms and elements as we are. In the mysterious world of quantum physics, humans and rocks are more alike than different! Rocks evoke the life force, and stir our imaginations as they connect with us through their own unspoken energies, reminding us of the immortality of time and of the concrete nature of the here and now.

"As Above"

Everything on Earth comes to us from the Universe. Our planet, our bodies, and everything we know are formed of atoms, the building blocks of all matter. Atoms are created within stars, each star with a nuclear reactor at its core. When stars complete their life cycles, their energies and contents are spewed out into the Universe, flooding space-time with new forms of matter that may end up billions and trillions of miles from where they started, perhaps streaming into the atmospheres of existing planets to create new life forms. Astronomer Carl Sagan said it best: "We are star stuff."

"So Below"

Everything on Earth is eventually turned under, recycled beneath the Earth's surface by something akin to a great plow, into a mystical place where the elements are broken down, heated, compressed, reformed, and uplifted in a kind of rebirth.

When trying to work with aspects of natural or "green" magick (and stone work is all about green magick), it is a good idea to first develop an understanding of the natural science that underpins the practices. In this case, by learning about what rocks and minerals are composed of and how they're created—in other words, by coming to understand their real-life correspondences—we're in an optimal position to use them in magickal practices.

First, a few definitions:

Atoms are the smallest building blocks of matter, and all ordinary matter consists of atoms. To get an idea of how small an atom is, take a pinch of sugar, then separate out one sugar crystal. If you were to cut that single crystal into a least 100 parts, each would be about the size of an atom.

Elements consist of matter that is made of a single type of atom. Elements, such as oxygen, carbon, iron, and silicon, cannot be broken down into other substances.

Compounds are formed by the bonding of two or more elements. For example, water is a compound formed by two hydrogen atoms and one oxygen atom. (You can confound your friends by referring to water as "dihydrogen oxide.")

Minerals are solid inorganic substances—either a free, uncombined element or an elemental compound. Minerals have specific molecular compositions and unique crystal structures. With a few exceptions such as mercury, they are solid. Examples include quartz (the Earth's most common mineral) and fluorite (the Earth's most colorful mineral).

Rocks are formed of two or more minerals and fall into three groups:

1. **Sedimentary rock** is formed underwater when sand, mud, and other materials are subjected to water and pressure over millions of years. Sandstone and limestone are probably the best-known examples. If you look at a natural sedimentary rock, you can usually see the tiny grains of sand, and sometimes trapped pebbles, shells, or other matter. When you stand on a bed or in a quarry of sedimentary rock, you're actually standing on an ancient, uplifted sea floor!

2. **Metamorphic rock** is formed deep under the Earth's surface when movements of the Earth's underground crustal plates create huge extremes of pressure and temperature over millions of years, changing existing rocks into new varieties. One of the most familiar and abundant metamorphic rocks is marble. Another is gneiss (pronounced "nice"), a metamorphic rock formed by the crushing and melting of granite. When you look at metamorphic rock in its raw state, you can see tiny mineral crystals and variegated colors, often with wavy bands running through the stone.

3. **Igneous rock** is formed when rock melts and becomes magma under the Earth's surface, then forces its way to the surface, where it may ooze out slowly between solid rocks or blast its way into the sky via a volcanic eruption. One of the best examples of an igneous rock is basalt, the most common rock found in the Earth's crust. In fact, most of the ocean floor is made of basalt, as is most of the northwestern United States. Granite is another important igneous rock. It is formed by the slow cooling of silica-rich magmas that move upwards from deep below the Earth. Most of North America's Sierra Nevada mountain chain is made of granite. Igneous rocks tend to be heavy and fine-grained.

   In the rock cycle, molten magma from the Earth's core rises to the surface, where it cools to form solid igneous rock. When igneous rocks are exposed at the earth's surface, they are eroded, by action of water, wind, glaciers, and so on, or weather to form sediments. These sediments are compacted and/or cemented to form sedimentary rocks. When existing igneous or sedimentary rocks are crushed and carried back down into the Earth, heat and pressure change them into metamorphic rock. Eventually rocks are carried back down into the Earth, where the heat melts them into magma. And the cycle begins again.

A **stone**, in building terms, is the hard, solid, nonmetallic mineral matter that is used as a building material. In terms of the stone magick that we're discussing here, "stone" is used as a kind of catchall term for crystals, gems, minerals, and so on.

A **gem** is a precious or semi-precious stone, which when "improved" (cut, polished, or engraved) becomes valuable or special in some respect.

A **crystal** is a piece of a homogeneous solid substance having a natural geometric form with symmetrically arranged plane faces. What does that mean in English? Crystals are minerals that share a common structure throughout, with their atoms literally arranged and lined up in identical fashion. The structure creates planes of weakness and the mineral tends to break along these planes, creating flat "faces." Think of the flat planes, angles, and points of a quartz crystal, and you'll be visualizing this. Fracture, on the other hand, is when minerals to break along non-planar lines. The conchoidal (seashell-like), fracture of obsidian is a good example of fracturing.

Finding Stones

As a magick user, you'll want to begin a collection of magickal stones, gems, and crystals, not only because they can be used for magick and divination, but because they're pretty, and fun to have. Keep a lot of stones in and around your house and you'll find yourself gifted with a profound sense of protection and well-being.

Where to find stones:

- Rock and gems shops.
- Natural history museums.
- Bead shops.
- Magick and New Age shops.
- Renaissance fairs and gem shows.
- Rock clubs.
- Online sources (try searching for lapidary shops and clubs).

You may be lucky enough to find stones in nature, which brings us to an important rule: Never walk by an interesting stone that puts itself in your path! If you collect stones in nature, be sure that it is allowed and make sure that you aren't on private or protected property. In the United States, for example, you cannot collect stones within a national or state park.

If you decide to become a rock collector, you'll want to assemble a kit of basic materials:

- Heavy gloves.
- Goggles.
- A rock hammer and chisel (always wear eye protection when using these!).
- Newspaper or plastic bags for wrapping specimens in the field.
- Permanent felt tip marker for labeling specimens in the field.
- A rock identification guide.

- ⓢ A magnifying lens.
- ⓢ Empty egg cartons (great for storing rocks and crystals).
- ⓢ A bottle of "liquid paper" for marking your rocks.

When you return home, wash each rock carefully to remove dirt, mud, and so on. Allow the rock to dry. Decide which surface is the rock's "top" and which is its "bottom," in terms of how you want to display it in your collection. Take a bottle of liquid paper and dab a pea-sized spot on the bottom surface of the rock. Allow the dot to dry thoroughly. With a ballpoint pen or a fine permanent marker, write the rock's identification number on the white spot. In a small notebook, write the number and make a corresponding entry about the rock.

Gargoyle Stones

As you've learned, most modern and medieval gargoyles are formed of either limestone or marble, while a few have historically been made of terra-cotta.

Limestone

Limestone is a carbonate rock, with more than half its weight composed of carbonate minerals such as calcite and dolomite, most of which come from the shells, bones, reefs, and fossilized remains of undersea animals. Carbonate rocks also include varying amounts of mud, quartz (and other kinds of silicon), iron oxide, and trace compounds.

Limestone comes in a wide variety of colors; most commonly it is gray or whitish gray. It may also be yellow, brown, or even black.

Red limestone

Red limestone is a special kind of fine-grained limestone that gains its red color from a high percentage of iron oxide. Limestone has a grainy appearance; if you look at a rough piece, you can literally see the grains of sand that have been squished together to form the stone. Most ancient stone monuments and carvings, at least through medieval times, are made of limestone, a hard, durable stone that is easy to carve. In magickal terms, limestone symbolizes strength, durability, and the spirit of guardians and ancestors. Like any stone, it also evokes the passing of time.

Marble

This stone has a variegated appearance—if you look at it with a magnifying lens, you can see the individual, tiny stones that have come together. Marble is usually white or a soft gray, but it can also appear black, green, blue, yellow, brown, or even pink. Marble is the noblest of artist stones. Its hardness makes it lasting and durable. It's also a workable stone and can be polished to a gorgeous, satiny finish. In fact, its name comes from the Greek *marmaros*, "shining stone." Magickally, marble is associated with strength and with protection against cold (physical and emotional). It also evokes qualities of change and transformation.

Terra-cotta

This stone is a kind of reddish clay that can be shaped and baked into a hard, stony substance. Legend says that the biblical Adam's name comes from *adamah*, literally "bloody clay;" this may go back to primitive Earth magicks, in which menstrual blood was often mixed with clay and/or used as an anointing material.[1] The reddish flower pots that we're familiar with today are made or terra-cotta. Clay represents the creative aspects of the Mother Earth and is also a symbol for human flesh (the gods were always picking up chunks of clay and creating living creatures out of them).

Other important Earthly stones:

Agate is associated with both Earth and Water. Available in an array of colors and patterns, it has long been credited with divine attraction and is said to gift the holder with persuasive speech. Agate creates a sense of calm, reduces fear, brings sleep, and lends strength, both to body and purpose.

Hematite is associated with the Earth Element. The polished mineral is a shiny, lustrous silver; in its rough form, it can be shaved and ground into a iron-based reddish powder known as "red ochre," used by ancient peoples as a red paint for mystical purposes. Hematite is used to stop bleeding. It offers protection in battle, increases alertness, and aids with divination and scrying.

Jet is another name for black anthracite coal that has been compressed into a form hard enough to be cut and polished. Coal is a kind of carbon; compress carbon over millions of years and you eventually end up with diamonds. Jet is associated with the Earth Element and with caves and the Underworld. Jet is highly protective; historically, talismans were used to repel demons and combat the evil eye.

Lodestone is associated with both Earth and Fire. It is a natural magnet; folklore says that it should not be carried during storms as it will attract lightening. Lodestone is likewise thought useful for attracting other things, including luck, money, or a mate.

Petrified wood is associated with Earth and Water. It soothes, supports patience, and provides a sense of calm. It has healing qualities, supports longevity, and can be carried as a charm against drowning.

Obsidian is associated with Earth, Fire, and Air. Known as volcanic glass, it is magma that cooled so fast that the minerals in the material had no time to form their normal crystalline matrix. Obsidian breaks with a conchoidal (shell-shaped) fracture and forms razor-sharp edges, making it an important tool stone for aboriginal peoples. Obsidian is black and glossy, and thin pieces appear gray and translucent. It is a powerful stone for grounding and centering, and has strong protective qualities.

Snowflake obsidian, an obsidian variation that includes white snowflake-like markings, also has grounding and centering capabilities. Even more, it is useful for supporting the mind and all kinds of mind magicks.

Tigereye is associated with Earth. It attracts money and is especially useful for warding against the evil eye, bad luck, and danger.

Creating a Stone Altar

As you begin learning more about gargoyles and stones, you might want to consider constructing a stone altar. The base could be a large, flat rock, or perhaps a piece of slate or flagstone purchased from a garden store or a stonery. You may be able to find a remnant of granite or marble countertop at a home store. A simple alternative would be to drape your usual altar with an altar cloth bearing a stone or brick pattern.

Your altar tools can also be adapted to stone. An obsidian athame would make a fine addition to your magickal toolkit. A panticle can be made from a piece of flat stone with a pentagram or other symbols painted on it. A fist-sized rock with a central well or depression can serve as a chalice, and small, flat stones make good candleholders.

Immerse a stone in a vial or jar of spring or rainwater for 1–2 days and you have "stone water" (sometimes called a stone elixir, or simply "charged water), imbued with the magickal qualities of the stone and ready for use in spellcraft.

The same process works with oils: for best results use a neutral "carrier oil"—an oil used to dilute essential oils. Carrier oils are generally cold-pressed vegetable oils. Examples include sweet almond, apricot kernel, grapeseed, avocado, peanut, olive, and walnut oil.

Being a stone lover, I also prefer to use stones to indicate all four Elements: a piece of basalt for Earth, a piece of pumice for Air, obsidian for Fire, and either an agate or a stone with a small "well" marking for Water.

Stone Divination

Divination is the magickal art of understanding the past, present, or future by interpreting sets of patterns, symbols, or meanings. Because of their size and nature, stones lend themselves to many kinds of divinatory practice. Note: When doing stone work, handle and work with the stones using your dominant hand.

The Pendulum

A pendulum is a heavy object suspended from a thread that, through its movements in response to a question, helps divine meaning.

The classic pendulum is shaped similar to an upside-down pyramid, with a point at the bottom. Fancy pendulums are available in magick shops, but many common objects also work well. You may prefer to work with a pendulum that you have made. An advantage of this is that your own energies will be infused into the materials. In terms of stone, crystals make excellent (and receptive) pendulums. Heavy stone beads also work well, as does a piece of seashell. Jeweled rings can be powerful pendulums, although metal acts as a conductor, affecting its ability to divine energy; copper and aluminum should be avoided for this reason.

For best results, the pendulum should be symmetrical and balanced. Use an inert natural thread, such as cotton, silk, and so on, to suspend it. You may also want to buy or make a small cloth bag for your pendulum. If your sewing skills are limited, simply wrap it up in a piece of nice fabric and tie the bundle shut with a piece of cord, again using natural fibers.

Hold the pendulum with the hand with which you write. Sit down with your legs uncrossed, rest your elbow on a table, and hold the thread or chain of your pendulum lightly between your thumb and index finger. Your elbow should be the only part of your body touching the table. Suspend the pendulum in midair about a foot in front of you.

Swing the pendulum gently back and forth to become familiar with the movement. Allow the pendulum to swing in different directions, then swing it deliberately in circles. When you have the feel of the pendulum, stop its movements with your free hand. Once the pendulum is still, ask it which movement indicates a positive, or yes response. Be patient until the pendulum responds. Thinking yes as strongly as you can will speed the process.

Repeat the process for the following responses: "no," "I don't know," and "I don't want to answer." Note that your pendulum will move in one of five ways: It may move backward and forward, from side to side, swing in a circle (clockwise or counterclockwise), or fail to move at all.

Once you understand how the pendulum will indicate answers, you can begin asking it simple questions that can be answered with a "yes" or "no." For best results, allow plenty of time, and don't try to work with the pendulum when you are tired, ill, stressed, or rushed. Your pendulum responses should remain the same throughout your life, and regardless of what kind of pendulum you use. Recheck them every so often, just to be sure.

Between uses, keep your pendulum in its bag or wrapping and store it out of direct light. It may periodically be charged on your altar or by exposure to the full moon.

Stone Gathering

For this, you'll need a large quantity (50–100) of several small stones, such as rounded pebbles or gravel and a bag in which to store them. The stones should either be all of the same kind (for the first method) or evenly divided into like quantities of two or more different stones (for the second method). For example, if you wanted 60 stones and wanted to use tigereye, agate, turquoise, and hematite, you'd need 15 of each. Note: you can buy strings of small stone chips in most bead supply stores.

Method one: Use the stones as a simple yes/no system. Ask your question aloud and imagine it in your mind's eye. Reach into the bag and close your hand around a number of stones. Take them out and count them: A negative number of stones means no, and a positive number means yes.

Method two: Ask and imagine your question as in method one. Pull out a number of stones and separate each kind into a pile. Count the stones in each pile; some will have more and some will have fewer stones. The correspondences of the majority and minority stones will give input about your question.

Stone Pulling

For this, you'll need a small drawstring bag and a collection of several stones, each of a different type. Here is my basic set:

- **Amethyst:** Healing; banishment of fear and anxiety; absorption of negativity; psychic qualities; wisdom and purity of thought.
- **Bloodstone:** Healing of wounds; aversion of disaster or misfortune; guards against deception; cleansing and purification; peace; understanding.
- **Carnelian:** Happiness; fulfillment of desires; energy; vitality; self-confidence; bold speech; health.
- **Citrine:** Clarity and transformation; bridge between intuition and logic; mental ability; health.
- **Fluorite:** Strong correspondence to psychic powers, psychic/precognitive link between planes of existence; also a strong healing crystal.
- **Hematite:** Cessation of bleeding; protection in battle; alertness; divination and scrying.
- **Jade:** Love; life; relationships; strength and power; expression of inner feelings.
- **Moss agate:** Divine attraction; aid to persuasive speech; truthfulness; good fortune; pleasant dreams.
- **Quartz points:** Energy, enthusiasm, strength, intuition.
- **Rose quartz:** Healing; softens flaming emotions; restores calm and balance.
- **Snowflake obsidian:** Shadow; limitations; inevitable progression of time; powerful divination stone.
- **Tigereye:** Attracts money, protection against evil.
- **Turquoise:** Clarity; purification; tranquility; second sight; protection against psychic attack; echoes the deep oceans; one of the most powerful of stones.

Put the stones into the bag. Now ground, center, and meditate on your question, or on the situation that you wish to understand better. Reach in hand and pull out a stone. Take a moment to do this, allowing the correct stone to "find" your fingers. Now pull it out, and consider the above correspondences to find your answer.

Stone Casting

Use the same set of stones that you used in "stone pulling." You'll need a large, flat surface on which to work, at least 3–4 square feet. You'll also need to identify the cardinal directions are—use a compass if needed. Take all of your stones into your hand. Ground, center, and meditate on your question or situation. Now, gently cast the stones away from you, as you'd roll a set of dice. You may then "read" the cast stones. There are several ways to do this, including:

- Have the stones fallen into a recognizable or meaningful pattern, or symbol?
- Have they congregated near one of the Directions, and therefore near one of the Elements?
- Which stones draw your attention, or your eye?

Use these impressions, along with your understanding of symbols, Elemental correspondences, and stone meanings to intuit meanings from the casting.

Stone Throwing

This is another simple yes/no method of stone divination. You'll need between three and 13 smooth oval or round stones—these can be simple "generic" stones, such as river pebbles. You'll also need a shallow box, around 12 x 16 inches or so. One of the box's largest panels should be removed; then, cut down the sides if necessary so that the open box is no more than 6 inches deep. Draw a line down the middle of the box's length. On one far end, inside the box, write "yes" on one side of the line and "no" on the other. Now, hold your stones in your dominant hand and cast them toward the yes/no end of the box. Note how many land on the "yes" versus the "no" side—there's your answer.

Stone Scrying

Scrying is the art of divining a present or future understanding by gazing into an object or substance. Fire, water, and mirrors are common mediums for scrying. In terms of stone magick, there are three standard types of scrying.

Scrying with a crystal ball is known as catoptromancy, catoxtromancy, or crystallomancy. Crystal balls can be somewhat expensive, but are a lot of fun to work with and a wonderful addition to anyone's *sanctum sanctorum*. To use the ball, place it in a holder so that it is immobile; ideally, set the holder and crystal on a black cloth or background. Ground, center, and allow yourself to enter a state of meditative awareness. Be calm and aware of opening your senses to experience whatever the crystal offers you. There are two approaches to your scrying session. One is simply to look into the ball, relax, and see what visions come. The other is to ask a specific question and then look for an answer.

A crystal ball.

Keep your crystal ball wrapped in a dark colored cloth wrap or bag between uses, and store it out of direct sunlight. For best results, don't allow anyone else to use it. Charge it periodically by leaving it exposed to the light of the full moon.

To scry with a shiny stone, you'll need a large stone with a shiny, smooth surface. A large piece of obsidian is ideal. Work with the stone in the same way and follow the same guidelines used for the crystal ball.

Many accomplished scryers use mirrors fashioned of obsidian—they are expensive, but if you can find one, it will be a real treasure. Follow the same guidelines as for the crystal ball or shiny stone (the shiny stone is simply another kind of mirror).

The sweat lodge is a kind of participatory prayer and divination using stones in a key role. Water is poured over hot rocks in a sealed tent to create steam. Participants, either nude or lightly dressed, sit in the tent around the rocks and inhale the steam. The combination of temperature, humidity, and elevated levels of carbon dioxide produces a state in which visions can arise. Note: This form of scrying may be dangerous and should only be undertaken with the assistance of an experienced guide.

Runes

Runes are another potent kind of stony divination. For stone runes, the Futhark symbols are painted onto clean, smooth, rounded rocks—river stones work well, but any smooth stone will do, and if you have the resources you could create amazing magick by awakening a set of precious runes in amethyst,

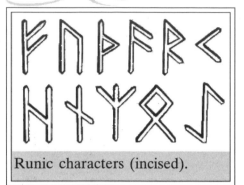

Runic characters (incised).

fluorite, turquoise, and so on. A permanent marker may also be used, and the stones sealed with a clear sealant or shellac. Traditionally, runes are stored in a reticule, which is a beaded, embroidered, or otherwise decorated drawstring bag.

Stones in the Tarot

The tarot (TEHR-oh) is a deck of 78 playing cards that evoke magickal symbolism and divinatory meaning. The cards are divided into the Major and Minor Arcana. The 22 cards of the Major Arcana are numbered and titled, The Fool (0), The Magician (1), The High Priestess (2), and so forth. The Major Arcana is arranged in a way that describes the classic heroic quest, or hero's journey.

The 56 cards of the Minor Arcana are divided into four suits: Pentacles, Wands, Swords, and Cups. Each suit has a traditional Elemental correspondence: pentacles correspond with the Earth Element (and thus with stones), while wands correspond with Air, swords with Fire, and cups with Water. Each suit includes 10 numbered cards, Ace through 10, and four court cards—Page, Knight, Queen, and King. Tarot decks are created with different themes, and these themes are used to illustrate the cards in the Minor Arcana. For example, you might work with an Arthurian Tarot, or a deck that was built around animals or trees.

Learning to read and use the tarot is a highly specialized magickal skill. It isn't so much a task of memorizing card meanings, as it is of opening oneself to the cards and allowing them to speak to you. If you develop interest in stone magick and find yourself interested in the tarot, pay special attention to the pentacles suit.

In his *Crystal, Gem & Metal Magic*, Scott Cunningham proposes the creation of a "stone Tarot," which uses a different stone to represent each unique tarot card.

Dirt Magick

Soil and earth, which are nothing more than ground-up stones mixed with organic matter, are powerful magick substances. When you travel or visit places of power, scoop up a small amount of earth, sand, bits of stone, etc. These can become strong additions to your workings. Soils from graveyards, ruins, thresholds, and crossroads are especially formidable.

Famous Stones in Antiquity

Gargoyles may appear humble, but they have quite the noble family tree!

The Blarney Stone

By Oranstar

It's probably the most well-loved stone in the world. Approximately 200,000 visit it per year and most sneak in a peck or two. But this stone doesn't kiss and tell.

It's the Blarney Stone.

The Blarney Stone overlooks the tiny village of Blarney, Ireland from its perch high atop Blarney Castle. Believed to be half of the famous Scottish "Stone of Scone" it is steeped in both history and legend.[2]

History tells us that Cormac McCarthy received the limestone block in 1314 as a gift for his prowess in battle. In 1446 Blarney castle was built and the stone was placed on the third story battlements. A little more than 100 years later Dermot McCarthy was forced to surrender his home to Queen Elizabeth I to prove his loyalty to the throne. In an effort to delay his surrender, McCarthy began making up elaborate stories as to why he could not give up his fortress. His excuses and promises of loyalty became jokes in the Queen's court. She was once overheard saying that she could not bear "more Blarney talk!" The term "blarney" has since come to mean a "friendly and charming way of talking which makes someone good at persuading people to do things."

Legend has it that the Blarney Stone was imbued with a special power well before it came to the McCarthy family. It is said that an old Witch was saved from drowning by a king. In return for her life she cast a spell upon a stone. This stone was at the top of a castle. The Witch told the king that he who kissed the magic stone would be given the gift of winning over all people with his words. For 500 years pilgrims have made their way to Blarney for the honor of kissing that same magic stone. For their troubles they may get a gift. This is the well-known "gift of gab" that many are said to have received.

Irish poet, Francis Sylvester Mahony, wrote this poem/limerick in honor of the Blarney Stone:

There is a stone that whoever kisses
never misses to grow eloquent,
he may clamber
to a lady's chamber
or become a member of parliament.

The Glastonbury Tor

By Estara T'Shirai

A tor is a very old hill, usually consisting of granite. A large outcropping is exposed to water and air, and gradually is weathered over millions of years into rock and eventually into gravel.

My obvious personal favorite tor is the Glastonbury Tor, standing as it does in a place sacred to my Patroness Morgan. In local folklore it has a rich history, being considered the gate by which *Gwynn ap Nudd* comes to the human world, and by which a brave person could reach the underworld, or *Annwn*. During Christian times it was identified with the Archangel Michael.

I can identify with tors (even ones that aren't in Glastonbury) in that I consider my own spiritual evolution to be a slow wearing away of what doesn't suit. It also reflects my (sometimes unfortunate) tendency to want to "stand alone" and not want anyone's help or company.

The Medicine Wheel

A medicine wheel is a circle-space that is marked out or defined with stones. The medicine wheel has a central feature, such as a stone cairn, medicine pole, or the like, and a series of radiating spokes that join the outer circular ring with the central feature. The term "medicine" is an aboriginal tradition that references the spiritual and/or healing aspects of stones. Native North Americans believe that medicine wheels are active and "alive," that they begin working immediately upon creation, and that they continue to function for as long as they are assembled. Some medicine wheels also have an archaeoastronomical purpose.

The kinds of stones, their number, and their size and precise arrangement varies among wheels and among different traditions. The famed Big Horn Medicine Wheel in Wyoming is 80 feet across and has 28 radiating "spokes" leading to a central cairn. In contrast, miniature "altar-sized" medicine wheels provide an alternative when space is limited.

In some cathedrals and other structures, gargoyles are set in a ring around a turret or tower, arguably creating something akin to a simple stone circle or medicine wheel, with the gargoyles representing spokes.

You can work with gargoyles, medicine wheels, and stone circles in a number of ways. You could use homemade or purchased gargoyle sculptures to create a stone circle of your own, possibly in combination with other stones. You could also incorporate gargoyles into specific points of a medicine wheel.

The Omphalos Stone

Most scholars use the term Omphalos to describe the sacred baetyl (var. betylos, betylus, or betyles) stone in the Temple of Delphi. This Temple was important to ancient Greece as a place of worship and, more importantly, as the home to series of Oracles at Delphi. The Greeks viewed the temple as the center of everything. Legend says that Zeus sent two eagles to fly across the world and they met at its center, the "navel" of the world and the site of the temple of Delphi. The word omphalos means "navel" in Greek. The Omphalos was also called "the stone of splendor," and was believed to assist with divination and allowed direct contact with the Gods.

The Omphalos stone, from the temple of Apollo at Delphi.

The actual Omphalos stone is shaped similar to an egg or a beehive and doesn't look anything like a navel. It may represent the phallus, or alternatively, a female womb-symbol. The Omphalos image frequently appears flanked by two doves, a symbol that represented the sexual aspect of the ancient Goddess. There were a number of these omphalos stones in Greece, the most famous being the one at Delphi. Likewise, there were the so-called animated or oracular stones, venerated as of divine origin or as a symbol of divinity.

Although the most famous Omphalos is found in Greece, the image recurs throughout ancient arts and writing. Other Omphalos stones have been found in temples in Rome, Iraq, Egypt, and Jerusalem. The idea of the Omphalos lives on in modern spirituality and even in literature. In her recent book,

Ancestors of Avalon, Diana Paxson fictionalizes the fall of Atlantis and the building of Stonehenge. The most sacred artifact of the inhabitants of Atlantis is their Omphalos stone, which is carried with them to their new home and which eventually redeems their society. It is portrayed as an object of unimaginable power.

The Philosopher's Stone

By S. A. Sherwood

The advent of J. K. Rowling's first book *Harry Potter and The Philosopher's Stone*, (British title—America's title is *Harry Potter and the Sorcerer's Stone*)

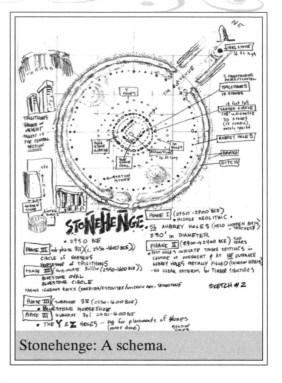

Stonehenge: A schema.

brought about a renewed awareness of the famed stone so diligently sought by alchemists, both true and false, throughout history. Legend tells that the stone turns lead into gold and grants its possessor immortality. Yet history reveals a long lineage of charlatans but only a few true alchemists. The charlatans never produced the stone and the alchemists kept the results of their work secret, leaving humankind to wonder whether the stone was just a myth.

Paracelsus, the 16th-century alchemist and founder of spagyrics, once said, "It is not proper to say much about the Philosopher's Stone or to boast about its possession. The ancients have indicated the recipe for those who have true understanding. However, they used parables to keep unworthy persons from knowing and misusing it." Is it any wonder then, that that the uninitiated should claim that the Stone is a fantasy?

But the Stone is no fantasy, and in truth, it is no stone at all. The recipe for its creation can be found in "The Emerald Tablet" of Hermes Trismegistus, and according to the mysterious alchemist known as Fulcanelli, in his work *Les Mystere des Cathedrales*, the Hermetic principles leading to its creation can be openly found in the Gothic cathedrals. Alchemist Cesare Riviera says of the

Stone, "...(it) does not appear to base and impure souls, but remains hidden in the celestial spheres of the inaccessible light of the Heavenly Sun." The question: What is this Stone that is not stone, the goal to which alchemists throughout the ages have devoted their lives? And the answer? The Philosopher's Stone is the creation of the light body, of consciousness perfected and reunited with the One Mind through the seven-step alchemical formula of purification.

The Rosetta Stone

By Oranstar and Moonwriter

The Rosetta Stone is a black basalt slab that is 45 inches long, 28 inches wide, and 11 inches thick (114 x 72 x 28 cm). The stone is believed to have been created around 196 B.C.E. apoleon's troops discovered it in 1799 near the Egyptian town of Rosetta. It features ancient Egyptian tributes to King Ptolemy V. The stone has three inscriptions: one in hieroglyphics, one in demotic, and one in Greek characters. It took thousands of years for scholars to decode the inscriptions, with Jean-François Champollion finally deciphering the meanings in 1822. His work led to the interpretation of other early Egyptian records. Today, the Rosetta Stone has a permanent home in London's British Museum.

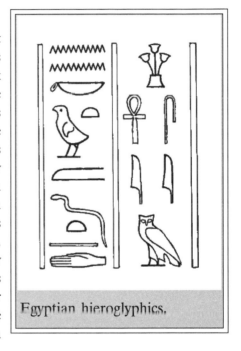

Egyptian hieroglyphics.

Stone Circles

A stone circle is a circle on the ground that is literally ringed with a perimeter of stones. Many stone circles were simply built as places of worship. Others were built along ley lines, lines of magickal power and energy said to crisscross the Earth and to link ancient monuments and places of power. Still, others were created for archaeoastronomical purposes; that is, their alignment coincided with, or tracked alignment in the heavenly bodies.

The Stone of Destiny

The ancient Kings of Scotland were crowned kneeling upon a flat stone, known as the Stone of Destiny, or sometimes, because of its location, the Stone of Scone. The 336-pound block of sandstone was 26 inches long, 16 inches wide, and 11 inches high. The Stone's only decoration was a small Latin cross, created by an unknown carver.

The Stone of destiny has a rich past. Legend says it came from the Middle East, arriving in Scotland around 850 C.E. and taken to Scone Castle, Scotland. Its history may go back to biblical times, where Jacob is said to have used it as a pillow. Another version suggests that the Stone was part of the ancient Irish Kingdom of Dalriada (c. 450–850 C.E.).

In 1296, Edward I removed the Stone of Destiny from Scone, placing it in Westminster Abbey, London. He believed that the action would give him control of Scotland. Unfortunately, his action only humiliated the Scots, and added to the enmity that brewed between the two cultures over the centuries. In 1950, Scottish nationalists stole the stone and placed it in Arbroath Abbey; however, they were forced to return it to Westminster. In 1996, the English people returned the Stone to the Scots, an action of great importance to Scottish independence. Today the Stone has found a new home in Edinburgh Castle.

Lia Fáil

By Kalla

A favorite historical stone is the Lia Fáil, one of two stones named the Stone of Destiny. According to myth, the Lia Fáil was brought to Ireland by the Tuatha Dé Danann. The stone was reputed to cry out in joy when the rightful king of Ireland stood on it. The stone is also said to bless the rightful king's reign with prosperity and longevity.

The Stygian Stone, "Stone of the Styx"

In Hebrew mythology, Jews claimed that King David found this stone when he began digging the foundation for his temple. The stone was said to have magickal powers that unlocked the Earth's living waters, the "fountain of the great deep."

The Sword in the Stone

Legend tells of the ancient, elemental sword Excalibur, forged in the Earth's fiery depths, raised into the sky, and imbued with magick and mystery by the Lady of the Lake, a guardian of ancient Avalon. Merlin himself retrieves the sword, then sinks it into a rock, where it awaits the one man who will be able to draw it from the stone: the true and rightful King of Britain. This mythic king turns out to be a boy: Arthur. He draws the sword and becomes King of England. He doesn't exactly live happily ever after, but it's a great story all the same. For an interesting version of the legend, try John Boorman's 1981 film, *Excalibur*.

The Tarpeian Rock

Found on Rome's Capitoline Hill, the Tarpeian Rock was sacred to an Etruscan goddess. Myth told of a treacherous woman named Tarpeia, who was crushed under the shields of a legion of soldiers betrayed by her. It subsequently became the custom for warriors to pile their shields up around the Tarpeian Rock after a victory.

Try This

1. If you like to draw and sketch, you might create your own set of tarot cards. First, familiarize yourself with the use and images on a standard tarot deck. Then, use medieval and gargoyle imagery to illustrate your own cards. For the Minor Arcana, consider the following suits:

   ◉ Earth: simple non-winged anthropomorphic or zoomorphic gargoyles.

   ◉ Air: winged gargoyles.

   ◉ Fire: demonic gargoyles.

   ◉ Water: water-spewing (functional) gargoyles.

2. Practice a method of stone divination for one month, recording your results.

3. Create a set of stone runes.

4. Visit a famous stone or stone monument near your home.

Part III: Especially for the Gargoyle Hunter

16
All Things
Gargoyle

Across the garden pool, the gargoyle
Stares at the cherub
Who shares this gothic courtyard.

The two of them bracket the brink of a pond
Pea-green and opaque
As an angel's smile. Leaves like little boats
Float on the glassy surface, ferrying forlorn thoughts
Back and forth.

The cherub reflects on regret, heaven lost
For an infinity of foolishness
And the gargoyle mourns freedom torn away
For an eternity of guarding goldfish.

Can a stone heart break?
The gargoyle's has, a shattering of granite
Under the weight of alien emotions.
When did love steal inside through slate-grey skin?

The gargoyle cannot recall,
But the slow march of moss over stone
Has grown far since the first breach of obdurate solitude.

The cherub has never looked up
From the lucent pool, cannot bear
To meet the gaze of paradise
And so
Will never see the gargoyle staring fondly near.

The gargoyle knows what has gone before
Yet has come to love these moments as they are;
The cherub only mourns the moments melted long ago.

Sorrow pools in strange places.
They may possess a certain grace
But peace will elude this place unless
What was written in stone might be unwrought.

They sit in silence, invisible from the garden gate
Unable or unwilling to make a change,
Peculiar companions in pain.

Birds may perch on them,
Butterflies may come and go
On their rainbow business among bright flowers
But still the two stone hearts
Will stand alone

One yearning for eternal joy, now lost,
One simply longing to go on.

Peculiar Companions
—By Elizabeth Barrette

While Europe is definitely the hub of Gothic era gargoylia, gargoyles and grotesques can be found all over the world, even in today's modern times. One has only to look! The following "Field Guide" will help you locate those gargoyles that you can still see today.

The Well-Prepared Gargoyle Hunter

Basic supplies:

- Camera (ideally one with a telephoto lens).
- Binoculars.
- Note pad and paper.
- Sketch pad (optional).
- This book!
- Hiking stave.
- Pith helmet (just kidding).

Tricks of the Trade

1. Gargoyle-watching is best done during autumn and winter, after the trees have dropped their leaves.
2. Ask the locals for locations of gargoyles, especially in old European cities, and in big east coast cities in the United States.
3. Do research before you go—today's Internet is a trove of detailed information telling you where the gargoyles are hiding. The books in the resource section will be useful, too.
4. Use binoculars or a spotting scope, otherwise there are many gargoyles you simply won't be able to see.
5. Be prepared to climb! Look for stairs and elevators to take you to the highest points of the building.

The following is by no means a complete, comprehensive guide—that would require a bigger book! But it will give you ideas of where to find some interesting gargoyles and grotesques, and with luck, at least one of them will be close to your home. If you're able to, head for one of the world's best gargoyle viewing spots: France, with more than 100 cathedrals, and New York, with more gargoyles per square mile than anywhere else in the United States and more cathedrals (18) than any city in the world.

Gargoyle Hunting in Australia

City: Melbourne

Building and location: Trinity College, University of Melbourne

Date seen:

Description: Six bronze grotesques crown the eastern side of the Evan Burge Building.

Dimensions:

Markings: The oddly shaped grotesques resemble large cylindrical pipes, each with a lifelike head on the end.

Your observations:

Special notes: This installation honors women and men who have made significant contributions to Trinity College and the wider community.

Gargoyle Hunting in Europe

Belgium

City: Brussels

Building and location: Cathedral of Saint-Michel (Cathedral of St. Michael and St. Gudula)

Date seen:

Description: Many gargoyles, including shrieking demons holding miniature people.

Dimensions:

Markings:

Your observations:

Special notes: Begun in the early 13th century, the cathedral was built atop an old Romanesque foundation and took 300 years to complete.

City: Brussels

Building and location: Town Hall (Hôtel de Ville)

Date seen:

Description: Gargoyles and grotesques, including singing and laughing men, a harpy, a mermaid, and at least one mouth-puller.

Dimensions:

Markings:

Your observations:

Special notes: First stone was laid in 1402. The building was destroyed in 1695 by French troops; only the tower and outside walls were saved. Restoration began immediately. The entire facade is decorated with 203 small statues representing the Dukes and Duchesses of Brabant who ruled between 580–1564.

France

City: Reims

Building and location: Cathedral at Notre-Dame de Reims

Date seen:

Description: Gargoyles and grotesques include dogs, cats, demons, birds, eagles, creatures, many chimeras (including a human/sphinx/ horse), rams, and a splendid griffin grotesque.

Ram gargoyle from Reims Cathedral.

Dimensions:

Markings:

Your observations:

Special notes: Includes original and restored gargoyles.

City: Paris

Building and location: Cathedral of Notre Dame

Date seen:

Description: Iconic "sitting gargoyle;" also dogs, cats, demons, birds, and eagles.

Dimensions:

Markings: One creature combines human, sphinx, and horse.

Your observations:

A functional gargoyle from Notre Dame.

Special notes: The gothic Cathedral at Notre-Dame is arguably the most famous cathedral in the world, and is well known for its "sitting gargoyle." Climb up the north tower to access a narrow walkway; from here you can the *Galerie des Chiméres* and see many gargoyles and grotesques at eye level. Most gargoyles have been restored or replaced. Much is 19th-century restoration work (dating to 1845) that repaired damage from the Revolution. The Cathedral is "home" to the fictional Quasimodo, hero of Victor Hugo's *Hunchback of Notre Dame*.

City: Chartres

Building and location: Chartres (Our Lady of Chartres) Cathedral

Date seen:

Description: Approximately 4,000 sculpted figures, including many gargoyles.

Dimensions:

Markings:

Your observations:

Special notes: The best single example of high Gothic arches in the world. The current cathedral is the sixth structure on the site, and was built in only 26 years on the foundation of the fifth cathedral, the latter destroyed in 1194.

Germany

City: Freiburg

Building and location: Cathedral of Our Lady (Minster, or city cathedral)

Date seen:

Description: A defecating person on the south side. Also a monstrous gargoyle.

Dimensions:

Markings:

Your observations:

Special notes: Construction spanned the 13th and 16th centuries. For the last century, the cathedral's upkeep has been funded by public donations. A likely permanent scaffold surrounds the structure to allow for continuous repair of sandstone sculpture and filigree.Climb 330 steps up the spire for a view of surrounding town and the Black Forest.

Ireland

City: Dublin

Building and location: Christ Church Cathedral

Date seen:

Description: Several gargoyles on exterior

Dimensions:

Markings:

Your observations:

Special notes: Built in 1030, it was originally founded as a Viking church, and subject to the Archbishop of Canterbury. It later became an Irish Church. Known today for having a "world record" 19 bells in its tower.

Italy

City: Milan

Building and location: Cathedral of Santa Maria

Date seen:

Description: Huge 15th century figures—*gigantii*—support water-spouting animal gargoyles on their shoulders, with water issuing from the animal's mouths. Also features traditional gargoyles, including a monstrous winged dog, a merman, and various chimeras.

Dimensions:

Markings:

Your observations:

Special notes: An elevator leads to the roof gives access to the gargoyles there. Some of the gargoyles are Baroque and date to the early 18th century.

City: Venice

Building and location: Basilica of San Marco

Date seen:

Description: On the upper level are early-15th-century *doccioni*—figures holding vases on their shoulders, from which the water flows.

Dimensions:

Markings:

Your observations:

Japan

City: Donjon

Building and location: Himeji Castle (built 1601–1614 C.E.)

Date seen:

Description: A unique Japanese-style gargoyle atop the castle

Dimensions:

Markings:

Your observations:

The Netherlands

City: Den Bosch (modern name for Hertogenbosch)

Building and location: Cathedral of Saint John (Sint-Janskathedraal)

Date seen:

Description: In a unique portrayal, frightening gargoyles appear to leap out at human figures straddling the flying buttresses. Others include human, monster, and animal forms, and at least one tongue thruster.

Dimensions:

Markings:

Your observations:

Special notes: The best location in Holland for viewing gargoyles dating from c. 1500 or the early 16th century.[3]

Scotland

City: Melrose

Building and location: Melrose Abbey

Date seen:

Description: Dragons, a pig playing the bagpipes.

Dimensions:

Markings:

Your observations:

Special notes: Originally built around 660 C.E. as one of the great border abbeys, the Abbey was burned to the ground in 1385 by Richard II's army. It was immediately rebuilt and endures today. The heart of "Robert the Bruce," a significant force in the abbey's reconstruction, is buried on the site.

Spain

City: Barcelona

Building and location: Sagrada Familia

Date seen:

Description: Snake, lizard, and snail grotesques

Dimensions:

Markings:

Your observations:

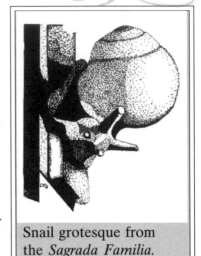

Special notes: Grotesques are lifelike and natural (non-stylized).

United Kingdom

City: Oxford

Building and location: University of Oxford (Oxford University)

Date seen:

Snail grotesque from the *Sagrada Familia*.

Description: Gargoyles and grotesques include angels, demons, monkeys, chimeras, gnomes, lion, royalty, drummer, jesters, a Bob Hope grotesque, a Ronald Reagan grotesque, England's king/queen/prince, wildman, carver figures, dragons, college faculty and staff, and dogs

Dimensions:

Markings:

Your observations:

Special notes: Many gargoyles—some are original, while many are restored. Founded as school for clergy more than 800 years ago.

City: Grantham

Building and location: Angel and Royal Hotel

Date seen:

Description: A defecating man

Dimensions:

Markings:

Your observations:

Special notes: When seen from the hotel's facade, you only see the man's face. Walk to the right to see his other end!

City: Patrington
Building and location: Church of Saint Patrick
Date seen:
Description: Various gargoyles, including a rendition of Samson and the lion.
Dimensions:
Markings: More than 200 human and animal carved heads.
Your observations:

Special notes: A wonderful example of the Decorated Gothic style. Has survived almost unchanged since its completion in 1410.

United States

State: Illinois
City: Chicago
Building and location: University of Chicago,; 5801 Ellis Avenue, Chicago, Ill. 60637; (773) 702-1234. *www.uchicago.edu*
Date seen:
Description: An angel is found on the building's corner. Various gargoyles, grotesques, and statuary are found on buildings around campus. Included are unusual birds (an albatross, a condor), a duck, eagles, alligators, a lion (as Moses) holding the Ten Commandments, an angel, dragons, devilish characters, rams, and a set of four chimeras indicating the freshman, sophomore, junior, and senior student. Rosenwald Hall includes animals representing the four continents: buffalo, bull, elephant, and lion.
Dimensions:
Markings:
Your observations:

State: New Jersey

City: Princeton

Building and location: Princeton University; Princeton, N.J., 98544-5264; (609) 258-3000. *www.princeton.edu*

Date seen:

Description: Many grotesques: One of the most famous is "The literate ape," an ape who reads and lectures from his position above a building entrance. Others include a tiger (the University mascot), Mother Goose, Cerrunos, Green Men, lion, a crab (because they walked backwards, crabs were an ancient symbol of misfortune), and many more. The biology building features grotesques of living animals (including a rhinoceros, ape, elephant, boar, frog, and crab), while the geology wing shows grotesques of fossils and dinosaurs.

Dimensions:

Markings:

Your observations:

Special notes: Widely referred to as a "modern-day Oxford," Princeton was originally founded as a Presbyterian seminary. Campus lore says that the "Literature Ape" gargoyle is lecturing on Darwin.

State: New York

City: New York

Building and location: Chrysler Building; East 42nd Street/Lexington Ave.

Date seen:

Description: Angular stainless steel gargoyles, all identical

Dimensions:

Markings:

Your observations:

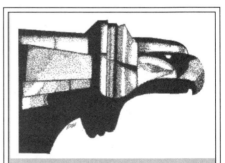

Steel Eagle (grotesque) from high atop New York's Chrysler Building.

Special notes: America's most Gothic modern building, with its height and soaring spire. The gargoyle's design was said to follow the original radiator cap and hood ornament of a 1929 Chrysler automobile.

State: New York

City: New York

Building and location: Cathedral Church of St. John the Divine ;1047 Amsterdam Avenue, New York, N.Y., 10025; (212) 316-7540. *ww.stjohndivine.org*

Date seen:

Description: More than 75 grotesques, but modern versions and grotesque interpretations of medieval gargoyles. One of the most interesting is a rendition of the Four Horsemen of the Apocalypse, with one rider carrying a bomb. Others include imps, tongue thrusters, a lion eating a man (harkens back to legends of giants), humans, bicephalic and tricephalic heads, Nelson Mandela, biblical stories, a mushroom cloud destroying Manhattan (a parable of the destruction of Jerusalem, including a destruction of the Twin Towers), Green Men, an angel, a dog, birds, and a cat biting its own tail.

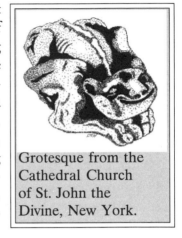

Grotesque from the Cathedral Church of St. John the Divine, New York.

Dimensions:

Markings:

Your observations:

Special notes: The world's largest cathedral. Begun in 1892, it was constructed in three phases over 120 years, and is yet unfinished—the result of financial problems, intervening world wars, and a shortage of craftsmen. Combines Romanesque, Byzantine, and Gothic styles. At 601 feet, the easternmost section of the cathedral is the longest in the world.

State: Oregon

City: Portland

Building and location: MacTarnahan's Brewing Taproom; 2730 NW 31st

Date seen:

Description: A row of modernistic, cast iron bulldog gargoyles fronts the building.

Dimensions:

Markings:

Your observations:

Special notes: Continuous with the roof guttering system, the gargoyles are fashioned from 1/8 inch black tubular steel and drain into rock-lined pits at the edge of the sidewalk.

State: Oregon

City: Portland

Building and location: Portland State University, Shattuck Hall; intersection of SW Broadway and College

Date seen:

Description: Wise owl terra cotta grotesques crown the top edges of the buildings; pigtailed girls gaze down from each entrance.

Dimensions:

Markings: Each owl sits atop a "Book of Knowledge."

Your observations:

Functioning bulldog gargoyle of tubular steel in Oregon.

Special notes: The red brick building was a Portland public school from 1915 until the 1960s. It is now a part of Portland State University.

State: Pennsylvania

City: Philadelphia

Building and location: University of Pennsylvania; 3451 Walnut Street, Philadelphia, Pa., 19104; (215) 898-5000. *www.upenn.edu*

Date seen:

Description: More than 450 grotesques can be found on the roof bosses of the college's quadrangle dormitories. They include students (human and animal), a boy-fish, a clown, various student athletes, a grim reaper, a gold maker, and various beasts.

Dimensions:

Markings: Many topics are featured, most reflecting college life. Several of the sculptures are of women.

Your observations:

Special notes: Begin in 1890, the images began with charcoal sketches; from these, a life-sized clay model was sculpted, then each was carved from a limestone block. Each grotesque-boss measures 14 inches square and each took three days to create and carve.

State: South Dakota

Building and location: Mt. Rushmore National Monument, Black Hills

Date seen:

Description: Mount Rushmore is arguably the hugest set of grotesques in the world, or at the very least, of carved heads.

Dimensions:

Markings: Features the granite faces of Presidents Washington, Jefferson, Theodore Roosevelt, and Lincoln.

Your observations:

Special notes: Carved by Gutzon Borglum and a crew of 400 stone workers between 1927-1941. The sculpture is eroding at a rate of 1 inch per 1000 years.

City: Washington, D.C.

Building and location: Cathedral Church of St. Peter and St. Paul (also known as the Washington National Cathedral); Massachusetts and Wisconsin Avenues, NW, Washington, DC, 20016-5098; (202)537-6200. *www.cathedral.org*

Date seen:

Description: A great many of the cathedral's gargoyles are representative of historical or biographical traditions, as in a large number of sculpted griffins. The group includes a baby, turtle, walrus, snakes, owl, cow, parrot, witch, cats, bear, elephants, human wearing a gas mask, another human holding a bomb, an Army mule, alligator, various devils, angels, pigs, elephants, lizards, dragons, locusts, a businessman, bats, roosters, mouth pullers, electrocardiogram (EKG) monitor, New Year's baby, griffins, pelican, cowboy, pig, tongue-thrusting Pan, crooked politician, "flower dog," wild boar, goat, weeping sea turtle, horse, rabbit, eagle, unicorn, thief, saber-toothed mother cat clutching a kitten, and a ram.

Markings: Many of the gargoyles were funded by private donations—including a grotesque of one donor's French poodle.

Your observations:

Special notes: The Washington National Cathedral (Washington D.C.) was begun in 1907 and finished in 1990. Perched atop Mt. St. Alban, the city's highest point, it occupies 55 acres in the center of Washington D.C., The cathedral's foundations reach 25 feet below ground. The masonry is self-supporting a la medieval fashion, and uses no structural steel. Built in the deco-rated Gothic style, the cathedral was created from more than 150,000 tons of glass, steel, and Indiana limestone. Most gargoyles have central pipes; all but two are part of the guttering system as functional waterspouts. The "gargoyle count" is around 112. Regardless, the Cathedral has more gargoyles than any other building in the United States. No two of the cathedra's gargoyles are alike.

Dragon gargoyle from
Washington National Cathedral.

Appendix A: A Glossary of Magickal and Medieval Terms

Acroterium: statues of animals placed on the roof corners over temples or special buildings to invoke guardianship or protection.

Allegory: a story, poem, or picture that can be interpreted to reveal a hidden meaning, typically a moral or political one.

Amulet: (magickal) an object that is magically empowered; talismans are often worn or carried.

Anthropomorphic: having human characteristics.

Apotropaic: supposedly having the power to avert evil influences or bad luck. Origin: late 19th century, from Greek *apotropaios,* "averting evil," from *apotrepein,* "turn away."

Apprentice: a person who is learning a trade from a skilled employer, having agreed to work for a fixed period at low wages. Origin: Middle English, from Old French *aprentis*, from Latin *apprehendum* "to understand."

Apse: a large semi-circular or polygonal recess in a church, arched or with a domed roof, typically at the eastern end, and usually containing the altar.

Arcane: understood by few; mysterious or secret. Origin: mid-16th century, from Latin *arcanus*, from *arcere,* "to shut up," from *arca,* "chest."

Arch: a curved symmetrical structure spanning an opening and typically supporting the weight of a bridge, roof, or wall above it; a structure of this type forming a passageway or a ceremonial monument: *a triumphal arch.* Origin: Middle English, from Old French *arche*, based on Latin *arcus*, "bow."

Archaeoastronomy: the investigation of the astronomical knowledge of pre-historic culture; the study of ancient monuments created to somehow track the movements of heavenly bodies.

Aristocrat: a member of the highest class in a certain society, especially those holding hereditary titles or offices; a group regarded as privileged or superior in a particular sphere. Origin: late 15th century, from Old French *aristocratie*, from Greek *aristokratia*, from *aristos*, "best" + *-kratia*, "power." The term originally denoted the government of a state by its best citizens, that is, the rich and wellborn.

Asperges: the rite of sprinkling holy water at the beginning of a spiritual event, particularly the Catholic Mass. Origin: late 16th century, the first word of the Latin text of Psalms 50(51):9, recited before Mass during the sprinkling of holy water.

Athame: (magickal) a dagger used in magickal rituals to invoke deities and define sacred space. Traditionally, the athame is double bladed and has a black handle; symbols may be inscribed on that handle and/or blade. Modern magick-users may create variations in the traditional form. The blade is only used symbolically, and it is not used to physically cut anything.

Augur: to portend a good or bad outcome; to foresee or predict; (in ancient Rome) a religious official who observed natural signs, especially the behavior of birds, interpreting these as an indication of divine approval or disapproval of a proposed action. Origin: late Middle English, from Latin, "diviner."

Banishing: a magickal working that dissipates, neutralizes, or removes unwanted negative energies or forces. Often used as a step in larger rituals; a spell that removes someone or something from the spellcaster.

Basilica: a large oblong hall or building with double colonnades and a semi-circular apse, used in ancient Rome as a court of law or for public assemblies.

Bestiary: a descriptive, illustrative, or anecdotal work on various real or mythical kinds of animals; typically a medieval work with a moralizing tone. Origin: mid- 19th century, from medieval Latin *bestiarium*, from Latin *bestia*, "beast."

Binding: (magickal) a spell that attracts something to the spellcaster; a binding action may also attach something to the spellcaster.

Bleacher: a person who bleaches textiles or other material.

Book of Shadows: (magickal) a term describing one's personal workbook or record of magickal craft.

Boss, roof: a piece of ornamental carving covering the point where the ribs in a vault or ceiling cross.

Bowdlerize: to remove material that is considered improper or offensive from a text, account, carving, especially if, as a result, it becomes weaker or less effective; something that is unbowdlerized is in its original untainted condition. Origin: A colloquial term from mid-19th century, from the name of Dr. Thomas Bowdler (1754–1825), who published an expurgated edition of Shakespeare in 1818.

Byzantine Empire: the empire in southeastern Europe and Asia Minor formed from the eastern part of the Roman Empire. It ended with the fall of Constantinople to the Ottoman Turks in 1453.

Carnival: a period of public revelry at a regular time each year, typically during the week before Lent in Roman Catholic countries, involving processions, music, dancing, and the use of masquerade. Origin: mid-16th century, from Italian *carnevale*, from Latin *caro, carn-* "flesh" + *levare,* "put away."

Cathedral: a church building that is the seat of the local bishop; the principal church of a diocese, with which the bishop is associated. Origin: Latin *cathedra*, "seat," from Greek kathedra.

Censer: a container in which incense is burned, typically during a religious ceremony.

Centaur: (Greek mythology) a creature with the head, arms, and torso of a man and the body and legs of a horse. Origin: Latin, from *kentauros*, the Greek name for a Thessalonian tribe of expert horsemen.

Center(ing): (magickal) a meditative technique that focuses on connecting one's own center (of gravity, of self) with the energy of the surrounding place and time.

Chandler: (historical) a dealer in household items such as oil, soap, paint, and groceries.

Chef-d'œuvre: a masterpiece; a seminal project created by an apprentice and presented to the master as proof of apprenticeship completion. Origin: early-17th-century French, literally "chief work." Also known in Latin as the *magnum opus*, where it is used in alchemical terms, to describe spiritual illumination and transformation.

Chimera or chimaera: a creature that is not of this world and cannot exist in reality; any mythical animal with parts taken from various animals; a thing that is hoped or wished for but in fact is illusory or impossible to achieve.

Circle: (magickal) when used in ritual, a sacred space that represents the intersection of all planes, retains energy cast during the ritual, and maintains a keep free of all outside influences.

Cleansing: (magickal) a magickal action that removes psychic or spiritual debris from a person, object, or area.

Clepsydra: an ancient time-measuring device that worked by a flow of water. Origin: late Middle English, via Latin from Greek *klepsudra*, based on *kleptei,* "steal" + *hudM´r,* "water."

Cloven: split or divided in two.

Colonnade: a row of columns supporting a roof or entablature.

Cooper: a maker or repairer of casks and barrels.

Corbel: a projection jutting out from a wall to support a structure above it; a kind of support (a structure such as an arch or balcony) on corbels. Origin: late Middle English, from Old French, diminutive of *corp* "crow," from Latin *corvus,* "raven" (perhaps because of the shape of a corbel, resembling a crow's beak).

Cruciform: of or denoting a church having a cross-shaped plan with a nave and transepts.

Cryptozoology(ist): the search for and study of animals whose existence or survival is disputed or unsubstantiated, such as the Loch Ness Monster and the Yeti.

Cubit: an ancient measure of length, approximately equal to the length of a forearm. It was typically about 18 inches (44 cm), although there was a long cubit of about 21 inches (52 centimeters). Origin: Middle English, from Latin *cubitum,* "elbow or forearm."

Cutler: a person who makes or sells knives and other cutlery.

Daub: a plaster made of mud, clay, twigs, straw, horsehair, pig bristles, and other materials; used to plaster over wattle, filling in the open spaces.

Demotic: the kind of language used by ordinary people; popular or colloquial speech.

Divination: the practice of seeking knowledge of the future or the unknown by supernatural means; a practice that was "of the Gods," literally "divine." Origin: late Middle English, from Latin divinatio(n-), from divinare, "predict."

Dualism: the division of something conceptually into two opposed or contrasted aspects; the religious doctrine that the universe contains opposed powers of good and evil, especially seen as balanced equals.

Entablature: a horizontal, continuous lintel on a classical building supported by columns or a wall.

Etymology: the study of the origin of words and the way in which their meanings have changed throughout history.

Extant: still in existence; surviving; particularly when pertaining to a manuscript that has endured over time.

Fable: a short story, typically with animals as characters, conveying a moral. Origin: Middle English, from Old French fable (noun), from Latin fibula, "story," from fari, "speak."

Farrier: a craftsman who trims and shoes horses' hooves.

Flying buttress: a buttress slanting from a separate pier, typically forming an arch with the wall it supports.

Freestone: rock that can be cut easily in any direction; in particular, fine-grained sandstone or limestone of uniform texture. Origin: from Old French franche pere, "excellent rock."

Fresco: a painting done rapidly in watercolor on wet plaster on a wall or ceiling, so that the colors penetrate the plaster and become fixed as it dries.

Furrier: a person who prepares or deals in furs.

Futhark: an alphabet also known as the runic alphabet, because it is typically copied onto runes. Origin: named for its first six letters: f, u, th, a (or o), r, and k.

Gargoyle: a stone waterspout or drainpipe carved in the form of a grotesquely carved face or figure, projecting from a roof gutter; carvings on the outside of buildings designed to direct water from the roof away from the base of the walls.

Gaul: an ancient region in Europe that corresponds to modern France, Belgium, the southern Netherlands, southwestern Germany, and northern Italy.

Gild(ed): Covered with a thin coating of precious metal, usually gold.

Glazier: a person whose profession is fitting glass into windows and doors.

Gnome: a legendary dwarfish creature supposed to guard the earth's treasures underground. Origin: mid-17th century, from French, from modern Latin gnomus, a word used by Paracelsus as a synonym of Pygmaeus, denoting a mythical race of very small people said to inhabit parts of Ethiopia and India ("Pygmy"); late 16th century, from Greek gnM'm', "thought, opinion" (related to gignM'skein, "know").

Gothic architecture: of or in the style of architecture prevalent in Western Europe in the 12th–16th centuries, characterized by pointed arches, rib vaults, and flying buttresses, together with large windows and elaborate tracery. The style included large stained glass windows and an uplifted design that brought large amounts of light into the structure.

Gothic era: the period in Europe roughly corresponding to the 12th–16th centuries, or, 1100–1500. (Note: The exact span of the Gothic era varies by plus or minus one century in varying sources.)

Gothic: of or relating to the Goths or their extinct East Germanic language, which provides the earliest manuscript evidence of any Germanic language (4th–6th centuries C.E.); of or in the style of architecture prevalent in western Europe in the 12th–16th centuries, characterized by pointed arches, rib vaults, and flying buttresses, together with large windows and elaborate tracery; (pseudoarchaic) belonging to or redolent of the Dark Ages; portentously gloomy or horrifying.

Griffin: a mythical animal with the head and wings of an eagle and the body of a lion, typically depicted with pointed ears and with the eagle's legs taking the place of the forelegs.

Grimoire: (magickal) a book of magic spells and invocations. Origin: mid-19th century French grammaire, literally "grammar."

Grotesque: a carved creature that resembles a gargoyle but doesn't have a drainpipe function.

Ground(ing): (magickal) a meditative technique that focuses on connecting one's own center (of gravity, of self) with the earthly place, as a way of "returning" from a ritual space and of dissipating excess energy safely back into the surrounding place and time.

Guild: a medieval association of craftsmen or merchants, often having considerable power; an association of people for mutual aid or the pursuit of a common goal. Origin: late Old English, probably from Middle Low German and Middle Dutch gilde, of Germanic origin; related to "yield."

Harpy: (Greek and Roman mythology) a rapacious monster described as having a woman's head and body and a bird's wings and claws, or depicted as a bird of prey with a woman's face. Origin: late Middle English: from Latin harpyia, from Greek harpuiai "snatchers."

Heraldry: the system by which coats of arms and other armorial bearings are devised, described, and regulated.

Hieroglyph(ic): a writing system in which a picture of an object represented a word, syllable, or sound; found in ancient Egyptian and other writing systems.

Hieros gamos: Literally, the "sacred marriage," an act of sexual intercourse between man and woman, or historically, King and goddess consort. In ritual, the *hieros gamos* is often symbolized by the dipping of the athame (a male symbol) into the chalice (a female symbol).

Indulgences: (historical; Roman Catholic Church) a grant given by the pope and purchased by the populace for remission of the temporal punishment in purgatory still due for sins after absolution. In other words, people paid to have their sins forgiven, hoping to enter a state of grace after death and avoid a quick trip to Hell! The unrestricted sale of indulgences by pardoners was a widespread abuse during the later Middle Ages.

Ley lines: (magickal) invisible lines of earthly energies. Ley lines are said to connect places of power, including the most significant archaeoastronomical observatories.

Liminal: of or relating to a transitional or initial stage of a process; occupying a position at, or on both sides of, a boundary or threshold. Origin: late 19th century from Latin limen, limin, "threshold."

Lingam: a symbol of divine generative energy, especially a phallus or phallic object worshiped as a symbol of Shiva. Origin: Sanskrit linga, literally "a mark or sexual characteristic."

Lintel: a horizontal support of timber, stone, concrete, or steel across the top of a door or window. Origin: Middle English, from Old French, based on late Latin liminare, from Latin limen, "threshold."

Mason: a builder and worker in stone.

Medieval: of or relating to the Middle Ages, the period of European history from about 500 C.E. to about 1500. Sometimes called "the Dark Ages." Origin: early 19th century, from modern Latin medium aevum "middle age" + -al.

Menagerie: a collection of wild animals kept in captivity for exhibition. Origin: late 17th century, from French ménagerie, from ménage, "to stay."

Mercer: a dealer in textile fabrics, especially silks, velvets, and other fine materials.

Mermaid: a fictitious or mythical half-human sea creature with the head and trunk of a woman and the tail of a fish, conventionally depicted as beautiful and with long flowing golden hair. Origin: Middle English, from mere (obsolete "sea") + "maid."

Millennium: a period of 1,000 years, especially when calculated from the traditional date of the birth of Jesus Christ.

Misericord: a ledge projecting from the underside of a hinged seat in a choir stall that, when the seat is turned up, gives support to someone standing. Origin: Middle English (denoting pity): from Old French *misericorde*, from Latin *misericordia*, from the stem of *misereri*, "to pity" + *cor, cord,* "heart."

Nave: the central part of a church building, intended to accommodate most of the congregation.

Norman: denoting, relating to, or built in the style of Romanesque architecture used in Britain under the Normans. Origin: Middle English, from Old French Normans, plural of Normant, from Old Norse Northmathr, "Northman."

Ouroboros: a circular symbol depicting a snake, or less commonly a dragon, swallowing its tail, as an emblem of wholeness, illusion, eternity, or infinity; the Ouroboros is an ancient symbol of alchemy. Origin: From Greek Ouroboros "snake devouring its tail."

Pagan: a person holding religious beliefs other than those of the main world religions; a person who follows an Earth-based form of spirituality characterized by the immanence of divinity and usually by a pantheon of deities. Origin: late Middle English, from Latin paganus, "villager, rustic," from pagus, "country district." Latin paganus also meant "civilian," becoming, in Christian Latin, "heathen" (one not enrolled in the army of Christ).

Pantheon: a hierarchy of spirits and deities within a magickal or spiritual system.

Parable: a simple story used to illustrate a moral or spiritual lesson.

Parapet: a low, protective wall along the edge of a roof, bridge, or balcony.

Parchment: a stiff, flat, thin material made from the prepared skin of an animal and used as a durable writing surface in ancient and medieval times; a manuscript written on this material.

Patron: (arts) a person who gives financial or other support to a person, organization, cause, or activity.

Pavoir: a person whose profession deals with laying tiled floors.

Pediment: typically surmounting a portico of columns; a similar feature surmounting a door, window, front, or other part of a building in another style. Origin: late 16th century (as periment): perhaps an alteration of pyramid.

Pentacle: (magickal) a five-pointed star used for magickal purposes; often called a pentagram. The pentacle is situated so that one point is upwards-facing and the star stands on two of its other points. Pentacles are often engraved on discs or platters, becoming panticles. In some traditions, initiates use the pentacle as a base on which to create a personal embodiment of spirituality, akin to the Native American medicine shield.

Pentagram: (magickal) see pentacle.

Petrified: organic matter that has been changed into a stony concretion by encrusting or replacing its original substance with a calcium-based, silicon-based, or other mineral deposit; a living plant, animal, or human that has become converted into stone or a stony substance in such a way; deprived of vitality or the capacity for change. Origin: late Middle English, from French pétrifier, from medieval Latin petrificare, from Latin petra, "rock."

Phallic: relating to or resembling the penis.

Pneumatic: containing or operated by air or gas under pressure.

Porter: a person employed to front the entrance of a hotel, apartment complex, or other large building.

Portico: a structure consisting of a roof supported by columns at regular intervals, typically attached as a porch to a building. Origin: early 17th century, from Italian, from Latin porticus, "porch."

Pottage: a thick soup composed of simple ingredients; thought of as a "poor man's" meal.

Quarry: a place, typically a large, deep pit, from which stone or other materials are or have been extracted. Origin: Middle English, from a variant of medieval Latin quareria, from Old French quarriere, based on Latin quadrum, "a square" (possibly referencing the cubic shape of cut stone blocks).

Rampart: a defensive wall of a castle or walled city, having a broad top with a walkway and typically a stone parapet.

Ridgeline: a roof's peak.

Romanesque: of or relating to a style of architecture that prevailed in Europe c. 900–1200, although sometimes dated back to the end of the Roman Empire (5th century). Romanesque architecture is characterized by round arches and massive vaulting, and by heavy piers, columns, and walls with small windows. Although disseminated throughout Western Europe, the style reached its fullest development in central and northern France; the equivalent style in England is usually called Norman. Origin: French, from roman, "romance."

Runes: small stones or pieces of bone, bearing runic marks, and used as divinatory symbols, that is, the casting of the runes. Runes were used by Scandinavians and Anglo-Saxons from about the 3rd century. They were formed mainly by modifying Roman or Greek characters to suit carving, and were used both in writing and in divination. Origin: old English *rk´n*, "a secret, a mystery"; not recorded between Middle English and the late 17th century, when it was reintroduced under the influence of Old Norse *rúnir, rúnar, "magic signs," or "hidden lore."*

Runic: a letter of an ancient Germanic alphabet, related to the Roman alphabet; a mark of mysterious or magic significance.

Saddler: someone who makes, repairs, or deals in saddles and riding tack.

Salamander: (magickal) a mythical lizard-like creature said to live in fire or to be able to withstand its effects; an elemental spirit living in fire.

Sanskrit: an ancient Indic language of India, in which the Hindu scriptures and classical Indian epic poems are written and from which many northern Indian languages are derived.

Satire (satiric): the use of humor, irony, exaggeration, or ridicule to expose and criticize people's stupidity or vices, particularly in the context of contemporary politics and other topical issues.

Satyr: (Greek and Roman mythology) one of a class of lustful, drunken woodland gods. In Greek art they were represented as a man with a horse's ears and tail, but in Roman representations as a man with a goat's ears, tail, legs, and horns.

Sphinx: (Greek mythology) a winged monster of Thebes, having a woman's head and a lion's body. It presented a riddle about the three ages of man, killing those who failed to solve it, until Oedipus was successful, whereupon the Sphinx committed suicide; an ancient Egyptian stone figure having a lion's body and a human or animal head, especially the huge statue near the Pyramids at Giza. Origin: late Middle English, via Latin from Greek Sphinx, apparently from sphingein, "draw tight."

Spire: a tapering conical or pyramidal structure on the top of a building, typically a church tower.

Statuary: any type of statue or carving.

Stonemason: a craftsman who prepares, carves, or builds objects out of stone.

Sylph: a spirit of the air. Origin: mid-17th century, from modern Latin sylphes, sylphi and the German plural Sylphen, perhaps based on Latin sylvestris, "of the woods" + nympha, "nymph."

Tanner: a person who tans animal hides, especially to earn a living.

Terra-Cotta: unglazed, typically brownish-red earthenware, used chiefly as an ornamental building material and in modeling. Origin: early 18th century, from Italian *terra cotta*, "baked earth."

Thurible: a censer. Origin: late Middle English, from Old French, or from Latin thuribulum, from thus, thur- "incense."

Tithe: one-tenth of annual produce or earnings, formerly taken as a tax for the support of the church and clergy.

Torc: a neck ornament consisting of an open band of twisted metal, worn especially by the ancient Celts. Origin: mid-19th century, from French torque, from Latin torqueo, "twist or bend," or torques, "collar" or "necklace."

Transept: (in a cross-shaped church) either of the two parts forming the arms of the cross shape, projecting at right angles from the nave.

Trope: a figurative or metaphorical use of a word or expression.

Tympanum: a vertical recessed triangular space forming the center of a pediment, typically decorated; similar space over a door between the lintel and the arch. Origin: early 17th century Latin from Greek tumpanon, "drum," based on tuptein, "to strike."

Undine: a spirit or nymph inhabiting water. Origin: early 19th century, from modern Latin undina (a word invented by Paracelsus), from Latin unda, "a wave."

Unicorn: a mythical animal typically represented as a horse with a single straight horn projecting from its forehead. Origin: Middle English, via Old French from Latin unicornis, from uni- ("single") + cornu "horn," translating Greek monokerM´s.

Vernal: of, in, or pertaining to spring.

Warding: (magickal) to protect with magick.

Wattle: woven twigs used to fill in the spaces between posts in a timber-framed house. Wattle was then plastered with daub.

Wyvern: a winged two-legged dragon with a barbed tail. Origin: late Middle English (denoting a viper), from Old French wivre, from Latin vipera.

Yeoman: (historical) a person qualified for certain duties and rights, such as to serve on juries and vote for the knight of the shire; a servant in a guilded trade or in a royal or noble household, ranking between a sergeant and a groom or a squire and a page. Origin: Middle English, probably from young + man.

Zoomorphic: having or representing animal forms or gods of animal form. Origin: late 19th century, from zoo ("of animals") + Greek *morph.* "form."

Appendix B: Template for Recording Fieldwork

When making your notes, consider the following:

- What is the sculpture made of?
- Does it have any specific history that you know of?
- Do you know its age?
- Who created it?
- What might its purpose have been?
- Does the building have any special history?

See the template on the next page. Photocopy it for multiple use.

Date and Time:

Location:

Type of gargoyle:

Size and description:

Sketch or diagram:

Notes:

Ideas for magickal use:

Certificate of Gargoyle Studies

DEPARTMENT OF ARCANE LORE

It is Hereby Certified that

_____

In recognition of completing a course of study and practice in the realm of Gargoyle theory, is granted the

An Apprentice in Gargoyle Academics

Awarded this ___ day of _____, 20___, with all the rights and privileges thereon given under the auspices of furthering Gargoyle Lore and Research

Prof. Moonwriter

Signed this day by Susan "Moonwriter" Pesznecker
Professor of Gargoyle Disquisition

Notes

Chapter 1

1. MacDonald, Sonya. "WU Libraries. Gargoyle Gallery." Quote attributed to Sturgis, Russel. *Sturgis' Illustrated Dictionary of Architecture and Building. http://library.wustl.edu/units/spec/archives/gargoyle* Dec. 5, 2005.

2. Alika. *A Medieval Feast.* New York: Harper Collins, 1983, p. 17.

Chapter 2

1. Goldberg, Jonah (producer). *Gargoyles: Guardians of the Gate*, 1995.

2. White, T.H. *The Book of Beasts, A Translation from a Latin Bestiary of the Twelfth Century.* Mineola, NY: Dover Publications, 1984, p. 75.

3. Goldberg, Jonah (producer). *Gargoyles: Guardians of the Gate*, 1995.

4. Benton, Janetta Rebold. *Holy Terrors. Gargoyles on Medieval Buildings.* New York: Abbeville Press, 1997, p. 102.

5. In her book, The First Fossil Hunters: Paleontology in Greek and Roman Times (2001), Adrienne Mayor presents evidence that ancient legends of monsters may be based on the discovery of dinosaur bones in central Asia, hundreds of years before the common era. Quoted in "Historical Base for Gargoyles." *http://northstargallery.com/gargoyles/aboutgargoyles.htm* 2001.

6. Goldberg, Jonah (producer). *Gargoyles: Guardians of the Gate*, 1995.

7. Walker, Barbara. *The Woman's Dictionary of Symbols and Sacred Objects*. San Francisco: Harper & Row, 1988, p. 257–8.

8. St. Bernard of Clairvaux, *Apologia ad Guilb. Sancti Theodroici abbat.*, ch. xi. *Patrol.*, clxxxii, col. 916.

Chapter 3

1. Friedman, John Block. *The Monstrous Races in Medieval Art and Thought*. Cambridge, MA: Harvard University Press, 1981, p. 9–21.

Chapter 4

1. Harding, Mike. *A Little Book of Gargoyles*. London: Aurum Press, 1998, p. 62-3.

2. Lindahl, Carl, John McNamara, and John Lindow. *Medieval Folklore. A Guide to Myths, Legends, Tales, Beliefs, and Customs*. Oxford: Oxford University Press, 2002, p. 93–4.

Chapter 6

1. Gies, Joseph and Frances Gies. *Life in a Medieval City*. New York: Harper and Row, 1969, p. 244–5.

Chapter 7

1. Bond, Francis Bligh. *Gothic Architecture in England*. London: B.T. Batsford, 1912, p. 400.

2. Goldberg, Jonah (producer). *Gargoyles: Guardians of the Gate,* 1995.

3. Translation from Ballade, "As a Prayer to Our Lady," in the collection known as "The Testament," as found in *The Complete Works of Francois Villon* (Ed. Anthony Bonner). New York: Bantam, 1964, p.68–69.

Chapter 8

1. "Cathedrals," from *Magazine* by Jump Little Children. Audio CD, released 1998.

Chapter 9

1. Rowling, Marjorie. *Life in Medieval Times*. New York: Perigee/Berkley Publishing Group, 1979, p. 156.

2. Rowling, Marjorie. *Life in Medieval Times.* New York: Perigee/Berkley Publishing Group, 1979, p. 167.

3. Gies. Joseph and Frances Gies. *Life in a Medieval City.* New York: Harper and Row, 1969, p. 92.

4. Gies. Joseph and Frances Gies. *Life in a Medieval City.* New York: Harper and Row, 1969, p. 89.

5. Gies. Joseph and Frances Gies. *Life in a Medieval City.* New York: Harper and Row, 1969, p. 235–6.

6. Benton, Janetta. *Holy Terrors. Gargoyles on Medieval Buildings.* New York: Abbeville Press, 1997, p. 60.

7. Rowling, Marjorie. *Life in Medieval Times.* New York: Perigee/Berkely Publishing 1979, p. 172.

Chapter 12

1. Newell, Mike (director). *Harry Potter and the Goblet of Fire.* 157 minutes, rated PG-13. 2005.

Chapter 13

1. Gies. Joseph and Frances Gies. *Life in a Medieval City.* New York: Harper and Row, 1969, p. 241.

Chapter 14

1. Walker, Barbara. *The Woman's Dictionary of Symbols and Sacred Objects.* New York: Harper & Row, 1988, p. 152.

2. Bray, Olive and D.L. Ashliman. "Hávamál. The Words of Odin the High One." *www.pitt.edu/~dash/havamal.html#runes* March 28, 2003.

3. Harding, Mike. *A Little Book of the Green Man.* London: Aurum Press, 1998, p. 12.

4. Sheridan, Ronald and Anne Ross. *Gargoyles and Grotesques. Paganism in the Medieval Church.* Boston: New York Graphic Society, 1975, p. 25-6.

5. *"Der Roman d'Abladane,"* in *Zeitschrift für romanische Philogie.* Halle, Germany, 1893, p. 215–32.

Chapter 15

1. Whitcomb, Bill. *The Magician's Companion. A Practical & Encyclopedic Guide to Magical and Religious Symbolism.* St. Paul, Minn.: Llewellyn, 1994, p. 517.

2. Herrick, Robert. *Works of Robert Herrick (Vol. II).* Alfred Pollard (Ed). London: Lawrence & Bullen, 1891, p. 73.

Chapter 16

1. Walker, Barbara. *The Woman's Dictionary of Symbols and Sacred Objects.* New York: Harper & Row, 1988, p. 337.

2. Gray, Martin. "Blarney Stone. Cork, Ireland." *www.sacredsites.com/europe/ireland/blarney_stone.html* 2006; Moynihan, Maura. "Welcome to Cork Kerry." *www.corkkerry.ie* 2005.

Chapter 17

1. Benton, Janetta Rebold. *Holy Terrors. Gargoyles on Medieval Buildings.* New York: Abbeville Press, 1997, p.130.

2. Benton, Janetta Rebold. *Holy Terrors. Gargoyles on Medieval Buildings.* New York: Abbeville Press, 1997, p.131.

3. Benton, Janetta Rebold. *Holy Terrors. Gargoyles on Medieval Buildings.* New York: Abbeville Press, 1997, p.132.

ex amino

Resources

Books

Anderson, William. *Green Man—The Archetype of Our Oneness with the Earth*. San Francisco: Harper Collins, 1990.

Basford, Kathleen. *The Green Man*. New York: D.S. Brewer, 2004.

Benton, Janetta. *Holy Terrors. Gargoyles on Medieval Buildings*. New York: Abbeville Press, April 1997.

————. *The Medieval Menagerie: Animals in the Art of the Middle Ages*. New York: Abbeville Press, 1992.

Billingsley, John. *Stony Gaze. Investigating Celtic and Other Stone Heads*. Milverton, UK: Capall Bann, 2001.

Blackwood, John. *Oxford's Gargoyles and Grotesques*. Oxford: Charon Press, 1986.

Bridaham, Lester Burbank and Ralph Adams Cram. *The Gargoyle Book: 572 Examples from Gothic Architecture*. Mineola, N.Y.: Dover, 2006.

Brunvand, Jan Harold. *The Study of American Folklore (4th Ed)*. New York: Norton, 1998.

Camille, Michael. *Image on the Edge: The Margins of Medieval Art*. Cambridge, Mass.: Harvard University Press, 1992.

————. *Image on the Edge: The Margins of Medieval Art*. Cambridge: Harvard University Press, 1992.

Crist, Darlene Trew. *American Gargoyles: Spirits in Stone*. New York: Potter Books, 2001.

Cunningham, Scott. *Cunningham's Encyclopedia of Crystal, Gem & Metal Magic.* St. Paul, Minn.: Llewellyn, 1988.

Davis, Francis A. and Russell Sturgis. *Sturgis' Illustrated Dictionary of Architecture and Building: An Unabridged Reprint of the 1901–2 Edition, Vol. II: F-N.* Mineola, N.Y.: Dover, 1989.

DeKirk, Ashley. *Dragonlore.* Franklin Lakes, N.J.: New Page/Career Press, 2006.

Friedman, John Block. *The Monstrous Races in Medieval Art and Thought.* Cambridge, Mass.: Harvard University Press, 1981.

Gies. Joseph and Frances Gies. *Life in a Medieval City.* New York: Harper and Row, 1969.

Haldane, Suzanne. *Faces on Places.* New York: Viking, 1980.

Harbison, Peter. *Ancient Irish Monuments.* Dublin: Gill & Macmillan, 1997.

Harding, Mike. *A Little Book of Gargoyles.* London: Aurum Press, 1998.

————. *A Little Book of the Green Man.* London: Aurum Press, 1998.

Hunt, Marjorie. *The Stone Carvers: Master Craftsmen of Washington National Cathedral.* Washington, D.C.: Smithsonian Books, 1999.

Illes, Judika. *The Element Encyclopedia of 5000 Spells.* London: Harper Element/Harper Collins, 2004.

King, Stephen. *Nightmares in the Sky.* New York: Viking/Penguin, 1988.

Lindahl, Carl, John McNamara, and John Lindow. *Medieval Folklore. A Guide to Myths, Legends, Tales, Beliefs, and Customs.* Oxford: Oxford University Press, 2002.

Matthews, John. The Green Man: Spirit of Nature. Newburyport, Mass.: Red Wheel/Reiser, 2002.

Pellant, Chris. *Rocks and Minerals (DK Smithsonian Handbooks).* New York: DK Publishing, 1992.

Randall, Richard H., Jr. *A Cloisters Bestiary.* New York: The Metropolitan Museum of Art, 1960.

Rowling, Marjorie. *Life in Medieval Times.* New York: Perigee/Berkley Publishing Group, 1979.

Sheridan, Ronald and Anne Ross. *Gargoyles and Grotesques. Paganism in the Medieval Church.* Boston: New York Graphic Society, 1975.

Walker, Barbara. *The Woman's Dictionary of Symbols and Sacred Objects.* New York: Harper & Row, 1988.

————. *The Woman's Encyclopedia of Myths and Secrets.* San Francisco: Harper San Francisco, 1983.

Wilkinson, Phillip. *World History (DK Pockets)*. New York: DK Publishing, 1996.

Yenne, Bill. *Gothic Gargoyles*. New York: First Glance Books, 1998.

Zell-Ravenheart, Oberon. *Companion for the Apprentice Wizard*. Franklin Lakes, N.J.: New Page Books, 2006.

Zell-Ravenheart, Oberon. *Grimoire for the Apprentice Wizard*. Franklin Lakes, N.J.: New Page Books, 2004.

Children's Books

Alika. *A Medieval Feast*. New York: Harper Collins, 1983.

Bunting, Eve. *Night of the Gargoyles*. New York: Clarion, 1994.

Coakley, Lena. *Mrs. Goodhearth and the Gargoyle*. Custer, Wash.: Orca Publishers, 2005.

Farber, Erica. *The Headless Gargoyle* (Critters of the Night , No 4). New York: Random House, 1996.

Macdonald, Fiona. *How Would You Survive in the Middle Ages?* New York: Franklin Watts/Scholastic Inc., 1995.

Pilkey, Dav. *God Bless the Gargoyles*. New York: Voyager Books, 1999.

Prelutsky, Jack. *Gargoyle on the Roof*. New York: Harper Trophy, 2006.

Smith, A.G. *Gargoyles and Medieval Monsters Coloring Book*. Mineola, N.Y.: Dover, 1998.

Snyder, Zilpha Keatley. *Song of the Gargoyle*. New York: Yearling/Random House, 1994.

Web-based Resources

"BatMUD." The Official BatMUD Site. *www.bat.org*, 2005. Accessed Aug., 2006.

"Encyclopedia Mythica." *www.pantheon.org/areas/bestiary/articles.html* 2005. Accessed July, 2006.

"Gargoyles." Gargoyles and Gargoyle Photographs. *www.stratis.demon.co.uk/gargoyles/gargoyle.htm* Oct. 15, 2002. Accessed August, 2006.

Arnold, Walter S. "Walter S. Arnold. Sculptor/Stone Carver." Walter S. Arnold/Sculptor -Virtual Sculpture Gallery. *www.stonecarver.com/gargoyles/index.html* 2006. Accessed May, 2006.

Arnott, Michael and Iain Beavan. "The Aberdeen Bestiary Project." Aberdeen University. *www.abdn.ac.uk/bestiary/bestiary.hti*. Accessed June, 2006.

Getson, Jennifer. "The Bestiary." *www.southwestern.edu/ACS/latin/team9/the_bestiary.htm* May 2, 2002. Accessed June, 2006.

Gray, Martin. "Blarney Stone. Cork, Ireland." *www.sacredsites.com/europe/ireland/blarney_stone.html* 2006. Accessed August, 2006.

Moynihan, Maura. "Welcome to Cork Kerry." *www.corkkerry.ie* 2005. Accessed August, 2006.

Royhandy. "Stoneskin Gargoyle Video." Broadband Reports.com. *www.dslreports.com/forum/remark,16451067~mode=flat.* Accessed August, 2006.

Film and Video

See Chapter 12.

Guided Magickal Study: Texts

Buckland, Raymond. *Buckland's Complete Book of Witchcraft (2nd Ed.).* St. Paul, Minn.: Llewellyn, 2002.

Zell-Ravenheart, Oberon. *Companion for the Apprentice Wizard* and *Grimoire for the Apprentice Wizard* (see above).

————. and Morning Glory Zell-Ravenheart, *Creating Circles and Ceremonies. Rituals for All Seasons and Reasons.* Franklin Lakes, NJ: New Page Books, 2006.

Guided Magickal Study: A Sampling of Online Resources

Note: Unless otherwise stated, cost refers to first year, level, or degree of study.

Avalon Center for Druidic Studies. *www.avaloncollege.org* Ages: 18 and older (some younger students admitted). Program: Baccalaureate and graduate-level Pagan and Druidic studies. Cost: $297 per 3-credit course; first level Awenydd program requires 36 credits. Certification: Diploma(s).

College of the Sacred Mists Online School of Wicca. *www.workingwitches.com* Ages: Unrestricted for 18 and older. 16–17 must have parental permission; under 16 may participate with a co-enrolled parent. Program: Celtic Traditional and Faerie Wicca. Cost: One-time enrollment fee $25, plus $20 per month. Certification: Certificate of degree achievement; potential ordination as priest or priestess.

Grey School of Wizardry. *www.greyschool.com* Ages: 11 through adult; 11-13 year olds require parental permission. Program: seven-level course of study in magickal practices and general wizardry. Cost: $18 for 11–17, $30 for 18 and over. Certification: Certificate of Journeyman Wizardry. Notes: The school neither teaches nor endorses any form of spiritual or religious practice, and the student body includes students of all faiths, including Christians.

Grove of Dana Online Druid College. *www.druidcircle.net/index2en.html.* Ages: 13 and older; separate program for younger students. Program: three-level program of self-study in Druidry. Cost: Free. Certification: Completion certificates.

Order of Bards, Ovates, and Druids (OBOD). *www.druidry.org* Ages: 16 and older. Program: Three-level program in Druidry. Cost: $401–634 for first level (Bardic). Certification: Certificate(s) of completion. Notes: Some classes may be college credit-transferable.

WitchSchool. *www.witchschool.com* Ages: 13 through adult. Program: Three-degree program in Corellian Wicca. Cost: First degree is free; second and third levels available for $5 per month, $30 per year, or $49.99 for a lifetime membership. Certification: Certificate(s) of completion.

Index

About the Author

After 25 years as a nurse—including two decades working with a research team studying human inner ear balance function—**Susan Pesznecker** returned to school in 2001, nourishing a lifelong desire to write and teach. In 2006, she will finish a double-MA program in English and creative non-fiction at Portland State University. Her writing interests include personal essay, memoir, and landscape narrative, while literature focuses include women writers, folklore, and composition theory. Sue's personal essays have been published in *Oregon Humanities* and *Oregon Quarterly.* Her interest in gargoyles began during a study of folklore and grew into a larger project, culminating in this book. In addition to writing, she teaches college-level composition, literature, and creative writing.

Of course, Sue also has a magickal side! As Moonwriter, she is an eclectic Pagan and a student of the Natural world, with interests including studies of Elemental magick, herbology, healing, Natural divination, cosmology, and Nature studies. She grows her own organic veggies and herbs, and loves to hike, camp, go rockhounding, watch birds, and simply hang out in the outdoors. As Professor Moonwriter, she is Dean of Students in the online Grey School of Wizardry, where she oversees a student body of more that 700 and also leads the Department of Nature Studies.

A fourth-generation pioneer Oregonian, Sue/Moonwriter has three wonderful grown children and lives in Milwaukie. She is currently working on several magickal and mundane writing projects. Lift your eyes west in the evenings, and you'll be watching the Moon right along with her.